LIGHT AND DARK

Volume Five of The Ambeth Chronicles

HELEN JONES

For my loves

PROPHECY

Child of Darkness, Child of Light,
Hair of flame shining bright,
Gate of oak, stepping through;
An ancient line is born anew.
Find the Dark, find the Light,
Then shall things be set to right;
For what is lost will be found,
In mist, in stone, underground.
'A Sword, A Cup, A Crown –
All hearts shall hold them pure.
Heart's love the Sword will lay down,
To rest in blood secure;
Heart betrayed the Cup will take,
Returned to an ancient home;
Cold heart the Crown shall stake,
For death before it is done.'

CHAPTER 1
SOMETHING STILL TO SALVAGE

Denoris, High Lord of the Dark, had a problem. Well, he had several, as far as he could see; a state of affairs that didn't make him happy. But there was one, at least, from which he might hope to salvage something. He urged his horse forward and she picked up speed, clods of earth coming up from under her hooves. The air was fresh with recent rain, green grass coated the hillsides and the land was beginning to wake as winter eased its grip. In the distance the tall pointed towers of Etras' keep rose, stark black against grey-blue peaks. The very edge of their world, or so it seemed, the mountains rising to inhospitable heights beyond. An appropriate place to find one who had been exiled.

But there had been no word from Etras since he'd left on his mission to capture Alma. He'd passed through the Gate a week ago, Denoris knew that much from the tracers, but hadn't returned. The only return signatures on the tracers were of the Light, and he knew to whom they belonged. Gritting his teeth he bent lower, clenching the reins. Alma. She'd eluded him once more. How, he had no idea. Etras was one of the best trackers who ever lived, and would have been ruthless. Her father had been a powerful lord in his own right, but she was half human —

her Channelling powers should only have taken her so far, surely. If only his fool of a son had been able to hold on to her, whatever power she possessed would have been his to control. Now all he had were the dregs of a plan, a missing friend and alliances that were shaky, at best. And the Crown, of course. That was something.

He slowed, nearing the entrance to the keep. A clap of sound made him look up. Two Watchers were entering the high tower, their leathery wings slapping together. One of them shrieked, an ugly broken sound that echoed from the stone walls. Denoris narrowed his eyes. Hmmm. Yes, there were still things to be salvaged here.

He pulled his horse to a halt. The huge wooden gates were ajar, the place seemingly deserted. He'd held a glimmer of hope that Etras might have returned — perhaps been injured and needed to heal. He knew something had happened to Artos, that he'd been found, stabbed, close to the Stone Gate. The healer hadn't wanted to give him too many details, but he'd exerted his will on her and she'd let slip that the Lord of Light had been wearing human-world clothing when she'd healed him. And that could mean only one thing – Artos had been looking for Alma as well.

He dismounted, put his shoulder against the huge gate and pushed, his muscles straining. Slowly it swung open, revealing an empty courtyard with burned-out torches still in the sconces, but no signs of life other than the shrieking Watchers in the tower above. He led his horse through the opening, her hooves clattering on the cobbles. He tied her reins to a post then turned, hands on hips.

'Hello!' he called out, his voice ringing across the yard. There was no answer. His nostrils flared and he took in a breath, his mouth tightening. Then he glimpsed a flash of colour, orange against a grey stone archway. 'You there!' He strode forward. 'I'm looking for Etras.'

A shape moved in the shadows, accompanied by the harsh sound of retching. Denoris paused. Had some sickness taken hold? The shape moved into the light, resolving into a young woman, human, wearing a loose orange robe. She was painfully thin except for the small mound of her stomach, which she was cradling, her long fingers pale against the coarse fabric of her dress. Her dark hair hung in strings around her face, which would have been beautiful if it wasn't so pasty, a faint tinge of green to her skin.

'My L-lord.' She turned away, retching, her body convulsing. Denoris frowned. He had no time for this. He put his hand on her shoulder. The young woman stiffened, then straightened up.

'My Lord, I-I'm sorry.' She wiped her mouth. 'I'm with child, and so—'

'Where is Etras? And the rest of the staff? Tell me.' He held her gaze. Her eyes glazed over, her mouth opening slightly.

'They have all left, my Lord.' Her voice was flat.

'Where is Etras?'

'He went away. He did not return.'

Denoris blew out a breath. So it was as he'd feared.

'What about those in the dungeons?'

A shudder passed through the young woman. He tightened his grip on her shoulder. 'I don't go down there,' she said. 'If you go down there, you don't come back up. We all knew that. We heard the screams.'

Denoris' frown deepened. Exiled or no, Etras needed to be more careful. Staff talked and rumours travelled. He needed no one to know what he had been trying to build here.

'Etras wouldn't let me go down there. He wanted this child, he wanted to—'

'Listen to me.' Denoris paused. Why was he doing this? Perhaps he was tired. 'You will go home now and forget you saw me.'

The young woman stared at him. He met her gaze, forcing his

will deeper, feeling the sweetness as it took hold, the euphoria of control over another.

'I will go,' she agreed, her voice still flat.

She turned. But instead of going back through the archway, she went to the outer gates and walked through them. Denoris raised an eyebrow. Ah well. It wasn't what he'd meant, but she might make it home. Or not. It was of no concern to him.

He took one of the torches from the wall, then struck a flint from his pocket against the stone. Sparks flew. Once the torch was alight, he took it and went to a door, set deep into the stone wall. The lock on it was broken. His mouth tightening, he pulled the door open and stepped inside.

Stone stairs twisted down into darkness. Denoris started down them, rage curling in the pit of his stomach. The dungeons seemed to be deserted, too; cell door after cell door stood open. Surely they wouldn't have—

There was a loud bang. Denoris stopped. Lifting the torch higher he peered further along the narrow passageway. At the end was a door, solid timber and iron with a small window grate, bolted from the outside. Another crash. The door shuddered, as though something heavy had hit it from the other side. Denoris moved closer.

A stench of rotting meat became apparent, and the sound of heavy snorting breath. Denoris smiled. So all was not lost. Not yet.

He reached the door and waited, placing his torch in a nearby sconce. The creature would catch his scent, he knew. What he wondered, though, was where Etras had put the others.

Metal-tipped claws clanged on the grated window. The door rattled on its hinges. Denoris drew his knife and moved closer. When the claws scraped across the grate once more, he stabbed forward into the fleshy palm. A strangled shriek came from inside the cell. The window remained clear and he peered through it.

Two Galardin were in the cell. One was slumped against the

far wall, its dark fur matted, its scales losing their sheen. The other was pacing, its huge shoulders hunched and curved. It bared its teeth and growled at Denoris, one clawed hand cradling the other. The remains of several others lay strewn around the floor in various stages of decomposition – the smell was so strong Denoris covered his mouth. Rage rose in him again. Yet another plan gone awry. Why would Etras have put them all in one cell? But he had, and they'd turned on each other. The ones that were left were of no use to him, unable to be controlled. There was only one thing to do.

Drawing his sword, Denoris slid the bolts clear. Then he opened the door and stepped into the cell. The attack came almost immediately. A raking strike whistled through the air where his head had been a second before. But he was ready. Ducking to the side, he turned and stabbed upwards through the unprotected stomach. The Galardin let out a strangled groan as it slumped forward onto the sword, which came out through its scaled back. Denoris pulled his blade free and the creature fell, bright blood spreading across the fouled floor. He went to the other Galardin, which was still slumped against the wall. It looked up at him, its dark eyes pools of suffering, tears matting the dark fur. Without hesitation he killed it. Then he wiped his sword on the carcass and turned to leave the cell, fury in his heart.

Once outside he crossed the courtyard, heading for an archway set into the stone wall of the keep. Stairs curved into the darkness above. As he ascended, shrieking came from above, accompanied by scraping sounds, like metal on stone. There was a strong odour of musk and burning, an animal scent of death.

The stairway ended at another stone archway, the top few stairs littered with straw and small bones, picked clean and white. Denoris drew his sword, holding it out as he stepped into the tower room. There was a leathery flapping, the air full of feathers and darkness, swirling around him. He gripped the sword tighter, ducking to avoid a swipe from a taloned wing. He was surrounded by nests, great baskets of straw and twigs and feather. Four of them covered almost the entire floor. There were chicks in two of them, their long beaks jabbing the air, their blind heads turning as they squeaked, revealing rows of needle-sharp baby fangs. But Denoris wasn't worried about them – the large raptors guarding each nest were the real threat.

Watchers came in many shapes and sizes, like the wurms Denoris had used to track Alma. But wurms were easily killed. He rather suspected the raptors would be more difficult to despatch. What he needed to do was control them. They would be in thrall to Etras, but Etras, darkness damn him, was gone. It was up to him to take the next steps in this game. He dodged another lethal swipe, careful not to damage the powerful wings, then stepped closer to the nearest beast. It reared up and back, wings flapping. But it wouldn't leave the chicks – he'd counted on that. He reached out, evading the snapping jaws, his sword still up in guard position, and grasped the long slender neck of the creature. It was leathery, the skin slippery under his grip and unpleasantly clammy. He swallowed his revulsion and focused his gaze on the red gleaming eyes. The creature gave in easily enough. Denoris' will broke through the thrall Etras had set, building a new set of commands. It seemed the creatures were telepathic, a hive mind. Control one, and you control them all. Good, that made things easier. The creature relaxed against his hand, the great beak coming forward to brush against his hair so he could smell the fetid breath. He sent his commands, waited to feel the acquiescence. There was a flap of wings, the scrape of talon on stone as the creatures left Etras' tower. Several would stay to guard the chicks until they were big enough to fly, but the rest he sent to his house in the hills. A surprise for Aeres. Denoris grinned at the thought of his elegant wife being confronted with the creatures roosting among her chimney pots.

He had plans for her, as well, once this game was done.

CHAPTER 2
DARK STAR

'Urgh, only the first week back and I'm already exhausted!' Colleen sat down at the table, sighing dramatically.

Sitting next to Sara, Alma giggled. 'Good to see you too, Colleen. Where were you yesterday?'

'Oh, my Monday schedule is a joke,' said Colleen, wrinkling her nose. 'Wish it was still summer.'

'Yeah, me too.' If only she knew. Alma's summer had been... eventful. It felt almost good to be back at school, a welcome dose of normal

'We missed you! Do not go away like that again.' Colleen popped a chip in her mouth, pausing to chew before continuing. 'Sara was lucky she had Josh to keep her occupied when she got back from France. We barely saw her.'

'That is so not true!' squealed Sara. Alma and Colleen both laughed. Alma already knew that things had become serious between Sara and Josh over the summer. The two girls had met up for a debrief almost as soon as Alma returned home. Still, she liked teasing Sara.

'That's not what I heard.' Alma nudged her. 'How will you cope, not seeing him for an hour or two?'

Colleen snorted. 'Oh, they'll just text endlessly.'

'That's not fair!' said Sara, glaring.

Colleen giggled. 'Actually, speaking of hot guys...'

'Were we speaking of hot guys?' asked Alma. They all laughed. Sara pushed at Alma and squealed.

'*Anyway*,' Colleen went on, 'there's a new guy in my English class and he is *totally* hot.' She pretended to fan herself.

Alma raised her eyebrows. 'Oh yeah?'

'Yes. He's tall, blue eyes and dark hair and, uh, god, he's just so—'

'Hot?' Alma giggled, amused by Colleen's over-the top-description. 'So, what's his name, this new super-hot guy?' She grinned, but Colleen looked mystified.

'You know what, I don't know.'

'Oh, come on!' Sara threw a chip at Colleen. 'That's not like you.'

'Well, I think it's something with a D. David? Declan? Or maybe an E?'

Sara breathed in sharply, glancing at Alma.

'Oh Alma, I'm so sorry, I wasn't even thinking!' Colleen said.

'About what?' Alma frowned, wondering whether both girls had lost their minds.

'About David?' Sara looked at her strangely. 'Had you forgotten?'

'Oh. Oh! Right.' Alma bit her lip. 'Um, no, I mean, I hadn't forgotten.' God. What was she supposed to say about David, her mysterious boyfriend who was supposed to have died earlier that year. Because it was actually her friend Caleb who had died, killed in Ambeth by her real boyfriend at the time, Deryck. She blew out a breath. 'Um, it's just, I had a lot of time to think about things, over the summer,' she said, her voice going up at the end of the sentence. 'So, I mean, I miss him, I always will, I guess,' she said, looking down. That part was true. 'But I'm ready to move on. So don't worry, I'm fine, really I am.'

Sara put her arm around Alma. Colleen took a noisy sip from her straw.

'What do you have this afternoon?'

'Erm, environmental studies, I think.' Alma said, glad the subject had changed.

Colleen raised her eyebrows. 'Really?'

'Well, yeah. I mean, I'm thinking about doing something to do with land management or environmental stuff when I go to university, so that's why I'm taking it.'

Colleen nodded then she looked at Sara. 'And you?'

'Media studies.'

'Me too! That's awesome! Oh my god!' Her eyes widened and she looked past Alma, who'd started on her sandwich.

'What's so good about that?' Sara sounded grumpy.

'Shhh! Oh!' Colleen had gone pink.

Alma frowned. What had got into her? Sara looked equally confused.

'Ohmygod he's coming over here!'

'Who's coming over here?'

'The guy!' hissed Colleen. 'The hot one, from my English class!' She sat up, fussing with her hair and smiling. Alma turned. A boy was approaching their table. He was tall, olive-skinned and handsome, his longish dark hair falling forward over eyes that were unusually blue. He moved with purpose, unlike the other boys slouching and posturing their way around the lunch room. It was the boy from the Foyer, the one Alma had seen the day before. She'd felt drawn to him, to his energy, but hadn't been sure why. There was something *so* familiar about him. She realised she was staring and turned back to her sandwich.

Sara elbowed Alma and jerked her head. Alma looked up. The boy was standing next to her. Across the table Colleen tossed her hair, but it was obviously Alma he'd come to see. He smiled, revealing straight white teeth, and Alma smiled back, unable to help herself.

'Hi,' he said. 'I'm Ethan. You're Alma, right?'

'Uh, yeah,' said Alma. He looked at her as though he was willing her to remember something. She could feel Sara vibrating with excitement beside her. Shaking his head, he broke eye contact and shoved his hands in his pockets.

'Can we talk, please? Just for a moment. I really need to speak to you.'

'Erm, okay,' said Alma. This was completely weird. Still, she had a fairly high tolerance for weird these days. She stood up, scratching at her bracelet. 'So, um—'

'Introductions!' she heard Colleen hiss.

'Oh, yeah. Um, this is Colleen, and this is Sara.'

'Hi.' Ethan grinned, then turned his attention back to Alma. 'Shall we?'

'Right, um, I'll see you guys in a bit.' Alma fell into step next to Ethan. What the hell was going on? As she walked away she heard Colleen say to Sara in a fierce whisper, 'I thought she didn't know him!'

'She doesn't, as far as I know.'

'Then what's going on? Huh, half Alma's luck...'

Then they moved out of earshot, to Alma's relief.

'Shall we go over there?' Ethan pointed to a deserted space near the wall, looking amused. 'It's just, it's probably better if no one can hear us, right?'

Alma frowned, rubbing at her arm again. 'Wait.' He stopped, and she could see the energy lines in him again, just as she had the day before. They were beautiful, dark and light twined together.

'Alma?'

She blinked and the energy lines disappeared. 'It's just, I feel like we've met before...'

'We have.' He nodded, another flash of smile. God, he was cute! But his smile faded as she didn't respond. 'Don't you remember me?'

Alma shook her head. 'No, I'm so sorry. I mean, you're so familiar but I just can't—'

'In the woods, Alma. That's where we met.'

Suddenly she got it. The blood drained from her face, her stomach dropping.

He put out his hand to steady her. 'I'm sorry, I thought you'd realised.' He was closer to her now, his voice low and urgent. 'Are you okay? Are you going to faint? It's just, your friends are watching us right now and if you collapse it's really not going to look good.' There was humour in his tone but the concern in his eyes was real. 'Come on,' he said, gently pulling her towards the wall.

When they got there she leaned on the cool bricks, staring at him. Energy lines flickered in and out as she tried to deal with her shock. *In the woods*. After the Harvest Fair. It all came flooding back. Caleb dying on the green, her flight through the woods to safety and the mysterious stranger who had saved her from the Dark Hunt.

'You... you saved me. Oh—'

He nodded.

Alma blushed, remembering how she'd clung to him, sobbing, on that terrible day. 'I never got the chance to thank you, for what you did.'

'It's okay,' he said. Her bracelet was warm against her wrist. She rubbed at it once more, her eyes widening as she realised what it meant.

'You-you helped me but... aren't you...' she paused a moment, 'Dark?' She winced as she said it.

'Your bracelet is giving me away, isn't it?' he asked.

Alma waited, her lips pursed.

'My father is Lord Cedran.' His mouth twisted, and Alma realised he was nervous about telling her. He looked so like his father, with the same golden skin and dark hair. Yet the eyes that shone blue were completely different from the stern stare of the Dark Lord.

'My father was Lord Galen.' It still felt strange to say it – she hadn't told anyone else about the revelations of the summer, not even Sara. But she felt as though she needed to tell Ethan, that it would be all right for him to know. She wasn't sure why. She wasn't sure about anything right now. 'But, I still… I don't understand. If you're Dark, why were you, why did you…?' Her voice broke and she looked away.

'I was running, too, in the woods that day. And I couldn't let them take you.' Alma's eyes filled with tears and she took in a gasping breath. 'Caleb was a friend.' He put his hand on her forearm. His touch was gentle and soft energy ran from his hand into her, soothing her distress.

'He was,' she said, a tear escaping down her cheek. 'The best.' Ethan was still touching her arm, his hand moving lightly on her skin. She blushed, breaking the contact.

'Um, so, what are you doing here?' she said, wiping her cheek.

He grinned, dimples flashing in his cheeks. 'Well, I go here. I think actually we have a class together.' Then his expression grew more serious. 'I am also here, Alma of the Prophecy, to help you find the Crown, the last piece of the Sacred Regalia.'

'What?' Alma slumped back against the wall, feeling as though she might slide down it. 'But y-you live here, right?'

His brows drew together. 'My mother's human and I live with her, though I do visit Ambeth pretty regularly. My father and I, we have an… unusual relationship.' There was no bitterness in his tone, just weary resignation, as though relating a truth long dealt with. Alma blew out a long breath – Ambeth and its convoluted history was sometimes too much to take. Yet here they were, children of Light and Dark, brought together. She realised it was the first line of the Prophecy – she'd always thought it referred only to her, to her human heritage. But now, of course, she knew she was not human, not fully.

'So you are... the Child of Darkness?'

Ethan nodded, his frown clearing. 'It looks that way,' he said, 'and, as you are the Child of Light, it kind of makes sense that we do this together.'

Alma glanced over to the table where her friends sat, only to see them turn their heads away quickly. She almost laughed – they had no idea what was really going on over here, nor would they ever. Ethan also glanced over, then met her grin with one of his own, as though he knew what she was thinking.

'So, will you work with me? I mean, we can go back to Ambeth together, maybe talk to Thorion about what to do next.'

Alma paused, not sure what to say. 'I... I still find it hard to go back there, you know? I've been a couple of times, to see Grandfather...' She looked down. 'I mean, I brought them the Cup, but it was just too painful. It wasn't just Caleb I lost.' She tucked her hair behind one ear, glancing at him. 'There are people I don't want to see.'

'I know about Deryck,' he said, 'and I understand why you'd feel the way you do. And, for what it's worth, he's not doing so well these days.'

'I don't care how he's doing!' Alma shook her head. 'After what he did to me—' She stopped, tears coming to her eyes.

'I'm sorry,' said Ethan. 'Forgive me, please. I'm no good at this stuff.' He hung his head.

'N-no, it's fine, I'm fine. I'm sorry, I didn't mean to snap.'

'We can do this together, Alma. I won't forsake you.' His handsome face was soft. In her heart, so bruised and battered, Alma felt a tendril of answering warmth. Reaching out, she took his hand.

'Together,' she echoed.

He smiled. He was so close to her and for a moment she felt that strange connection again, as though her energy was reaching out to him, sparks crossing the space between them. Then she realised she was staring. She dropped his hand, blood hot in her cheeks.

He put his hands in his pockets and leaned against the wall. He was still smiling, though.

CHAPTER 3
WARNING SIGNS

Deryck wandered through the darkened gardens. He'd been drinking already, a few goblets of wine before he left his father's apartments, but it had made no difference to his mood. He paused at one enclosed space. Bright striped cushions were scattered across the grass. Alma had brought him here. He pushed away the thought of what he'd done to her, the bruises on her wrist. And how she'd forgiven him, afterwards. His heart clenched and he reached for the stone that hung from his neck, letting darkness wash away the pain of her memory, leaving him with only the sweetness.

A couple came stumbling through an opening in the hedge, both of them laughing, arms wrapped around each other. They tumbled onto the cushions. The girl's high-pitched giggle was annoyingly familiar. It was Lissa. Deryck knew he hadn't treated her well, their brief relationship ending in disappointment for her. But he hadn't been able to give her what she wanted. He didn't care at all that she was kissing someone else now. In fact, he was happy for her – one less thing to think about. He started walking again.

As he neared the Palace, he could hear voices and laughter.

Hands in pockets, he fell in with the people meandering along the Long Walk, ignoring the smiles and glances thrown his way. He entered the Foyer, then the Great Hall, the guards bowing as he passed. It barely registered. The Hall was crowded. It had been two months since Alma had returned the Cup, and more of the great families from the hills seemed to arrive each day, all of them keen to see it. The apartments behind the Palace were full almost to bursting.

Beautiful faces flashed past as he moved through the crowd. The huge lanterns were lit, glowing overhead, the scent of roasting meat and perfume in the air. He still didn't know why he'd ended up there. The band were excellent, as they usually were, and there was good food and drink to be had, but none of it touched the bleakness inside him. He saw a few people he knew – he nodded to Tomas, Ellery's boyfriend. Tomas nodded back and smiled. He was nice. It was good that his sister had found some-one, though she seemed oddly distant of late. Sometimes, in the night, he thought he heard her crying out, but whenever he went to find her, she was never there. Everything seemed strange, lately. Darkness knew he was bored, waiting around for whatever his father wanted to do next, for Thorion's punishment, for Alma to come back to him, like he knew she would. Touching his tallus stone, he let the dark energy run through him, its silken touch familiar as a caress, her red hair and blue eyes in his mind.

'ELLERYYYY.' THE WORD SLITHERED THROUGH THE AIR, A snake hiss. Ellery froze as a hand descended on her shoulder, warm through the silk of her shawl. She turned to see the grin-ning face of Rindor, son of Lord Nevros. He was dark and hand-some, like his father. Silver glittered in his long black hair, and on the deep burgundy of his tunic.

She stepped back, pointedly removing her shoulder from his

increasingly familiar grasp. He lifted his hands, his grin widening. 'What? Aren't you pleased to see me? Have you forgotten me so soon?'

'I've forgotten nothing,' said Ellery. Where was Tomas? He'd gone to get them drinks. He should be back by now. However, she could handle this. 'You seem well,' she continued, inclining her head, taking another small step back. Her hands clenched into fists, but she lifted her chin, meeting his gaze.

'As do you. You're as beautiful as I remember.'

Ellery's nostrils flared. She tried not to think about the last time she'd seen Rindor, in the gardens a couple of years earlier — his grasping hands, her pleas for him to stop, the ripping sound as he tore her dress... She hadn't told her father; he would only have blamed her for what happened. She'd sworn to herself that next time she saw Rindor, he would pay. But here she was, without a knife. Damn.

'Well, it's been... good, seeing you.' She hated herself in that moment. What a lie. There was nothing good about seeing him. She forced a smile, remembering a time when she'd thought he was the handsomest boy in Ambeth, thrilled by his attention. How young she'd been, and how naïve. Her eyes narrowed and his grin faltered, just for a moment.

He bowed. 'And to see you. Let's not leave it so long before the next time, hey?' And, before she could stop him, he reached for her hand, raised it to his lips, and kissed it. He winked at her, turned, and entered the crowd. Ellery stood still, her hand slick where he'd kissed it, fighting back tears. He wouldn't win, she wouldn't let him! She summoned up the darkness she knew dwelt in her, drawing on it as her feelings hardened, sliding back down to the place inside where she kept all her hurt. She scanned the crowd, looking for Tomas, seeking the light he brought.

∼

Tomas, drinks in hand, took a hasty step back as a figure clad in smoke-grey chainmail pushed past him. The light from the overhead lanterns picked up silver glints in the mail, flashing from the red stones embedded along the sleeves. Shit. That was close. The figure paused and turned to him. Tomas swallowed. Oh no.

'Are you here with friends tonight?'

The hunter's eyes were dark like his hair, which was long and tied at the nape of his neck.

Tomas took in a breath, standing straighter. 'I am,' he said, hoping his voice wouldn't shake. It held.

'Then I suggest you stay with them.'

Tomas' brows drew together. 'I mean no offence, but why is that?'

The hunter raised an eyebrow. 'Because we have business here in the Hall tonight. And we do not need anyone—' he curled his lip '—getting in our way.'

Tomas nodded. 'Fine'. He was tense as a wire, though. His fingers were numb where they wrapped around the goblets.

'Is that for the Lady Ellery?' The hunter inclined his head to the drink.

'Yes.'

The hunter's lip curled again. 'You're riding above your grade, there. Be grateful that she is here tonight with you.'

'I have no quarrel with the Hunt,' Tomas said, stung by the remark. 'And I do not take your meaning.' He did, though, of course he did. He knew every time he looked at Ellery, every time eyes were on them, that she was leagues above him, and not just because of who her father was.

'Lesser sons of lesser lords are the type we use as prey,' hissed the hunter, leaning closer. 'And we ride, later tonight. I give you this warning as a gift. Take it.'

Tomas said nothing, though his mind was whirring. The Dark Hunt rarely came to the Hall, preferring to spend their nights riding in chaos and darkness. But he'd heard rumours that a recent hunt hadn't gone well, that there had been casualties and the prey had eluded them. They weren't allowed to hunt within the Palace, so they could only be in the Hall for one reason. They were recruiting.

The hunter nodded, fixing Tomas with a dark glare, then moved on through the crowd. Tomas let out a breath, his legs trembling. Rage burned in him at the hunter's remarks. The crowd parted and he saw Ellery, her dark head turning as she scanned the crowd. When she saw him her face lit up and she beckoned him over. He went to her, counting his lucky stars once more.

~

'NICE NECKLACE, PRETTY BOY.'

Deryck turned, frowning. He was near to the pillars that ran down the side of the Great Hall, the alcoves filled with people laughing and drinking. Something landed with a thud at his feet. He looked down to see a gauntlet of dark chain mail, jewelled with deep red stones. His frown deepened. He bent and picked it up, taking it to a nearby table and dropping it among the glasses and half-empty plates.

'I think you dropped this?' He kept his face deliberately tight; no smile, no fear, nothing to betray him. He had no desire to become prey.

'Maybe I did, maybe it just fell.' Simeon. Leader of the Dark Hunt. He sat, one arm along the back of the padded seat, long dark hair around his face, half sneering, half smiling. His armour was jewelled and silvery black, like the gauntlet. 'And I asked you about your necklace.'

'What about it?' All at once Deryck didn't care what they did to him. Besides, they knew who he was. He might be younger than they were, but his father would destroy them all if they harmed him. His sister had ridden with them, once, although the circumstances had been different. He tried not to think about that day, about Alma, a bright figure against dark green, running across the fields. Yes. Kill him, hunt him, whatever. He didn't care anymore.

Simeon laughed. 'You just don't see many of them, that's all.' When he smiled his face lit up, became friendly. 'So tell me, son of Denoris, do you ride? Do you hunt? Will you follow the moon with us?'

Deryck's breath caught, his heart pounding, even against the stupor of his stone. These were the ritual words. They were asking him to join the Hunt. Once he was in there would be no turning back. The Hunt rode for the Dark if required, doling out punishment, as they'd tried to do that terrible day at the tournament. The rest of the time they rode for their own pleasure, dangerous and wild, flashing across the hills in pursuit of those unfortunate enough to be marked as prey. He still for the life of him had no idea how Alma had escaped them. He was glad she had. But to join them? Membership was for life, however long that might be. He raised an eyebrow.

'Why me?'

Simeon laughed, as did the others at the table, all of them, men and women, similarly garbed in dark silver and red jewels, like smoke and blood. One of the young women, her dark hair in two long braids, leaned forward, her cleavage pressing against the deep V-neck of her top. 'Maybe we like pretty golden boys,' she said, her voice husky. Deryck swallowed.

'Or maybe that's just you, Floria.' Simeon shot her a glance and she sat back, pouting. He returned his focus to Deryck. 'I hear you're a good rider, and we know you're a vicious fighter. So, if you're interested, come ride with us. No commitment necessary. Yet.' He drew out the last word. 'What do you say? Shall we take you and your magic stone on a journey?'

Deryck stared at him, nettled by the reference to his fighting. But it was no secret, what he'd done. Killing another boy in front of half the population of Ambeth tended to get around, to stay news. And if it was the stone they wanted? He supposed it matched their look, black with red sparks within. He really didn't care. By the darkness, he needed something new in his life.

'I will ride. I will hunt. I will follow the moon with you,' he said. There. It was done.

Simeon raised his eyebrows. The rest of the table fell silent. 'Is that so?' he said, his voice softer. 'Well, son of Denoris, you are welcome among us. Move along!' he snapped at the rider sitting opposite him, who obligingly shuffled along the bench seat. Simeon held out his hand. 'Come, sit with us. Now we drink, but later tonight, we ride.'

'Hope you can keep up,' said Floria as Deryck sat down, shooting him a wink. He felt a familiar stirring in his loins as he met her gaze. Well, at least it might be interesting. He picked up a goblet and took a drink. He touched his stone once more, his eyes closing. Beneath the table, a foot twined around his leg and he slid lower in his seat. Yes, interesting.

CHAPTER 4
RECKLESS HEARTS

Across the room, Tomas frowned as he watched Deryck join the Hunt at their table. That could only mean one thing. But would Deryck really be so reckless? Ellery had told him about Deryck, about how he'd lost his love, but surely he was stronger than that?

'What's wrong?' Ellery took one of the drinks from his hand, a smile on her face.

Tomas opened his mouth and then closed it again. The hunter who'd approached him before was lounging against a column just a few feet away. When Tomas caught his eye he nodded, once, his dark gaze fixed on him. Right. Tomas got the message. This was not the place to discuss the Hunt, not when they were watching him. Damn! Tomas returned his attention to Ellery, whose smile had disappeared.

'Nothing,' he said, kissing her on the cheek. 'When we've finished these, would you like to walk with me in the gardens?'

Ellery blushed, her long lashes lowered. Tomas's heart clenched. He still couldn't believe she'd chosen him. She was wearing green tonight, an emerald shade that matched her eyes, the silk and velvet hugging her slender curves. She kept her shawl clutched around her, despite his efforts to take it from her and hang it up, saying she was cold. He would warm her, if he could. There were times when he wanted to wrap her in his arms and keep her safe forever.

'That sounds nice.' She glanced up at him. "Father's away tonight, so I can stay out later.'

Tomas grinned, taking a gulp of his drink. Ellery giggled. She put her goblet to her lips and tipped her head back, downing the lot. She put the goblet down on a nearby table, her green eyes glazing over. 'I'm ready to go,' she said, laughing again.

Tomas didn't need to be asked twice. He put his own drink down and took her arm, twining it through his own. 'Then let's go, my lady.'

DENORIS ENTERED THE DARKENED ARENA BENEATH THE HUMAN city, ancient dust rising beneath his boots. His machine waited, the glow from the stolen Crown suspended at its centre picking out glints of silver wire and twisted metal. The dark pool at its base swirled endlessly, a vortex of black. He stepped into the space beneath the Crown, spreading his feet and bracing himself. He took a deep breath, blew it out and gripped the metal poles either side of him. Light flared in the dark space. He gritted his teeth as the whirlpool spun faster, a snaking thread of darkness coming up to meet it.

Later he lay in the dust, fumbling for the tallus at his throat, the last tendrils of dark energy dissipating as they left the chamber, heading out to cause more chaos in the human world above. He was trembling and sweating. It was getting worse, the effects lasting longer each time he used the machine. Darkness knew he needed the girl! He couldn't sustain this for much longer. Once he had Alma, he would put her in the machine every day, get her to channel the powers of this place and increase the spread of darkness in the human world. If only Etras had managed to get her, to put the damned tallus on her! She would be here and married to Deryck already if he had. He closed his eyes, sighing as the tallus' dark energy spread through him, washing away the ache in his muscles, restoring his energy, soothing his agitation. He had once told Deryck it had taken him a century to master the stone – indeed, he'd hardly used it in the years since. But now, as his plans came to fruition, with the Balance tipping in favour of the Dark, he found he was turning to it more often again, needing its restorative power. He sometimes felt as though it were changing him, crystallising his brain cells, its strands of darkness snaking their way inside. But he couldn't give up using it now. He needed the girl, that's all. Once he had her, and the machine was working every day, then he could rest.

He got up, brushed the dirt from his jacket and hitched up his jeans. It was time to go back to Ambeth and see what his children were up to. Ellery hadn't seen the machine as yet – perhaps he could introduce her to it soon. Darkness knew she needed to be brought back into line, and his current methods didn't seem to be working.

Soon enough he was back at his house by the river. The thought of the bed upstairs, with its spare lines and cool linens, was tempting. But he had things to do and could not tarry. With his armour strapped on once more and frustration building in his heart, he stepped through the Gate back to Ambeth.

THE GARDENS WERE DARK AND COOL, BUT ELLERY WAS WARM, leaning into Tomas as they wandered the twisting paths. He thought for a moment about forgetting what he'd seen and taking her to a space he knew, where they could talk and kiss and share the night. He pushed the urge down. He had to tell her, for

Deryck's sake. He'd seen how Ellery's brother had changed, and knew she was worried about him.

'I need to talk to you.'

He felt Ellery stiffen. 'You do?'

'Not like that. Nothing like that,' he said. 'It's about Deryck.'

'Deryck?'

They passed beneath an archway of stone into a high-hedged space, one of the many that made up the sprawling gardens. There were tales that the gardens changed, that the layout never stayed the same. He wasn't sure about that, and yet, no matter how many times he walked through them, there always seemed to be somewhere new to find.

'He's not... bothering you, is he?' Ellery looked up at him, her eyes wide.

'No, no. Did you see him this evening?'

'In the Hall?'

'Yes. With the Hunt.'

Ellery rolled her eyes and let go of his arm. 'Typical. Was he picking a fight with them – Wait – I would probably have noticed that. What was he doing?'

'Well, I'm not sure, but... it looked like he was joining them.'

'Really?' Ellery narrowed her eyes, tilting her head. 'Huh. Okay. Well, Father won't like that.'

Tomas frowned. 'What?'

Ellery shrugged. 'Well, he's the favourite. Father will think he's wasting his time.'

His frown deepened. Did she not understand? 'Ellery, this is the *Hunt*. Eric told me they lost two members just the other week, fighting in the hills. They... your brother could be killed. Aren't you worried?'

The sarcastic expression slid away from Ellery's face, replaced by sorrow. She swallowed before speaking. 'I worry about Deryck all the time. About what the stone is doing, how he's doing, after losing Alma. He—' she shook her head. 'Honestly, the Hunt is the least of my worries. I mean, I've ridden with them myself—' she frowned '—not that I'm proud of it, but they know who our father is. There's no way they would let anything happen to him.'

'But—'

'Honestly. Don't worry about it. I'm not.' She put her hands on his arms, reaching up to kiss him. He kissed her back, giving in to the moment. Finally they parted. He smiled as he touched her face, gently.

'Shall we walk some more?' His voice was unsteady.

Ellery glanced up at him through her lashes. 'I know a place, deeper in the gardens. More private.'

'Sounds good. Will you show me?'

She took his hand and gently tugged him along the path, laughing as she picked up the pace. The pathway was hung with lanterns and they ran through pools of light and shadow. It felt, to Tomas, almost like flying.

DENORIS SAT IN THE SHADOWS, THE GARDENS RUSTLING AROUND him, his mind as dark as the evening. He thought again of Etras, felt a momentary pang at the loss of his old friend. Perhaps it was for the best, though. Etras had always been... reckless. Which had its purposes, but not in a game as intricate as this one. Not with his end goal: Dark on both thrones, his son and daughter in power, and the human world under his thrall. And the Channeller. His mouth tightened. Always she eluded him, thwarting his plans. He slammed his fist down onto the stone bench, but all that did was bruise his knuckles. His disquiet, and the feeling that things were not, for the first time in a while, going his way, persisted.

At the sound of voices he moved deeper into the shadows. One never knew what one might hear, alone in the gardens at night. He recognised one of the speakers. Ellery. He snorted. Probably cavorting with that boyfriend of hers again. Well, he had plans for her that did not involve a lesser son of lesser nobles. He heard what Tomas was telling her and he stiffened, rage almost blinding him. *Deryck.* Joining the Hunt. Well, he would see about that. He waited until the voices passed, then rose from the bench. On impulse, he followed them. It was time to remind his daughter where she stood. Then he would deal with his son.

~

ELLERY CLOSED HER EYES, THE DAMPNESS FROM THE GRASS seeping through her dress. This was heaven, or something like it. She and Tomas were lying beneath a tree, the tangled branches making patterns like black lace against the sky. Small lanterns were scattered around them, like fallen stars on the grass. She pressed against Tomas, wanting him closer. Oh, she liked him so much. If only her life wasn't so complicated. She pulled away from the thought as his arms tightened around her, his kisses becoming deeper, her hands sliding down his back and lower still. He gasped and raised his head. She saw the gleam of his teeth as he smiled. Then his mouth was on her neck, moving down to her shoulder, his hands sliding the fabric of her dress down. She stiffened.

'What is it? Shall I stop?' He lifted his head, a lock of dark hair escaping his ponytail and curling against his cheek.

She shook her head. 'No, it's not that.' She couldn't move, though.

He tilted his head, half smiling, half frowning. Then his smile slid away as his gaze went to her shoulder.

'Ellery, who has hurt you?'

Movement returned. She swallowed, pulling her dress back up over her shoulder, covering the bruises there.

'It's nothing. I-I was just out riding and I fell and—'

'Those are finger marks.' His hands, so gentle, slid the fabric from her shoulder once more, moving it further down her arm. He bent and kissed the marks one by one, his lips warm on her skin. She sobbed, unable to help it, at how gentle he was. He cupped her face in his hands and kissed her.

'Tell me,' he said again. 'Let me help you.'

'I don't... I can't talk about it.' She turned her head away, her heart breaking.

Tomas rolled off her, sitting up. Ellery, cold to the bone, did the same, her head hanging so all she could see was her skirts, his long legs in breeches tucked into leather boots. She tried to focus on them – the shine in the dark brown leather, a small scuff on one toe, the way they wrinkled around his ankles. But they blurred so much she couldn't see them anymore. And Tomas was there, his arms around her once more.

'Hey, it's all right. You don't have to tell me.'

She rested her head on his chest, soft wool beneath her cheek. The sound of his heartbeat was calming. She took a moment, wanting to enjoy it before he had to let her go again.

'M-my father. He's not been the same since, well...' It was a release to say it. 'And I'm fine now.'

Tomas tensed against her. 'Your father! But he has no right—'

Ellery lifted her head. 'He has every right. And you know it. Who would stop him?' He stared at her, looking so sad and worried her heart twisted in her chest.

'But your brother. Can he not—'

'Deryck can't do anything.' Her mouth tightened. 'I mean, I think sometimes he wants to, but he's just so, I don't know, distant.' She sighed. 'Please,' she said. 'I don't want to spoil the evening. You're the only thing, the only one–' She couldn't go on.

Tomas bent to kiss her once more. 'I'm here for you,' he murmured against her mouth. 'You're not alone.'

'Ellery.' The voice was sharp, coming out of the darkness. She and Tomas came apart as though stung, scrambling to their feet.

'Father.' Ellery bowed her head.

'My Lord.' Tomas bowed, though Ellery thought he might have hesitated for a moment. She loved him for it.

Denoris nodded to Tomas, his expression reserved, then took Ellery by the arm. She flinched as his fingers pressed into her bruises. Her father's nostrils flared, his mouth tightening. She didn't dare look at Tomas.

'Come, daughter. The hour is late and you should be at home.' His tone was mild but the pressure on her arm was enough for her to know he was angry.

'Of course.' She smiled at her father, patting his hand, proud that her lips were not trembling. 'I didn't realise the hour.'

'Well, then,' said Denoris, sounding slightly less stern. 'Bid farewell to your companion and let us go.'

Ellery turned to Tomas. His fists were clenched. She swallowed before speaking. 'Thank you for a lovely evening. I'll see you later.'

Her father snorted, tugging at her arm. She had no choice but to go with him. As he led her out of the garden she turned to look back. Tomas was still standing there, gilded by lantern-light, his face so full of sorrow she could hardly bear it.

She held back tears as her father pulled her across the court-yard outside the apartments. Lanterns either side of the double doors illuminating the iron thorns, sharp like the pain in her heart. He said nothing to her as he pushed the door open, but his grip on her arm was like a vice as he guided her across the small foyer to the front door of their apartment. It opened, her father's steward stepping to one side to let them in. Inside it was warm. The door to her father's study was half open, golden light spilling across the tiled floor. It looked peaceful, a haven against the night. She knew it was not.

'Sit,' he said as they entered the room, finally letting go of her arm. She resisted the urge to rub it, even though it ached, bone-deep. Her father fixed her with a green glare and she went to one of the armchairs and sat down, though she didn't relax against the soft cushions.

'You're not wearing your tallus stone.'

Her mouth opened and closed. 'I... er... it's valuable, Father. I didn't wish to lose it in the gardens.'

'The chain I had made for it is strong. You wouldn't lose it, if you didn't take it off. Were you planning to take it off? Or anything else?'

Ellery's face burned like fire. 'What?' she whispered.

'With that boy.' Denoris went over to his desk, his shadow flickering across the carved dragons, their jewelled eyes catching the light. He unstoppered the decanter there and poured himself a drink. 'I saw you. In the gardens with him.'

'Father, I—'

'I don't mind that you amuse yourself,' he went on, taking a drink. 'But you must remember who you are. Who your family are. I have plans for you.'

Ellery's stomach lurched. 'What plans?'

'Change is coming,' Denoris said, waving his glass at her. 'Power will shift, and alliances need to be made. The Dark do not marry for love if there's an advantage to be gained. And you, daughter of the most powerful Lord of the Dark, are a valuable asset.'

Ellery's eyes stung. An asset. That was all he thought of her. Not a daughter. She'd had no illusions about her worth to him, but to hear it put so plainly hurt. Her heart clenched as she looked at him, armour clad, golden and handsome, leaning against his desk. If only he loved her as she did him.

'What about what I want?' She said it quietly, not wanting to anger him, even though she could feel her own anger beginning to build.

'What do you want?' He sounded scornful. 'Love? You see what love does. You see what it's done to your brother, what it did to your mother.'

'M-my mother?' Ellery went cold, tears forming in her eyes at the thought of the small gravestone in the nearby village. She doubted her father even knew it was there.

'Yes.' He waved his glass. 'She wanted love, even though I told her, I *told* her, I couldn't give it to her. And look where it got her.'

Was he drunk again? She could probably count on one hand the number of times he'd ever mentioned her mother to her, and certainly not in any detail. More in a you're-mad-like-she-was kind of vein. Her anger intensified at his casual manner.

'Where did it get her, Father?' She kept her voice meek, her eyes down, even though she wanted to get up and smash the drink in his face. Yes, let him tell her. He didn't know she already knew what he'd done, leaving her mother to die in the woods, to give birth alone.

Denoris looked down into his drink. 'It made her mad,' he said softly. 'If she hadn't followed me—'

Ellery waited, her heart pounding. 'Followed you? Where?'

Denoris said nothing. His hand went to his neck and he pulled his tallus stone from under his armour and closed his eyes. He shuddered, briefly, then sat straighter. His eyes came open and fixed on her, clear and fierce. She tensed.

'Love, Ellery, is dangerous unless returned, unless you're equal in every way. Only then can it work. And love—' he stood up '—is not what you're going to get from that boy. Do you understand me?'

Ellery pushed down her anger, her sorrow. She would never tell her father about her mother lying cold and alone in a graveyard far from home. He would probably rip the grave up and raze the chapel while he was at it. It would remain her secret, a cold hard stone in her heart. But Tomas...

'Don't hurt him.'

Her father came to her, swift like a snake striking. He leaned over her, an arm either side of her resting on the chair.

'I shall do what is necessary, daughter, to ensure the success of our plans. You would do well to remember that I expect the same of you.' His face was so close to hers she could feel his breath. She felt sick, wishing she could squirm away. She swallowed, and his green eyes tracked the movement. Her mouth opened and he shook his head.

'Do not say another word. Play with your boy, if that's what you wish. For now. Do you understand I'm being lenient with you?'

She nodded.

His mouth curved in a smile. 'Good. Next time I see you, I expect you to be wearing your tallus stone. Do not disobey me again.'

She nodded again, sure she was going to throw up. Her father stared at her a moment longer, then stood up. 'Leave me.'

She got to her feet, her legs shaking, and left the room.

CHAPTER 5

SECRETS SHARED

Alma slung her bag on the sofa, then switched on the kettle.
'Tea, mum?' she asked. Eleanor was sitting at the
kitchen table, reading the paper. She looked up.

'Why, hello, Alma, how was your first week at school? Recovered yet?' Her tone was dry

Alma stuck her tongue out as she opened and closed
cupboards, getting mugs and sugar.

'Not so bad, I guess.' She turned, leaning on the counter with
her arms folded.

'So what will you do now? Head out to the park?'

'What?' Alma frowned. 'Er, I don't know.' She hadn't been to
the park since her return from Wales. She hadn't wanted to be
anywhere near the Gate, or be reminded of the last time she was
there, of her hands thick with soil as she buried Deryck's keep-
sakes and letters, her heart breaking. It had been different in
Wales – she'd been able to handle it there. Sort of. She knew she
had to face it at some point, though, if she wanted to see her
grandfather. She realised her mother was staring at her.

'What?'

Eleanor sat back, folding the paper, still holding Alma's gaze. 'I think you should see your grandfather.'

Alma's mouth dropped open. *'What?'*

'He always wanted to know you. And now I know you've been there–' her voice faltered '–you should go again. See him. Get him to tell you about your father.' Her blue eyes were bright with unshed tears.

Alma shook her head. She swallowed. 'Oh, Mum.' She paused. 'I've already seen him. He knows. That I know.' The words fell out before she could stop them.

Her mother raised her eyebrows. 'You have? Where?'

Eurgh. Alma made a face. How to explain this one? Thinking fast, she decided to stick with a half-truth. 'Er, during the summer. I didn't mean to cross over, but I had the chance to and so, I did.'

Which was true. She hadn't planned any of it, thinking she'd never be back in Ambeth again. But since the events leading up to her finding the Cup she'd gone back through the Stone Gate several times to see Artos. Even though it terrified her to be in Ambeth, and she didn't stay long, she wanted to see him, to make sure he was all right. He'd almost fully healed from Etras' attack, but she was still worried about him. Plus, it was lovely to get to know him. She pushed the thought of Deryck from her mind.

The kettle was boiling and Eleanor went to pick it up, pouring water into the mugs and stirring in the sugar. 'Did you use the Gate near your grandmother's house?'

Alma's jaw dropped.

'What do you mean? How do you...?' she squeaked, staring at her mother.

Eleanor grinned. 'You know I was there with your father. He showed me, one day when we were out in the hills.' Eleanor added milk to the tea, stirring it.

'Oh.' Understanding washed over Alma. *Of course.*

'But how did you find it?' Eleanor continued, handing Alma

her tea, her tone conversational, like she wasn't blowing Alma's mind.

Alma blinked. 'Er, well, it was kind of an accident. I was out walking in the hills, then I saw the stones and went through and realised I was in Ambeth. Lucky I had my bracelet on,' she said, holding up her wrist. 'So, I thought I'd go down to the Hall, just to see, and well, I saw him there, and I told him I knew. And well, I saw him a few more times after that.' Great. More lies. What a load of nonsense. But, despite all they'd already shared, Alma wasn't ready to tell her mother about the whole Prophecy/Chosen One thing. And definitely not the Channelling thing. She tensed, grimacing slightly, but her mother just nodded, taking a sip of her tea.

'I would have told you about the Gate,' she said, 'if I'd known you wanted to go back there. But you just seemed so against it.'

'Well, I was,' said Alma, still unable to believe how calmly her mother was taking it all. 'But sometimes you can't turn your back on something. At least, that's what I've found.'

Eleanor smiled. 'Well, I'm glad.'

'You are?' The surprises kept coming. Alma sat down on the sofa. 'I mean, I wasn't sure if you would be, you know?'

'It's right that you should know about Ambeth. It's part of you, after all.' Eleanor shook her head. 'It was only my own fear, you know, that stopped me from letting you go through to see him.'

'Oh, Mum.' Alma's mouth twisted and she felt teary, thinking of her mum, so young, losing Alma's father and having to deal with it all by herself. No wonder she'd found it easier to forget, to push it aside.

'So, why don't you go tonight? Dinner isn't for an hour yet.'

Alma gripped her mug. It was burning her fingers, but it helped her keep focus. 'Er, maybe. You don't know, I mean, is there another Gate near here?'

Eleanor tilted her head to one side. 'Is it that boy?'

Alma looked away. She heard her mother sigh.

'It is, isn't it?'

Alma squeezed her lips tight and tried not to roll her eyes. 'What?'

'I know you were hurt.'

'I don't want to talk about it.'

'I'm not asking you to. All I'm saying is, don't let that hurt stop you from knowing your grandfather. Don't let it keep you away.'

But her mother didn't get it. Out in the mountains, at the Stone Gate, she'd felt safer. Beran or, once he'd recovered, her grandfather, would meet her there, taking her back to the Palace and straight to his quarters, where they could spend time together without her having to see anyone else. She wasn't even sure whether Thorion knew she'd been coming across. But to cross at the Oak Gate? Apart from the memories it held, she worried that Deryck had put a trap there or would be watching it, waiting for her to come through. Or worse, his father.

'I'll think about it,' was all she said.

'I hope you do.'

Alma nodded, picking up her tea and taking it upstairs to her room. She needed to be alone and think about everything. She was also still shaken by her meeting with Ethan. Even though they'd exchanged numbers and parted with a promise to catch up and talk about what they were going to do next, Alma still wasn't even sure if she wanted to look for the Crown. But, she realised, she did want to see Ethan again.

She put her tea down on the bedside table and flopped back on her bed, staring at the ceiling. It was all very well for Thorion to have sent Ethan to help her, but she hadn't the faintest clue where to find the Crown. She remembered the hours she'd spent in the library with Caleb, the pale sun turning his hair to gold as they'd looked through crumbling scrolls and old notebooks. Her eyes prickled and she squeezed them shut. How the hell was she supposed to go back there, sit at the table where they'd sat, act as though everything was all right, while the ache of his absence pulled at her like a rotten tooth in her mind. Maybe Merewyn could help, she thought, reaching for her phone. It buzzed in her hand as she picked it up and she jumped, almost dropping it. The screen lit up with a message. From Ethan.

U want to go to the park later? Hot chocolate, I'm buying. What do u say?

Shit. What should she say? She held her phone close to her chest, her heart pounding. Despite her fear, she was tempted. And a big part of that was because of the connection she'd felt between them. She knew Ethan would keep her safe, no matter what. It was strange to feel that way, after only meeting him twice, but she couldn't shake how it had felt in the woods, when she'd thought all hope was lost, and he'd helped her. So maybe she should go and meet him, hear what he had to say, at least.

She began to type.

CHAPTER 6
A NEW DAY

Thorion woke and rolled over, his hand reaching across the bed. But it was empty. Frowning, he turned the other way. She was there, silhouetted against the rising sun. Adara. Her chin in her hand, she gazed out of the window, perfectly poised – it was hard to believe she was the same one who had arched above him in the cool dark of the night, crying out as he'd felt his own release. Happiness surged through him, that they'd found their way to each other after all they'd been through. Smiling at the memory, Thorion rose from the bed.

'What is it you see, my love?'

She turned, the first rays of the sun shining golden around her. 'Beauty,' she replied.

He came to stand next to her, meeting her hazel gaze with his own. 'As do I, beloved.' He touched her face and she leaned into him, warm silk against his skin. Desire surged. 'Come back to bed, my lady. There is time still, before we have to start the day.'

'COME IN, MY LADY. IT'S NICE TO SEE YOU AGAIN.'

Ellery smiled, warmed by Mari's welcome. The woman's home was a calm refuge from the darkness of her own life. 'It's nice to see you, too,' she said, ducking under the low doorframe as she entered the small stone cottage.

'Come through,' said Mari, leading Ellery to the bright work-room at the rear of the house. It was much as Ellery had seen it the last time she was there. A scattering of gems lay on a silk scrap next to curls of metal on the worn workbench, a stool pulled up to it. Through the large windows the forest loomed, the trees soft with spring green. Mari patted another stool, next to a bookcase. 'Come, sit,' she said. 'Shall I make tea?'

'I'm afraid I can't stay long. Sorry.' Ellery perched on the stool, her hands twisting in her lap. No one knew she was here – she'd told her father she was going for a walk. Deryck was shut away in his room as usual.

'Ah.' Mari nodded, pressing her lips together.

Ellery frowned, then felt bad. If it wasn't for Mari...

'I have to thank you,' she said. Her voice was rough and she cleared her throat. 'For last time.'

Mari tilted her head, birdlike, her eyes catching the light.

'For telling me about my— about Grace.'

The other woman's expression softened. 'Oh my dear.' She came closer. 'Did you...?'

Ellery nodded, close to tears. 'I did.' She'd gone to see her mother's grave in the small churchyard, just where Mari had said it would be. She closed her eyes for a moment, trying to shut out the thought of her mother in labour, alone and afraid, left in the woods by her father. Rage pulsed through her, her resolve against him hardening. This was the first step in getting out from under his control. She opened her eyes. Mari stepped back, her lips parting.

'Er, my lady. Shall I show you the necklace?'

'If you would, please.'

Mari went to a small cupboard set into the wall, unlocking it with a key she pulled from her pocket. She retrieved a small silk pouch before closing and locking it again. She turned to Ellery.

'Here it is.' She pulled the drawstring mouth of the pouch apart, tipping the contents onto her palm.

It was perfect. Ellery had worn her tallus, both for comparison's sake and to appease her father, though she'd been careful to choose a high-necked gown, not wanting to take any chances with it touching her skin. The necklace in Mari's palm was a perfect match – the black stone, red glinting in its inky depths, cradled in a silver mount of twining ivy leaves so delicate they almost seemed to tremble.

'Oh!' She lifted her gaze to Mari, who was smiling. 'It's perfect. You're a genius, I mean, you have no idea how much—' She stopped short. She was rambling. The relief coursing through her was overwhelming. She hadn't realised what a weight her tallus had become. She took in a breath, collecting herself. As nice as Mari was, she didn't need to know any more about why Ellery needed the necklace. 'It really is perfect. Thank you.'

Mari placed the necklace back in the pouch before handing it over. Ellery stood, tucking it carefully into a deep pocket in her skirt. She reached into her other pocket, feeling for the small bag of gold. 'What do I owe you?'

Mari swallowed, looking away for a moment before meeting her gaze. She lifted her chin slightly. 'It's a gift.'

Ellery's brows drew together. 'A gift? What do you mean? I can pay you for it.'

'My dear, please. Let me give it to you. In memory of your mother.'

Ellery's stomach dropped. 'I can't possibly—'

'Please,' Mari said again. 'When your mother, when she was here, when she'd passed, well,' she paused, pursing her lips. 'She had some jewellery with her, a couple of rings and a necklace. You were gone with your father, of course, and there was no way of getting them to you, you understand, so it was thought best that they be buried with her. But I always felt sad, that they couldn't have gone to you. And, well, it seems to me you might need this necklace for reasons of your own. So please, take it as a gift. From your mother, via me.'

Ellery couldn't speak. Her mouth was open, her lips moving, but sound seemed to be locked inside her by the ball of pain in her throat. The tears that had threatened before now spilled from her eyes. Mari was standing straight, but the hand resting on her workbench was clenched, the knuckles white. Twice now she'd risked herself, risked what Ellery might do, who she might tell, to give her something of her long dead mother. Ellery finally found her voice.

'Thank you,' she whispered. She wiped her cheeks. 'You have no idea—' She stopped again. She couldn't involve Mari in her pain, even though her kindness was another cut of the blade. 'I have to go,' she whispered. 'I'm sorry, I'm so grateful – I just, I don't—'

'My dear.' Mari came closer, laying her hand on Ellery's arm, just as she had on her previous visit. The other woman's touch was warm, a lifeline in the storm that was threatening to consume her. 'If you ever need anything, come here. There will always be a place for you.'

Everything was blurry. Ellery nodded. 'Thank you,' she whispered again, knowing it wasn't adequate, that it could never be, for what Mari had given her. On impulse she reached out, hugging Mari briefly before letting go and turning, running from the cottage with her hand to her mouth.

'*ARE YOU INSANE?*' THE WORDS SLICED THROUGH THE AIR.

Deryck didn't back down, his mouth tight and shoulders square. His father was standing behind his desk, the carved dragons vibrating as he struck it with his closed fist. Deryck tried not to wince. The last vestiges of his hangover clung on, despite the effects of his tallus stone. The Hunt had kept him drinking deep into the night. He had a vague memory of stumbling through the darkened gardens, Floria holding him up until he reached the apartments. He'd woken up alone, though.

'I don't know what you mean.'

His eyes widened as Denoris came around from behind his desk. His father was in full armour, dark leather strapped to his muscular frame, black cape billowing behind him. 'If you think,' he said, pointing a finger at Deryck, 'that I'm going to let my son, my *only* son, join a ragtag group of lesser nobles to hunt the hills like a bunch of lunatics, you are sorely mistaken! I have plans for you, and they do not involve joining the Dark Hunt!' His father's voice rose to a roar.

'It's too late. I've already spoken the ritual words.'

'Then you will unspeak them.' Denoris was almost nose-to-nose with him, his green eyes narrowed, fists balled at his sides. Deryck clenched his own fists.

'I cannot. And, I don't want to.'

Denoris raised his arm and Deryck took a step back. 'Hit me, Father, and I swear, I'll hit you back.'

Denoris snarled. 'You dare, do you?'

'I'm bored!' Deryck shouted. 'Bored of waiting for Alma to come back to me. I'm starting to believe she never will, so maybe it's time for me to do something else. At least the Hunt want me with them.' As he said the words he realised, painful as it was, that they were true. She wasn't coming back to him. The thought deflated him and his head drooped.

'Deryck.' He lifted his head, surprised. His father's mood seemed to have changed.

'What?'

'Don't lose hope.'

Deryck screwed up his face, shaking his head. 'What hope is

there, Father? If she was coming back, she would have been here by now. I have to face it.'

'She has been coming back.'

'What?' Deryck whispered the word. It was as though he'd just been punched in the gut.

'She's been coming back. I've told you this already, remember? Only a few times, to meet with her grandfather. Who is, as you know, dealing with me on this matter.'

Oh. Of course. She'd been to see her grandfather. He paused. He was still shaken by the revelation that Alma was Galen's daughter, that she wasn't fully human as he'd thought her to be. 'So you've spoken to him?'

'About the match? Yes, of course. I wouldn't lie to you about this. I know what it means to you.'

Deryck hesitated. He hoped his father wouldn't lie to him. Not about something as important as this. But his father was capable of just about anything when it came to getting what he wanted. His mouth twisted before he spoke. 'Well, that's good, then.'

'It is.' His father frowned. 'And I doubt she would want you endangering yourself with the Hunt and their obscure vendettas. I have more planned for you than you know.'

'You've used them.' The words slipped out. Denoris blinked. Deryck ploughed on. 'You were happy for them to try and catch her, that day.'

'It was your sister who called them, not I,' Denoris replied.

'Still, you would have been pleased, if they'd got her.' Deryck reached for his tallus, not liking the pain of the memory.

Denoris sat on the edge of his desk, one hand rubbing his chin. 'So she's still prey, then?'

Deryck went cold. 'What?'

'The girl. She evaded them once. The Hunt do not give up, not until the prey is dead or the chase called off. You would hunt her, if she crossed their path?'

'No! Never!'

Denoris raised an eyebrow. 'Well. Perhaps it's for the best that you've joined them, after all. You can keep them away from her.' He fixed Deryck with his green gaze. 'If you must ride with them, do that at least.'

'So you won't stop me?' Deryck's hand closed around his stone and a pulse of darkness ran through him.

Denoris shrugged. 'You've taken the vow, I suppose. And if it keeps you busy, stops you moping around the place, then I'll allow it. For now.' He glared at Deryck. 'But only on the condition that you keep them away from the girl.'

Deryck nodded. He opened his mouth to speak but his father hadn't finished. 'And remember, this isn't forever. Once you're reunited with the girl, there will be other things for you to do.'

THE STUDY DOOR CLOSED WITH A BANG AS HIS SON LEFT THE room. Denoris blew out a long breath. That was a complication. He was angry with himself for missing it – he was never normally one to let a detail slide. He blinked, reaching for his tallus, letting dark energy move through him. With it came anger at his daughter. Stupid girl, calling the Hunt like that! Now they were involved, he didn't fancy Alma's chances if she crossed their path again, and he needed her alive, not dead.

No, he needed to sort this out. And, while he was at it, it was time to get his daughter settled. Let her become someone else's problem. He went to the door and called for his steward.

He was tired, more tired than he could remember being in all his long years. But there was much yet to be done.

When his steward appeared, panting, he told him his instructions. The man disappeared once more. Leaning on the doorframe, Denoris smiled.

The game was still in play.

CHAPTER 7
STARS COLLIDE

'M um, I'm going out.'
'But your dinner's almost ready and—'
'To the park.'

Eleanor stopped stirring the pot on the stove and turned to Alma, who was waiting at the kitchen door. 'The park? To see—?'

Alma nodded. 'Yes.' She grinned. 'And I'm not going alone.' She wasn't. It hadn't taken her long to reply to Ethan. *Okay,* she'd written. *Sounds good.*

And we can cross over?

Not sure, she'd messaged back.

Buy you a hot chocolate and we can talk about it?

Eleanor frowned. 'But, who—'

'I'll explain later. So can I go then? I won't be long.'

Eleanor nodded. 'You've got an hour.'

There was a knock at the side door. Alma darted into the kitchen and gave her mother a kiss on the cheek. 'Thanks, mum.' She went back into the hallway and opened the door. Ethan stood there, hands in pockets, dark hair falling forward over his eyes. He was wearing a sweatshirt with jeans and leather laced boots. Alma took a breath, her stomach swirling.

'Hi.'

'Hey.'

'Um, so—' A hand touched her arm and Alma realised her mother was behind her. She turned to her. 'Um, Mum, this is Ethan.'

Ethan held out his hand. 'Pleased to meet you, Mrs Bevan.'

'Oh, just call me Eleanor.' She came around Alma and took his hand. 'Mrs Bevan makes me sound so old.'

Ethan grinned. 'Shall we go, then, before it gets too dark?'

Eleanor raised her eyebrows.

'Yeah, we should get going, hey?' Alma stepped outside, turning to wave to her mother, who mouthed the word 'Cute'. Alma scowled, shaking her head.

Eleanor laughed and closed the door.

'So, how are you?' asked Ethan as they walked down the street. The evening was cool and clear, the sun beginning to set.

'I'm fine,' said Alma. She was still embarrassed by how she'd clung to him in the woods. It was strange, like they'd already been intimate even though they didn't really know each other. She followed him through the narrow gate to the field, trailing her hand over the old oak tree, the energy beneath the rough bark buzzing against her finger. She headed down the slope towards the road. Ethan waited for her to catch up. As she fell into step with him he glanced at her.

'Um, I know this is a bit—'

'Weird?' said Alma. They both laughed.

'Yeah, weird,' said Ethan, hands in pockets. He had dimples when he smiled, and Alma liked them. She realised she wanted to see him smile more often.

'But it doesn't have to be,' he went on. 'I mean, I know how we met, we both know what happened, but now we're here and... maybe we can just start again?'

Alma nodded. 'I like that idea,' she said. 'Especially if we're supposed to be working together.'

'So, any ideas?' Ethan asked as they walked beneath the stone bridge, his voice echoing under the cool arch.

'Nope, not a clue,' said Alma. They emerged on the edge of the park and started across the rolling grass, heading towards the small café. He walked close to her; not close enough to touch, but only just. She liked that, too. 'But that's no different from any other time.' She laughed. 'I never had any idea about where to find the Sword or the Cup, either – just ended up in the right place at the right time.'

'Really? Huh, that's cool.'

They reached the café and Ethan turned to her.

'Hot chocolate?'

Alma nodded. 'Yeah. Thanks.'

He grinned. 'And then you can tell me more about your uncanny ability to find things without even looking.' He held the door for her and they went in, ordering their drinks at the small counter. 'Shall we sit in or out?'

'Oh, out. It's a wild sky tonight.'

'What?' Ethan tilted his head. One corner of his mouth crooked up.

'Huh.' Alma didn't know where to look. She hadn't meant to let that slip, not yet. 'Er...'

'C'mon.' Ethan shepherded her outside, holding the door again, and they found a table near the hedge, away from the other customers. Alma sat down and Ethan took the chair opposite.

'Okay,' he said. 'Tell me about your "wild sky".'

Alma leaned her elbows on the table, looking up for a moment. How was she going to explain this? She decided to go with the truth. He knew about Ambeth, at least, so that was a start. 'Well, you know who my father is, right?'

'Galen?'

Alma nodded. 'Well, as I understand it, he could feel the energy of the land and sense where the Balance was off. His brother could as well. Together they could actually affect the energy of a place – restore it, if it had been damaged.'

Ethan raised his eyebrows. 'Wow.'

'I know, right? Well—' She stopped speaking as the waitress came out with their drinks. Alma reached for her mug of hot chocolate and took a sip, licking chocolate sprinkles and cream from her lips, her eyes closing in enjoyment. When she opened them Ethan was watching her. She blushed. He smiled – more dimples – lifting his mug to her.

'To working together.'

Alma clinked her mug with his, laughing, then took another sip. It was good hot chocolate. 'So anyway,' she said. 'It turns out I can do it, too.'

'Do what? Oh! Um, right, the land sensing thing. Really? You can do that?' He leaned forward.

'Yep.' Alma took another gulp of hot chocolate. 'Grandfather is helping me understand my "gift".' She grinned, making air quotes with her fingers. Ethan smiled too, his eyes reflecting the glowing sky. 'I'm something called a Channeller. It's pretty rare, actually, so he's pleased.'

'And what about you? Are you pleased?'

Alma sat back, cradling her mug, enjoying the warmth of it in the cool dusk. 'Um, yeah, I guess I am,' she said finally. 'It's nice to have something from my father, other than the red hair.' She took a handful, laughing a little. 'I wish I'd known him, you know? But at least I can talk to Artos about it.'

'So is that why you said it was a "wild sky?"' He looked up, as did Alma. The sky was a gleaming gold shading to blue. Feathery deep purple clouds moved across it, and the first few stars were coming out. Alma closed her eyes.

'I can feel it,' she murmured. 'It's something about the air, and the way it moves, and the clear colours. It's all in balance.' She opened her eyes to look at him. 'I've always loved this time of day anyway.'

'Huh.'

'What?'

'Oh, it's just this is my favourite time of day, too. The in-between time.' He half laughed, looking down. 'Sorry, that sounds a bit—'

'No, that's what I think, too,' said Alma. 'Like, anything's possible.' She looked away, feeling shy once more. What was wrong with her? 'Um, so...' She cast around, wanting something else to say. 'What about you?'

Ethan shook his head. 'What about me?'

'Do you have any powers from your father?' Then she blushed, wondering if it was too soon to ask. But he'd asked her. God, she really needed to calm down. Her skin felt as though it were on fire.

'Not really. I mean, nothing special. Not like you.' Ethan held her gaze and something passed between them, intense and warm. Then he broke the moment to glance at his watch. It was a nice watch, chunky dark metal against his wrist.

'We should go soon, I guess.' His mouth twisted. 'Are you okay to go through now? Thorion will want to know that we're together, er, you know, working I mean.'

'Oh! Right,' said Alma, distracted by his mouth as he talked, the shadowed cheekbones, the way he'd said 'together.' Then her eyes widened. 'What, through the Gate?' She looked across the park to where she knew it waited, indistinguishable now in the dusk, the trees one long dark mass at the edge of the grassy field.

'Well, yeah. We have time,' he said, looking again at his watch. 'Just a quick visit. My father doesn't like me to come across without seeing him, so I'll have to say hello. Then we can find Thorion—' He broke off. 'What's wrong?'

Alma had her hand to her mouth, the other one tapping on the table. She glanced at the trees again, remembering a silver heart tied with bright silk to one of them, letters left among leafy branches. She took in a shuddering breath.

'Hey.' Ethan reached across the table and gently touched her tapping hand.

'I just don't want to see him.' It came out as a whisper.

Ethan nodded. 'I get it. We'll go quick, through the woods and straight to the Palace. You can come with me to my father's, if you like.'

Alma shrank back in her seat.

Ethan shook his head, making a face. 'Right. No, not a good idea, I agree. Not yet, anyway.'

'Not yet?'

'Well, I'd like you to meet him someday. I mean, he's not that bad. Not like some of the others, you know.'

'Um, okay.' Alma picked up her hot chocolate again. It had gone cool but the sugary sweetness of it helped, making her feel more grounded. Energy lines were pulsing in and out all around her, a bright glow in the trees marking the Gate. Shit. She needed to pull herself together. 'I just don't know if I can do it. The Gate... I mean... what if there's something...?' She started to tap again, pulsing lines all around her.

'Hey.' His gaze was serious and she found, if she focused on it, that she could control the energy lines, like holding reins in her mind. 'I promise I won't let anything happen to you,' he said. 'If there's a trap, or he, or anyone, is there, I'll help you. Trust me. You can do this.'

Tears prickled at her eyelids. 'Promise?'

Ethan's expression softened. 'Of course. You're safe with me.' He stood up, holding out his hand. 'Come on, let's get this over with.'

Alma hesitated, then took his hand and stood up. They headed for the Gate.

'Can you cross by yourself?' Alma asked after a moment, wanting to distract herself from what was about to happen. It felt surreal, as though it was happening to someone else, someone who wasn't worried about Dark Lords and homicidal ex-boyfriends who wanted her back.

Ethan nodded. 'My father showed me how, a few years ago. He wants me to be able to choose where I want to live.'

'Really?' Alma thought about the Dark Lord Cedran, how fierce he'd seemed, the way he'd looked at her in the Great Hall when she was named as the Child of the Prophecy. It was hard to imagine him acting like anyone's father.

'Yeah. Like I said, he's different. I think you'd like him.'

'Well, um, okay.' Alma didn't know what else to say. She wasn't sure about that at all. But there was no more time to talk about it. They'd reached the Gate,

The oak trees were dark against the multi-hued sky. Two trees, no different than the others. Except they were. Alma could see the power between them, the energy twisting that she now knew denoted a Gate through to Ambeth. She swallowed, letting go of Ethan's hand.

He caught it again. 'Shall we go through together? That way I can't lose you.'

She smiled despite her fear, liking the way he said it, the feel of his hand, the calluses and soft warm skin on her own.

'Okay.' And all at once, she felt as though she could do it. As though he really would keep her safe. She pushed thoughts of Denoris, of Deryck, of dark creatures in the wood from her mind.

She took in a deep breath and closed her eyes. Her bracelet, already warm, began pulsing against her wrist. She felt an answering pulse of energy through her feet.

'Whoa! Is that you?' Alma opened her eyes to see Ethan looking at her with something like awe.

'Is what me?'

'That pulsing.'

Alma nodded. 'It's always like that for me.'

He smiled. 'Let's go, energy girl.'

She giggled despite herself and they stepped forward, passing through the Gate together, hand in hand.

CHAPTER 8
ANOTHER WORLD

'Simeon.'

'Lord Denoris.' The leader of the Dark Hunt inclined his head, one hand on the knife at his hip. His eyes were bright, watchful, the jewels on his armour glittering like blood in the firelight.

'Thank you for coming to see me. Will you sit?'

Simeon nodded again, then took a seat. 'Is this about your son, my Lord? I can assure you, the Hunt only takes on riders who choose—'

'It's not about Deryck. Not yet. There's another matter I wish to discuss.'

'Indeed?' Simeon raised an eyebrow. He settled himself back in the chair, resting one ankle on his opposite knee. His gaze flicked to the bottle on the nearby table. It came back to rest on Denoris.

The Dark Lord suppressed a frown. He needed this, so he would play the game, for now. He got up and went over to the table. He unstoppered the bottle, filled two goblets and handed one to Simeon. 'Let us drink together.'

After a pause, Simeon took the goblet. 'Thank you.' He didn't drink, though.

'Tell me, Simeon, about the girl. At the fair. The one you lost.'

'My Lord?'

Denoris pursed his lips before continuing. 'Galen's daughter.'

'The half-breed. What of her?' He leaned forward, the goblet between his fingers. 'I hear your son still has feelings for her. Are you sure this isn't about him? He's sworn to the Hunt now, and personal... attachments must be put aside.'

Denoris snorted. 'Deryck will do as he's told. No, this is about the girl, and her alone. You were called to hunt her, yet you failed. Is there a penalty for such things?'

Simeon's eyes narrowed slightly. 'There is not. The girl is still prey, until we catch her. We're accountable only to ourselves. And we do not let our prey escape.'

'But you did, in that instance.'

'We were waylaid by the King and his guards.' Simeon's expression darkened. He stared into the goblet as though he could see the scene replaying there. 'As you well know, my Lord. Your daughter was there, too, trying to keep up.'

There was scorn in the words. Denoris suppressed a smile. Good. He was getting somewhere. He went to his desk, relaxing back into his chair. 'Really? As I heard it, my daughter acquitted herself quite well. But that's not the issue here. You were asked to perform a service. You failed. I wish to know what you will do now to redeem yourself. As I see it, you're beholden to me until the deed is done.'

Simeon shifted in his seat. A line formed between his brows.

'You should know, my Lord, that the Hunt do not submit to any Lord of Ambeth.'

'You are the Dark Hunt. You ride for the Dark.'

Simeon's gaze narrowed. 'We ride for the thrill of the Hunt, and the Dark are the only ones who choose to avail themselves of our... services. Once we rode freely across the worlds.'

'Is that so?'

'It is.'

'And what about a Lord of another world?'

'My Lord?'

Denoris paused. This was a gamble. He'd not spoken openly of his plans to anyone other than Gwenene and, to a lesser extent, Cedran and Etras. He preferred the element of surprise wherever possible. But at the same time, he *needed* this.

'Would you submit to a Lord of another world? One who would let you ride beyond the Gates once more? What if someone could give you that freedom again?'

Simeon said nothing, his dark gaze on Denoris. Then he lifted the goblet to his lips and drank.

'Well, I suppose for such a lord, we might consider it.' He drew the words out, wine dark on his mouth. 'If he, or she, existed.'

Denoris waited. The hook was baited. And it was taken.

'So, what would we have to do, to gain such freedom?'

Denoris considered his next words. He knew he had him, but he still needed to be careful, just for a little while longer. 'Only this. Protect my son. And, when you do capture the girl, bring her to me. Unharmed.'

'Unharmed?' Simeon twirled the goblet between his fingers, looking into the swirling depths. Then he drank again. 'And you would be grateful?'

Denoris raised his own goblet, drinking deep.

'I would.'

'YOU ALL RIGHT?'

'Yes, fine. You?' Ethan, still holding Alma's hand, was breathing hard, sweat on his brow. Of course. She remembered how it used to be for her, the sickness of crossing. Gently, so he wouldn't notice, she pulsed energy into his hand. His expression cleared and he straightened up, smiling at her.

'Yeah. Let's go.'

The familiar path stretched before them, twisting through the woods to the field beyond. Pain started in Alma's chest, her breath quickening. She swallowed, letting go of Ethan's hand and wiping her palm on her jacket.

Head down, she started along the path. He said nothing, just kept up with her, his presence warm at her side. She was trying not to cry, to focus and just get through. Memories crowded in from all sides. The tree Deryck had pulled her behind for a kiss, the first time he walked her to the Gate. Caleb, smiling, dressed in green and brown, waiting for her the first time she crossed over. She could hardly bear it, almost running as they crossed the meadow towards the Gardens. It was early Spring, green misting the bare branches, the evergreen hedges dark against the blue sky. 'Not the Long Walk,' she muttered. 'I know another way.'

When they reached the edge of the gardens she turned, making her way along a dark hedge taller than she was. She reached a small archway and went through. Ethan followed, hurrying to catch up. They emerged into a small square garden with high hedges all around, benches set around a scrap of lawn and a single sculpted tree in the centre. An archway opposite led out. Alma made straight for it, but Ethan caught her arm.

'Hey,' he said, frowning. 'Alma, it's okay. Can we... will you talk to me, for a sec?'

She stared at him then nodded. 'Sorry.'

'Come on, let's sit down.' Alma let him pull her over to one of the benches and sat down. She put her face in her hands and leant forward, trying to slow her breath. Energy lines pulsed in and out. Ethan put his hand on her back and they stopped, the world returning to normal.

She turned to him, managing a weak smile. 'Sorry,' she said again. 'It's just, I don't want to see him.'

Ethan looked at her, his head tilted to one side, blue eyes shrewd. 'What did he do to you?'

'Other than killing Caleb?'

'No, I know about that,' said Ethan. 'Of course I do.' His voice was gentle.

'He broke my heart,' she said. 'And despite all that, despite what he did, there's a part of me that still cares about what happens to him. And that sucks.'

'Alma—'

'He came to take me again,' she went on, sitting up. 'This past summer, when I was in Wales. He came through a Gate to find me, wanted me to come back here with him, to be with him again like we were before.'

Ethan's face stretched with shock. '*What?* Was he serious?'

'Of course he was.' Alma chewed on her lip. 'And you know what the worst part was?' Ethan shook his head slowly.

'Part of me, a very small part, wanted to go with him.' Her voice was barely a whisper. 'I hated myself for that, because at the same time I was so angry, you know?'

'I'm sorry.'

'No, it's fine now. I-I don't want him. I never would go back to him. But for a time, for a while, he was... wonderful. Huh.' She realised it was important Ethan knew she wasn't going back to Deryck. She also knew what that meant. He smiled at her, just a half-smile, and all at once she wanted to touch him, touch his face.

'I won't let anything happen to you.' He started to lean in closer, his hand sliding on her back. She took a breath. Then footsteps came along the path and she jumped, her head turning. Ethan stood up.

'Stay here.' He went towards the gap in the hedge and stuck his head through, then looked back at Alma. 'It's all right,' he said. 'Just another courtier.' She nodded, making a face. Damn. That was very nearly a moment. Then more footsteps came along, crunching on the gravel. She got up from the bench to stand near Ethan, tense with fear. But this time it was a familiar face.

'Grandfather!' Alma stepped through the hedge. Artos turned at the sound of her voice, his face lighting up as she ran to him for a hug.

'Alma, my dear, this is a joyous surprise!' He smiled at her, his silver gold hair shining in the sun. 'I wasn't expecting you today!' He looked concerned. 'Are you all right, has something happened?'

'No, no, I'm fine,' said Alma. Then she remembered Ethan. 'Grandfather, I'd like you to meet someone.' Ethan came to stand next to her, bowing. Artos raised his eyebrows at Alma and grinned. She smiled back.

'Ethan, this is my grandfather, Lord Artos,' she said. 'Grandfather, this is my friend Ethan. He's—'

'Cedran's boy, if I'm not mistaken,' said Artos, extending a hand to Ethan, who took it, giving him a hearty handshake.

'That's right, sir,' said Ethan.

Artos looked at Ethan for a moment, appraising him. He seemed to approve. 'So, what brings you both to Ambeth today?

'Well, we're here to see Thorion, actually,' said Alma.

'And I owe my father a visit,' added Ethan.

'Shall we go to the Hall? I'm heading that way anyway. Luncheon is about to be served and I think your father will be there, Ethan, as will Thorion.'

'Sounds good.' Ethan nodded, starting along the path with Artos.

Alma didn't move. Her heart was pounding, her breath coming fast, her arms wrapped around herself. Ethan stopped and turned, as did Artos. His dark brows drew together. Artos, however, came back to her, putting his hand on her arm.

'Ah, of course. How about, instead, I arrange for lunch in my rooms? You can both join me, if you would like.'

Alma blew out a breath. She nodded but couldn't speak. For a moment she just wanted to turn and run, back through the woods to the Gate and home. But her grandfather, his face soft with kindness, was waiting.

Ethan held out his hand. 'Come on. You'll be fine with us.' He turned to Artos. 'Thank you, sir, but if it's all the same, I'll find my father. Plus, I can speak to Thorion, let him know we need to talk to him.'

Alma took Ethan's hand, not at all sure she would be okay. She tried to come across when it wasn't busy, wanting to avoid crowds. Not just because of who she might see, but because of her notoriety in Ambeth. Most people knew who she was, what she'd done, and she still struggled with their attention. But done was done, and at least she could make her escape to her grandfather's apartment.

Holding Ethan's hand, she started walking. Her grandfather fell into step on her other side. The three of them made their way towards the Palace looming above the gardens, its white walls shining in the pale sunshine. The guards were there as usual, opening the doors to the steady stream of people heading inside for lunch. Alma stayed close to Artos and Ethan, walking between them as they entered the Foyer, pretending it was all cool. Ethan had let go of her hand, but she could feel him, his steady strength comforting.

'Ethan!' A voice called across the Foyer and all three of them turned to see the magnificent figure of Lord Cedran approaching, clad in dark grey armour. Despite the armour he looked quite different to the forbidding warrior Alma remembered. His handsome face was smiling, revealing the same dimples as Ethan. Alma rubbed at her wrist, her bracelet burning hot.

'My Lord.' Ethan bowed his head to his father, who nodded in return.

'I was not expecting you today. How is your mother?'

'She is well, sir, and sends her regards.'

'Does she indeed? I'm glad to hear she's well. Please give her my regards as always.' His gaze moved to Alma and Artos, a question forming on his face.

'Uh, father, you know Lord Artos, of course, and this is his granddaughter, Alma.'

'From the Prophecy.' Cedran came up to her. He nodded to Artos, who returned the gesture, then fixed Alma with his dark gaze. She tensed, resisting the urge to shrink into her grandfather's side. Artos put his hand on her back, just above her waist, and she felt a small pulse of energy from him, of pure love. It calmed her enough to return the Dark Lord's smile.

'Lord Cedran, it's a pleasure to meet you,' she said.

'It's always a pleasure to meet a friend of Ethan's,' he replied. 'Will you be joining us for lunch?' He was polite, pleasant, but Alma couldn't relax totally.

Artos stepped in. 'No, Cedran, though I thank you for the invitation. Alma will be lunching with me today, in private.'

Cedran marked her again with his dark eyes, as though he was looking into the heart of her. Alma met his gaze, lifting her chin, and was rewarded with a half-smile.

'Well, then, I shall take my leave. Alma, I look forward to meeting with you again. Come, Ethan, let's go.'

'Alma, I'll come and get you, okay? Once everything's um, arranged.'

Cedran looked sharply at his son, his eyes narrowed slightly. Ethan glanced back at Alma, raising his hand in farewell as they walked away.

Alma turned to her grandfather, who was eyeing her shrewdly.

''Shall we go?' was all he said, offering her his arm. She took it, grateful to be getting out of the Foyer. As they started up the stairs, Artos hugged her arm to his side.

'Ethan seems very nice.' There was a question in his tone

Alma blushed. 'He's a good friend.'

'Is that all?' Artos sounded amused.

'Um, well, we're sort of working together now. Thorion asked him to help me, you know, with the last bit.'

'Ah, the search for the Crown. Yes, he's spoken of this to me.' They'd reached Artos' rooms. Artos opened the door, leading Alma into the little foyer and surprising a flustered-looking Beran. He rose to the occasion, taking Alma's jacket and arranging for lunch to be delivered all in one breath it seemed. Before she knew it, Alma was sitting on the comfortable sofa in her grandfather's sitting room, letting out a long breath as she sank back on the cushions. It was quiet and warm, with a fire crackling in the grate, and she was beyond grateful to be there. Her room was on the floor above – perhaps she should take a chance, drop in there. It had been a while since she'd seen it and she missed it, her starry ceiling and fluffy bed. She felt she could handle the memories there now. Maybe if Ethan was with her, anyway. She sat bolt upright at the thought.

Artos poured them both a drink and looked at her curiously.

'Are you all right?' He handed her a cup filled with cordial.

'Um, yes, fine.' She took a sip of her drink, letting it cool her burning cheeks. But there had definitely been a moment there, in the garden.

Artos settled down opposite her, looking at her expectantly. 'So you will look for it?'

'What – the Crown? It looks that way.' Her mouth twisted.

Artos laughed, sitting back. 'Sorry, my dear. It is just, you're so like your father. That's just the face he made when he had to do something he didn't really want to.'

Alma grinned. 'I know. I mean, I never really did much to find the other two pieces. It just sort of... happened.'

'And Ethan's going to help you?' Artos waggled his eyebrows.

Alma giggled. 'It's not like that. I mean, I don't think it is. I don't know...'

'I just want you to be happy, dear one. But what is it with you and the Dark? There are many nice young men of the Light, you know.' Alma blushed and he chuckled. 'Just think about it, my dear. I'd be happy to introduce you to a few.'

'Grandfather!' she squealed. 'Enough!'

There was a rattling noise and Beran returned, pushing a trolley filled with plates of food. He laid them out on the low table then left. Alma leaned forward, filling her plate, her stomach growling. She knew dinner was waiting at home, but food in Ambeth somehow tasted better than anything she'd ever had. Filling her mouth with pastry, she tried not to think about what Ethan was doing, or how his hand had felt, wrapped around hers.

CHAPTER 9
A NEW INTERPRETATION

'And is Dana keeping well?' Cedran fixed Ethan with a questioning look. He leaned back against the padded seat, one arm stretched along the back of the alcove. The Hall was getting busier, more people coming in to have their lunch. "Will she come to visit me, do you think?'

Ethan finished chewing his bite of sandwich and swallowed. 'Mum's the same as always,' he said, shaking his head. 'You know, she just likes to be at home. Um, I'm not sure if she's ready to come here yet. I can ask her again, I guess.'

Cedran nodded. 'So she is not... socialising?'

Ethan frowned. 'She goes out once in a while,' he said. 'Just with friends, you know, for coffee. That's all.' Cedran fixed him with a long stare. Ethan leaned back and folded his arms.

Then the Dark Lord smiled. 'Good,' he said. 'And the wards I placed on the house – they're holding?'

'No trouble so far.' Ethan took another bite of his sandwich. It was always the same whenever he saw his father – all he wanted to know about was Dana, what she was doing, that there were no other men in her life. It infuriated him – his mother was fragile enough as it was, without Cedran still wanting to be part of her life. But at the same time he was glad his father still cared. He knew what had happened to other human consorts of the Dark.

'So tell me about Alma,' said Cedran. 'How did you meet her?'

'She's a friend. From school, you know. And of course we have Ambeth in common. That's how we met – I set off her bracelet.' For some reason he didn't want to tell his father how they'd really met, running from the Dark Hunt after Caleb's death.

'A friend? Really?' Cedran was grinning now. 'Is that what they call it these days?'

'Dad!'

Cedran chuckled. 'I don't mind, Ethan. She is Galen's daughter after all, a fine match for you. Although...' His expression became more serious as he leaned across the table to Ethan, who was struggling between annoyance and the fact that his father was right. 'I hear that Denoris' son still carries a torch for her. I would stay out of his way, if I were you.'

'Dad, she's just a friend,' insisted Ethan. 'And I know about Deryck. She wants nothing to do with him, and I've promised her my protection if he bothers her.'

Cedran smiled again, leaning back. 'Oh really? Well, I hope she appreciates your... er, protection. Just as a friend, of course.' He gave Ethan a knowing look.

Ethan shook his head, blowing out a long breath. Okay, so he did want more than friendship with Alma, if he was being honest. There was a connection between them he couldn't explain. She felt familiar, as though he'd known her for years. Taking a drink from his goblet he looked around the Hall. He saw the tall figure of Thorion and lifted his hand to wave.

'Um, father, if you'll excuse me. I need to speak with Thorion.' He regretted the words as soon as he spoke them. Not much got past his father and, judging by the frown on his face, he wasn't going to get away without an explanation.

'What about?'

'Um, oh, well, he kind of asked me to sort of, look out for Alma and, well, I just wanted to let him know—'

'Ethan, do not play with me.' His father's face was suddenly like cut stone, his eyes a dangerous glitter. Ethan swallowed. He felt like he was ten years old again, caught in a wrongdoing. He had no choice but to tell the truth.

'Right. Okay, well, here it is.' Cedran folded his arms and sat back, waiting. 'Well, actually, Alma and I, we're looking for the Crown. Together.' He grimaced, waiting for his father to explode.

The muscles in Cedran's folded arms flexed. 'Is that so?' he said softly, his eyes never leaving his son. 'Well, then, perhaps I need to speak with Thorion as well.'

Damn.

The High King came towards them and Ethan got to his feet, as did Cedran. They both bowed, though Cedran's was stiff.

'Ethan, well met,' said Thorion. 'Are you well?'

'He is,' replied Cedran. 'And I'm wondering if we could speak privately.'

Thorion glanced at Ethan, who made a face. The jig was up.

'Of course,' Thorion said, courteous as always. 'In fact, it's overdue that we speak, Cedran. There are things we need to discuss.'

'So it seems.' The Dark Lord was also polite, but Ethan knew he was angry.

'Shall we go to my rooms?' Thorion continued. 'I can arrange for lunch to be served, unless you've already eaten.'

'We've already eaten. But yes, I think a more private setting would be suitable for this discussion.' The two Elders circled each other, Cedran's jaw tense, the King's eyes changing from blue to grey.

'Then it is agreed.' Thorion turned, heading for the Foyer. Cedran fell into step beside him, Ethan following behind. Double damn! This was going to be awkward at best. He trailed behind the King and his father as they ascended the private staircase to

Thorion's quarters, arriving at the double doors. Thorion opened them, leading them into a small vestibule, then through to a spacious sitting room. Two couches and several chairs were grouped near the large fireplace, sunlight streaming through the arched windows. 'Please,' he said, turning to Cedran and Ethan. 'Make yourselves comfortable.'

Edric, Thorion's steward, appeared through another doorway. 'My Lord. I was not expecting you back so soon. All is well?' He looked at Cedran and Ethan.

'All is well indeed. I have decided to lunch in my chambers, that's all.'

'The Lady Adara is still out,' said Edric. 'Though I expect her back later.'

'Thank you.' Thorion nodded to Edric. 'See that no one disturbs us for a while.'

Edric bowed and left the room. Ethan sat on the sofa, Thorion taking a chair opposite, but Cedran remained standing, his arms folded.

'I owe you an apology, Cedran.' Thorion's tone was mild, his hands flat on his thighs. Ethan looked from the High King to his father, trying to conceal his surprise. Cedran's expression was unreadable.

'What if something had happened to him, Thorion? What would I have said to his mother?'

Ethan's mouth tightened.

'You're right,' Thorion replied. 'I should have told you what was happening. Although, I would point out, it was Ethan's choice to make.'

'Do not talk to me of choice, Thorion! I know how it works,' snapped Cedran. Ethan stepped in, wanting to head off the seemingly inevitable argument.

'Father, I was the one who came to Thorion,' Ethan interjected. 'After Alma came back with the Cup, and what happened to Caleb... well, he was my friend, and I wanted to help, to do something. Thorion didn't *make* me do anything!'

'Is this true?' said Cedran.

'It is, though I should have informed you sooner. Once again I can only ask your forgiveness.' Thorion, his eyes now fully grey, frowned slightly.

Cedran regarded him for a long moment before nodding. 'Fine. But why did you agree to let him help her?'

A line appeared between the King's brows. 'Ethan offered his help, Alma needed it. I have no problem with him working with her.'

'But as my son, surely you could see I might wish to use him for the Dark?'

'Did you? Are you of the same opinion as Denoris? That the Dark should work separately from the Light? Surely we both want the same things?'

Cedran's lips tightened and he folded his arms. 'I can see that having the Regalia returned is a good thing, yes, but to what advantage for the Dark? We hold no power here—'

'You're part of my inner circle! Is that not power enough for you? What is it you want, Cedran?'

'I want what most of the Dark want!' Cedran's voice rose. 'To rule with the Light as we used to. And you ignore this at your peril.'

'What are you saying?' Thorion got to his feet, facing the other Elder. 'Is there something you wish to share with me?'

'Only that there are those among the Dark who will stop at nothing to get what they want! And the girl is part of it!'

As Ethan watched the two Elders argue back and forth, his anger grew, especially at the mention of Alma. This was *his* choice to make. Plus, they were missing something important.

'Excuse me!' he called out but was ignored, so he tried again. 'Father, Thorion!' Both lords stopped to look at him. 'This was *my* choice to make! And, have either of you considered that it's right there on the wall, in the Prophecy?'

Thorion and Cedran looked confused.

'What is, Ethan?' asked Thorion.

'*Child of Darkness, Child of Light?* Alma is the Child of Light, I'm the Child of Darkness, right?'

Astonishment dawned on both faces. Ethan hid a smile. Seriously, had they not realised?

Cedran spoke first. 'But... we were given to understand that there would be only one child of the Prophecy. That it referred to Alma's human nature. Though, of course, she's not fully human—' He broke off and looked at the High King. 'Thorion?'

An expression of understanding came across Thorion's face. 'Ethan, by the Light, I had never considered such a thing! But yes, now that you say it, of course it makes sense! But, then, why haven't you been involved from the start?'

'Well, I have, kind of.' Ethan looked down, then took a deep breath. 'Remember, after the tournament, when Alma was running?'

'Through the woods – yes, I remember.' Thorion's face twisted. 'I thought it a miracle, we all did, that she managed to escape. Wait... are you saying that you—'

'Yes. I helped her. That's how we first met. So, um, yeah, I wasn't being honest with you, Dad.' Ethan almost wanted to laugh at their shocked faces. 'I, er, threw the Hunt off her scent then helped her get to the Gate. She'd given up, you know. She was just lying there, waiting for them – I've never seen anyone cry like that.' The desire to laugh left him as he remembered that day, how much pain she'd been in. He'd wanted to help her, to make her better, more than anything.

Thorion shook his head. 'Then we owe you a debt of gratitude larger than I could have imagined,' he said. 'I'm glad that you were there for her, that you could help her when we could not. I did not realise...'

Cedran turned away, his fists clenched. Thorion glanced at Ethan. Then Cedran turned back to them, his eyes bright. 'Ethan, you did the right thing, helping her,' he said finally. 'I did not agree with what happened that day, any of it.' His voice was heavy with meaning. Thorion and Ethan looked at him in amazement.

'What?' He held his hands wide. 'Just because I'm Dark, does not mean I, too, do not wish for the Regalia to be returned. Of course I wish the girl had chosen our side, but it cannot be helped. Still, I wouldn't let anyone else know of your role that day in helping her escape.'

'Your father is right, Ethan,' said Thorion.

'Well, it's nice to see we agree on something, Thorion,' said Cedran.

'So you're okay with me helping Alma?' Ethan held his breath.

Cedran nodded. 'It's not you helping her that I have a problem with, Ethan. I already told you, she is Galen's daughter and as such a fine match for you—'

'Dad, please!'

'As I was saying, ' continued Cedran, 'my main issue was that I didn't know.' His voice softened. 'You are my only child, Ethan. You and your mother are... important to me. So I need to know if you're involved in anything that might be dangerous, that's all.'

'Thanks, Dad.' Ethan knew his father cared, but it wasn't often he said it. 'I should have told you, but—'

'I do not spend as much time with Denoris as I did,' Cedran went on. 'Our interests do not align as they used to. You can trust me, my son. And Thorion, I swear to you I that I am no longer involved in his schemes.'

Thorion regarded him steadily. 'I thank you, Cedran.' The King stretched out his hand. Cedran took it. 'And I hope you can accept my apology for not keeping you informed of Ethan's movements. He is your son, and you should have known.'

'Thank you,' said Cedran. 'I do. However, I would ask that, if there's anything more you think I should know, you won't keep it from me.' His mouth quirked up in a half-smile.

Thorion, his eyes now sliding back to blue, simply nodded.

'And now, I must go. I have a pressing appointment to keep. Ethan, I will see you again soon, I hope. Please remember me to your mother.'

'I will, Father.' Ethan stood up, about to bow to his father, but he was shocked when Cedran pulled him into a hug instead.

'Take care of yourself, and of Alma.' He released Ethan and left the room, closing the door behind him.

Ethan stood there, stunned by his father's display of affection. Then he felt Thorion's hand on his shoulder.

'Would you like a drink?'

'Yes. I mean, thank you, Lord Thorion.' He sank back down onto the sofa. Thorion handed him a goblet, the metal cool against his hand. He took a sip, surprised to find it contained wine. He looked at the High King, who nodded.

'I thought you could use something a bit stronger. Don't tell your father, though.' He winked.

Ethan burst out laughing, taking another mouthful. It was very good wine.

'So, it's going well between you and Alma?' Thorion sat down, relaxing against the cushions.

'Oh, not you, too,' muttered Ethan. Then, remembering himself, he said, 'Sorry, Lord Thorion. But really, we are just friends.' No matter how much he might want it to be more, there was no way he was admitting that, not yet.

'Of course, that's what I meant,' said Thorion. 'So, any ideas on the Crown?'

'Oh, Alma says she has none, but that she never had any idea about the Sword or the Cup either.' He laughed. 'So we should be okay.'

Thorion shook his head, smiling. 'Well, all I can do is leave you both to it. But remember, if you need any help, you can come to me.'

'Thanks, er, thank you, Lord Thorion.' Ethan took another drink, enjoying the warmth spreading through him. He closed his eyes, leaning his head back on the sofa, smiling to himself. Thorion's voice intruded on his thoughts.

'So, shall we send for her?'

'What?' Ethan opened his eyes, felt his cheeks flushing. He cleared his throat and leaned forward to put his goblet down.

'Alma.' Thorion grinned at him. 'I'd already asked Artos to join me this afternoon. Shall I send for him to come early, with Alma?'

'Oh, well, you know, I should probably take her back soon, er, you know, but not on my account, er—' He stopped, realising he was babbling. Judging by the humorous glint in Thorion's eyes, he knew it, too. But he was keen, all of a sudden very keen, to see Alma.

LORD CEDRAN MADE HIS WAY ACROSS THE FOYER, DEEP IN thought. It had been a morning for revelations. First Ethan showing up unannounced with Galen's daughter, then admitting that he was helping her. And he was still unsure how he felt about the new interpretation of the Prophecy.

He half smiled at the thought of Ethan telling them both what had been so obvious, yet they had all failed to see. That there were two Children of the Prophecy, and one of them was his son. He passed the last few stragglers leaving lunch and strode out into the gardens.

He hadn't been lying about the urgency of his meeting, but he needed time to think. For there was one detail he'd omitted, when speaking with Thorion.

The meeting was with Denoris.

CHAPTER 10
OH, ALL THE FEELINGS!

'Alma!'

Stepping into the King's sitting room, Alma was enveloped in strong arms, the scent of incense and green leaves surrounding her.

'It's so good to see you,' the King said, pulling back. She looked up into his glorious face.

'Uh, it's good to see you too,' she said, blushing. Thorion could always do this to her. Her blush deepened as she noticed Ethan sitting on the nearby sofa, smiling at her.

'And Artos! Well met this day, my friend.' Thorion released her, going to her grandfather and shaking his hand. The King was glowing, vibrant; Alma couldn't remember ever seeing him look so well. He turned, one arm out. 'Have you met Ethan? He's—'

'Cedran's son. Yes, we met earlier today.' Artos went to Ethan, who was on his feet, bowing. 'Oh, no need for such formality.' Artos smiled, clapping him on the back. 'Did you enjoy your lunch? And is your father well?'

'He is,' said Ethan.

'Though somewhat surprised to find out about him helping

Alma,' said Thorion. 'It seems that Ethan is full of surprises, actually. We have much to be grateful to him for.'

'Oh yes?' A gentle voice chimed in.

They all turned to see Adara enter the room. She was armour clad, in dull golden leather, her curls pulled back from her face. She went straight to Thorion, who put his arm around her, pulling her in close to kiss. Alma's eyes widened and she glanced at her grandfather, who nodded, smiling.

'Alma,' said Adara, coming over to give her a hug. 'So lovely to see you again.'

'And you,' said Alma, hugging her back. 'But, um, this is... different.'

Adara laughed. 'Just because I'm usually in robes, doesn't mean I can't fight,' she said. 'In fact, my empathy is coming in quite useful. I've been working with the arms master to see if I can predict where a fighter will strike next,' she went on, turning to include the rest of the room.

'And?' Thorion sounded intrigued.

'Oh, well, it's very interesting,' she said. 'I can tell you later. For now, I wish to hear what you've all been doing. But first, let me get changed.' She left the room, graceful as ever, the door closing behind her.

It was silent for a moment, then Artos spoke. 'So what is it Ethan has done?'

'What, apart from catching me and his father off guard with a new interpretation of the Prophecy?' Thorion grinned and Alma raised her eyebrows.

Adara came back into the room, immaculate in olive green silk, the gentle lady once more. She took Thorion's arm and he smiled at her, stealing a kiss. Ethan came and sat next to Alma. She glanced at him through her hair.

'The Prophecy?' said Artos, looking mystified.

'Yes,' said Thorion. 'As he pointed out to us, Alma is the Child of Light, he is the Child of Darkness. I know,' he said. A confounded look crossed Artos' lined face. Adara gasped, her eyes wide. 'It amazes me that none of us saw it before.'

'The Seer said... she said that help would come from the Human Realm. I suppose we all assumed... Well, I never.' Artos rubbed his chin. Then he bent his gaze on Ethan and Alma. 'So the two of you, together. It makes sense, I can see it now. But then, why—'

'Why wasn't he there from the start?' Thorion shook his head. 'He was, Artos. It was Ethan who helped Alma escape the Hunt that day.'

'What?' Adara and Artos exclaimed together.

Alma glanced again at Ethan, wanting to take his hand, though she knew she couldn't. But at the same moment he reached across, his warm fingers twining with hers briefly before letting go.

Artos came over to Ethan, dropping to one knee. 'I am forever in your service,' he said, his voice rough with emotion. 'That you were there for her, when I couldn't be, when no one else could be.' He bowed his head.

'Grandfather!' Alma reached for Artos, but Ethan was already up, helping the Elder to his feet.

'It was my pleasure,' Ethan said. 'I wouldn't have seen her harmed then, nor would I now. So please, I can't—'

Before he could finish Artos gathered him into a bear hug, slapping him on the back. When he released him Adara was there, kissing him on the cheek, her gentle hand on his shoulder. He went red, his hair flopping forward.

Artos laughed, taking his hand and clasping it in his own. 'You're forever part of our family, Ethan, for what you've done. If there's ever anything you need, just ask.'

Adara smiled, her golden eyes bright. 'It is a great thing,' she said in her soft voice. 'We're all grateful.'

Alma, her heart full, looked down at her hands, not knowing what to think. This was big. But if she stopped to consider things, she realised she felt the same way, that she would stand up for Ethan if he needed her. She remembered how he'd made her feel in the woods, how she'd cried on his shoulder, not wanting to leave the safety of his arms. It made her blush. She looked up to see Ethan, still surrounded by Artos, Adara and Thorion, smiling at her. She smiled back.

LATER, THEY ENTERED THE WOODS TOGETHER. ETHAN WAS close to her again, so close she could feel his calm energy. Yet he wasn't close enough. She wanted to touch him, rolling her hands into fists so that she didn't. She wasn't sure why – she had a feeling he wouldn't mind, but there was something holding her back. So instead she ran ahead of him, jumping over a rock in the path, darting around the shimmering green trees.

'Alma.' She stopped, turning as he came up behind her. 'Are you all right?'

'Yeah, fine.' Her heart was beating faster, and she was short of breath but, sure, she was fine.

'So... it was okay today, right?'

'It was.' She smiled at him, wanting to see him smile again. He did. 'And, thanks.'

His eyes narrowed and he shook his head slightly. 'For what?'

'For um, for understanding, I guess. About... you know.'

His expression softened and he moved closer to her, and it was as though everything slowed down. She could feel and hear everything – the leaves rustling around her, the birds singing, the passage of small creatures in the undergrowth, the forest pulsing with life and energy. 'I wouldn't let anything happen that you didn't want,' he said.

She looked down, not sure if she was ready for this. In fact, she knew she wasn't. Everything was still too fresh, too raw, the woods still filled with echoes of Caleb and Deryck, bright shadows from the past.

'Thank you,' she said, eventually, taking a step back. 'Shall we, er...?'

He seemed to get it, though she thought she saw regret in his blue eyes. 'Yeah, I guess we should get back. You can do the time thing, right?'

'Um, yeah.' He was still close enough that she knew if she just reached out and put her hand on him he would be hers, but she couldn't do it. Not yet. So instead she stepped back again, turning away. 'About the same time as when we crossed?' she said, over her shoulder.

'Sounds good.' He came up beside her again and she felt... safe, she realised. That's how he made her feel.

She wondered, then, how she made him feel.

CHAPTER 11
DARK WATERS

There was a place in the gardens where Cedran liked to sit, a small pavilion next to a curving pond. It was a romantic place. The little carved wood pavilion reflected in the calm waters of the pond, its edges softened by delicate reeds. He'd dreamed of sitting here with Dana, the soft breeze lifting her long hair, her blue eyes gazing into his. But it was not to be. He leaned on the balustrade, looking down at his reflection. Hearing footsteps crunching on the nearby gravel path, he turned his head.

It seemed his time for thinking was over. Denoris and Gwenene approached, arm in arm. Denoris' expression was dark and Gwenene, talking in a low voice to him, looked concerned. Cedran narrowed his eyes slightly, staying still. He needed to be careful now. Ethan's involvement with Alma, whatever form it took, would bring him into conflict with what Denoris wanted. And, if forced to choose between them, he would choose his son.

He deliberately shifted his weight so the wooden floor creaked, announcing his presence. Denoris looked up first, his emerald eyes glaring, then softening to something close to warmth as he saw Cedran.

'Well met, Cedran,' he called. Gwenene smiled in greeting, lifting one pale hand.

'Well met, Denoris, Gwenene,' replied Cedran.

They entered the pavilion. Gwenene let go of Denoris and sank down gracefully onto one of the benches overlooking the water, reaching to trail her fingers through the silvery depths. She seemed weary and preoccupied, Cedran noted, as he held out his hand to Denoris.

'Were you waiting for us? I had thought we would meet at my apartments.' The Dark Lord looked tired as well; there were dark circles under his eyes and his golden skin was more lined than usual.

Cedran shrugged. 'It's a fine day, and this is as good a place to meet as any.'

Denoris raised an eyebrow. 'I suppose.'

Cedran waited. But Denoris didn't seem inclined to speak. Instead, he went to sit with Gwenene, his gaze distant as he stared across the water.

Cedran frowned. The morning's events had shown him that he needed to reconsider his position, to act with care. Normally, he would take time to ponder, working through all scenarios before making a decision. But time was not something he had in this instance.

'So, how go the plans, to get the girl? Do you even need her anymore, after what happened?' Being direct usually worked for him, though Denoris was more difficult than most to deal with. Still, he was as close to equal with him as any in Ambeth.

But, to his surprise, it was Gwenene who answered. She snorted. 'The girl. Lucky, that's all she was. If Etras—'

'Etras? Last I heard he was on his estate, building an army. What does he have to do with all this?' A card played, but one he felt he could give up. He knew Etras had disappeared – his own people had informed him of it. He also knew this would throw Denoris into disarray.

Denoris laughed briefly, then shot a look at Gwenene, who turned away. 'Etras is gone. And you'd know that, too, if you had better spies.'

Cedran deliberately ignored the jibe. 'Is that so? Do you know what happened to him? Where he would have gone?'

The Dark Lord's blond brows drew together. 'I do not. Do you?'

'It has been many years since I've had dealings with Etras. Is that not the case for you?'

Denoris stared at him, then sighed. 'I asked for his help with something, but he has not returned.'

Cedran frowned. This was news. And he had a feeling it involved the girl.

'Help? With what?'

'Nothing.' This was Gwenene, her tone sharp. 'This is not a place to discuss our plans.'

'Perhaps,' Denoris said. 'But I would ask you this, Cedran. Will you still stand with us, when the time comes?'

Cedran knew he needed to tread carefully here. 'I am of the Dark, Denoris,' he said. 'And my loyalty is unchanged.'

Denoris considered him for a moment. 'But you no longer believe that the Dark should take power.'

'I believe there's need for change. As to the form it takes, perhaps I'm of a different mind to you these days. That doesn't mean I do not remain loyal.'

Denoris snorted. 'Well, that is as may be. However, it's not why I asked you to meet.'

'No?' Cedran folded his arms.

'No.' Denoris got to his feet. 'I am here to propose an alliance between our houses.'

Cedran narrowed his eyes. 'Are we not already allied?'

Denoris regarded him steadily. Cedran could almost see his suppressed rage simmering beneath his skin. 'I wish to make it official, if you're amenable. I offer my daughter's hand, for your son.'

Cedran swallowed, fighting to hide his surprise. 'In marriage?'

'No, for a dance at the maypole,' Denoris snapped. 'Yes, of course for marriage!'

Gwenene put her hand on his arm and he glanced down at her. Cedran took the moment to regroup, to gather his scattered thoughts.

'Is she not rather young for marriage? I mean no offense, but surely there are other ways—'

'She is old enough,' Denoris said. Gwenene's mouth tightened and she looked away.

Disquiet curled in Cedran's gut. 'Ethan, however, is not.'

'They are the same age.'

'Ethan has grown up in the human world, where they do not see marriage as we do,' Cedran said. 'While I'm honoured by your offer, I cannot speak for him in this instance, and certainly not without consulting his mother. She depends on him, and I know she would not approve.'

'You would take the decision of some human over that of—'

Cedran didn't let him finish. 'She is not "some human." She is my wife, and the mother of my son.'

'Yet she has never set foot in Ambeth.'

Cedran drew in a breath through his nostrils, his shoulders curving forward, fists clenched. 'That is her choice to make.' He growled the words.

Denoris stepped forward, but Gwenene quickly got to her feet, sinuous in silk and lace, and stepped between the two Dark Lords.

'Enough.' She placed one delicate hand on Cedran's chest, the other on Denoris. Despite her slender frame she was strong as steel. 'I told you he wouldn't go for it,' she said to Denoris. 'We can take over without his help, if that's what is required.' She darted a blue glance at Cedran, sly as a cat.

'Take over?' The tendril of disquiet bloomed into full-blown concern.

'Why yes.' The words were spoken lilting, wild, as though she were releasing something long held back. 'The human world is at a tipping point – it's only a matter of time.'

'Until what? This is not what we planned.'

'Things change, dear Cedran,' she went on. 'The past comes back to haunt us, the girl evades the hunter and the world twists in the balance. As it moves, so must we.'

'Gwenene, I've told you—' Denoris tried to reach for her, but she pushed him away, her fingers digging into his armour.

'Hush, hush my love,' she said. 'He won't give you his son, as I knew he wouldn't, and so we must make our own way, just the two of us, as it has always been, and the Dark will rise and take the thrones, and all will be as it should be.'

Her voice was keening, like that of a wild bird caught in brambles. Cedran remembered her outburst in the Hall when the Cup came back, and Denoris dragging her away before she could attack Alma.

'It was always Light and Dark on the thrones, not just Dark.' Cedran kept his voice steady, his gaze on her. 'You risk the very Balance if you take them both! Surely that's not what you want, for the human world to fall.'

'Humans – what are they worth? Their petty conflicts and short lives are meaningless in the great scheme of things.' Denoris stepped back from Gwenene's hand, brushing it away. She glanced at him, then wandered back to the bench, sinking down to trail her hand in the water once more.

Cedran blinked. 'Humans sustain us with their very energy. Every life brings something to the Balance. Surely you don't seek to destroy it?'

'I do not wish to destroy it, rather... tilt it, more in our favour,' said Denoris. 'I want the humans' energy, the power they give us. Cedran, we can do anything – imagine how it would be.'

'You would take them over?'

'Of course. A benevolent ruler, immortal, from another world. They will bow to me, clamour to give me their everything.'

'And what of the Light?'

'They will bow to me, to us as well.'

Cedran shook his head, his shock profound. He'd always known Denoris to be passionate and headstrong, his intelligence knife-sharp. But this, this was something different.

'I offer you one last time, Cedran,' Denoris continued. 'A chance to align with us, for your son to hold power in Ambeth, alongside my daughter.'

'I cannot commit my son to marriage, not yet. Though I am with you, as I have always been.'

Their plans had been so simple, once. Capture the girl, find the Regalia, use the leverage to bring the Dark back to an equal footing in Ambeth. But Alma had eluded Denoris, time and time again. Cedran, dread curling within him, wondered whether it had driven him mad.

Or made him a mindreader. 'Is it because he is already spoken for?' Denoris played with a lacing at the wrist of his armour as he spoke. But the rage was still there; fire burned in his green eyes as he glanced at Cedran.

'Spoken for? He is not.'

'Yet I know he was seen today. With Galen's daughter.'

Every sense prickled, every nerve screamed danger. Cedran lifted his chin. 'News travels fast, it seems.' He paused for a beat. 'They are friends from school. A happy coincidence that they found out they were both from Ambeth.'

Denoris narrowed his eyes. 'Well, perhaps you might mention to Ethan that my son is still very much interested in Alma. And that therefore, so am I.'

'I will, I suppose, if it comes up,' Cedran said, feigning disinterest. Inside, however, he was on the defensive. If Ethan wanted

Alma, then he should have her, regardless of what Deryck, or Denoris, wanted.

'Good. I will hold you to that, as I will to your... co-operation, going forward. There is still a place for you with us. If you want it.' Before Cedran could respond, Denoris took Gwenene by the arm and the two of them left the pavilion. Gwenene turned to smile at him as they left, her eyes wild.

Cedran blew out a breath.

He had several options, none of them easy. He needed to withdraw and consider them all. But first, he needed to make sure that Ethan and Alma were safe.

DENORIS ENTERED HIS APARTMENT, RIPPING HIS CLOAK FROM his shoulders and throwing it against the wall. He'd left Gwenene at her apartment in the care of her housekeeper, who'd administered a soothing draught. She'd not been the same since the Cup's return, talking in her sleep of Davies, of love and sorrow, until Denoris thought he would explode with jealousy and rage. She would return to him, he knew that, but time was of the essence. And now Cedran, refusing his daughter's hand! It was a good match, any fool could see it – the children of two of the most powerful lords of the Dark. Why were things unravelling, despite his best efforts? Still, there were some things he could control, and Cedran was not the only member of the Dark with a son. There were those who would marry his daughter just for her tallus stone, for darkness sake! He headed along the corridor to her bedroom. If Cedran's son was not available, she needed to be made ready to be seen, to attract the next suitor.

He opened the door.

'Daughter, I wish you to—' He stopped dead.

Ellery, sitting at her dressing table, turned, her eyes and mouth wide. She hastily reached out, but Denoris was faster.

He picked up the tallus necklace by its chain, the silvery leaves catching the light as it swung from his hand. He looked at it.

Then his gaze travelled to the identical necklace already around her neck.

CHAPTER 12
OF SECRETS AND CLOUDS

'How was the park last night?' asked Eleanor. Taking a break from clearing away the breakfast dishes, she leaned on the counter, cup of tea in hand.

Alma was still buzzing from her trip through the Gate with Ethan. She was sitting cross-legged at the kitchen table, still in pyjamas, the autumn sun striping through the French doors. 'Yeah, it was good.' She bit into her toast, the butter coating her tongue, almost humming with contentment.

'Ethan seems nice.'

Eleanor brought her tea over to the table and sat down, pinching a piece of Alma's toast.

'Hey! I mean, yeah, he's all right. Where's Dad and the boys?'

Eleanor grinned. 'He's taken them to soccer practice. And you don't get to change the subject that easily.'

Alma gave her mum a look. Then she sighed, running a hand through her hair. She was tired of having secrets, anyway. 'Fine. He is nice, and he's also—'

'Just a friend?'

'Oh! Well, yeah, that.' Alma blushed. 'But that wasn't what I was going to say.'

Eleanor tilted her head, her mug halfway to her mouth.

'No, um, he's like me, Mum. He's half from Ambeth.'

Her mother's eyes widened and she leaned forward. 'Really?' For a moment she almost looked like the teenager she'd been when she'd met Alma's father. The two photos Alma had of them together were among her most treasured possessions. 'Quick, tell me!'

'Yeah, his father is, um, Dark.' Alma made a face 'But he's not like that, I mean, he's so nice and we went through the Gate together and grandfather likes him and, well, he makes me feel safe.'

It all came out in a rush.

Eleanor's smile, which had slipped at the mention of the Dark, widened once more.

'He makes you feel safe? Well, that's good to hear. And that your grandfather likes him.' She nodded, then reached out a hand to Alma. 'Just be careful, okay? Don't be hurt again.'

'I know, Mum, I get it. But it's not like that with him.' It wasn't. Alma couldn't explain it, but she knew Ethan would never hurt her. 'Anyway, I think I might meet him today, again, at the park.'

'Sounds nice. Just make sure your homework is done first.'

There was silence then as Alma finished her toast and Eleanor drained the last of the tea from her mug. But Alma knew she needed to ask. She had always wondered.

'Mum?'

'Yes?'

'D'you... Would you like to come with me? One day, I mean,' she added, seeing her mother bite her lip. 'If you want to.'

Eleanor sat back. 'My time there is over,' she said, eventually. 'It ended when I lost your father.' Her voice shook on the last word

Alma felt awful. 'I'm so sorry,' she said. 'I really am.' She was, for so many reasons.

'It's fine,' said Eleanor, wiping her eyes. 'I'm just happy for you, that you have someone to share it with now.' She smiled a watery smile.

There were footsteps and the side door banged. Graham came into the kitchen, all smiles, rubbing his hands together.

'Right, trouble one and two are out of the way. Guess that just leaves you to sort out, Alma,' he said, ruffling her hair. He walked around the table to kiss his wife. 'And then we can be alone,' he said, affecting an accent as he twirled an imaginary moustache. Eleanor pretended to slap him with the tea towel.

'Oh you!' She giggled, blushing as she got up and put the last of the dishes away. Alma rolled her eyes, grabbing her phone and sending a text to Ethan. Her mum was right, she thought as she typed. It was a relief, finally, to be able to tell someone.

'FATHER, I CAN EXPLAIN- OW!' ELLERY SQUEALED AS HER father reached out and pulled the necklace from her neck, snapping the chain so it flicked into her skin. Her breath caught, terror taking her as her father's face tightened with rage.

'What is this?'

Her mouth opened and closed but she couldn't find the words. Denoris advanced on her, the two necklaces dangling from his hands, his broad shoulders curved forwards. He was like a snake about to strike, his green eyes glittering. She pushed her chair back, the legs scraping on the stone floor as she stood.

'I asked you a question, daughter. What–' he shook his hands at her '–is this?'

'It's not what you think.' Her hands were shaking and she clasped them together in front of her skirt, taking a step back.

'It's not what I think? So you haven't, for some reason, chosen to disregard the gift I gave you, a gift of great power, of acknowledgement as my blood? Is that what I'm thinking?' His voice rose to a roar.

Ellery trembled all over, though she stood her ground. She felt instinctively that if she cowered away it would make things worse, though she wasn't sure how.

'Please – ah—'

Her father dropped the necklace with the snapped chain to the floor and took her tallus stone in his hand. Pain streaked through her, black lightning agony, and she screamed from the force of it. She crumpled to the ground, writhing, wrapping her arms around herself as she curled up. He dropped her tallus on her dresser and the pain stopped, though the aftermath rang through her. She struggled to stand, gasping for breath.

'Father, I swear, it was only to keep it safe.'

'Silence!'

Denoris stepped on the fake tallus necklace, grinding it beneath the heel of his boot. Ellery winced, thinking of the hard work Mari had done. Then he hit Ellery, hard, an open handed slap across her face that stung. Her head snapped to the side and she half fell onto the chair, her dark hair tangled across her face.

'Father—'

He hit her again. She cried out as he pulled her from the chair and shook her like a rag doll. Someone was banging on her bedroom door, calling out – it sounded like Deryck, but it was hard to tell. She sobbed, fighting to breathe, her heart breaking as her father continued to beat her.

'You're just like your mad mother!' he shouted, knocking her to the ground. 'Never doing what I ask!'

Ellery rolled over on her back, scrabbling against the floor as she backed away from him. She could taste blood in her mouth and her shoulder was agony. She glared up at him. 'What are you going to do? Leave me in the woods to die, like you did her?'

Denoris stopped, his face going white. The muscles in his arms tensed and flexed. Ellery cowered back. He bent down, grabbed her by the front of her gown and lifted her to her feet. Her face was wet, tears and snot mingling with blood. Denoris dragged her towards her dressing table, her feet tangling in her gown. Holding her up he reached to his belt and brought out a knife. Ellery's eyes widened.

'Father, please.'

He pulled her to him, his face so close to hers she could see the flecks of gold deep in his emerald eyes.

'Put the necklace on.' He ground out the words.

Ellery hesitated. She didn't want to do it. Denoris brought the knife to her throat. The door to her room flew open, banging on the wall.

Deryck stood there, his mouth and eyes wide. 'What the hell is going on?'

Ellery knew she must look bad – she could feel the cut on her lip starting to swell and one eye closing as the flesh puffed around it.

'Your sister needs to do as she is told,' replied Denoris. His eyes and the knife did not waver. 'Ellery, put the necklace on, or I will cut your throat here and now.'

'Father, no!'

'Deryck, stay out of this. Use your stone and you will see that I am right.'

Gasping in pain and fear, Ellery saw Deryck touch his stone, his face shutting down. She closed her eyes for a moment, fresh tears warm against the stickiness on her cheeks. Maybe she should let her father kill her. Then it was as though a voice whispered in her head, soft and gentle, full of love. 'Stay alive, beautiful girl. For both of us. You still have a part to play.'

The love in the voice was like nothing she'd heard before. Maybe she was going mad. All at once, though, she didn't want to die. She opened her eyes, her vision blurry. The blade still pressing into her neck, she carefully reached out and picked up the tallus. She tried to put the necklace on, struggling to get it over her head. Finally her father sighed, tucked the knife back in his belt and took the necklace from her, undoing the clasp. Gulping and gasping, dizzy with pain, she managed to stay still as he placed the chain around her neck, lifting her hair to fix the clasp.

As soon as the stone touched her bare skin she was above the pain, floating on a cloud of bliss. As though from a distance she saw her father touching her face where he'd hit her, his expression unreadable. He murmured something, his hand drifting over her dark hair. It sounded like, 'You're so like your mother,' but she wasn't sure. Deryck leaned against the doorframe, his face blank. Her father led her over to the bed and laid her down, lifting her legs gently, stroking her hair so it fanned out around her on the pillow. She smiled at him, only faintly feeling the pain in her lip. Her father bent his head to kiss her, his lips moving on hers, and she sighed. He stood up, blood on his mouth, and beckoned to Deryck.

'Come and kiss your sister.'

Deryck moved towards her, a half-smile on his face. Ellery tried to frown but couldn't, as though she were surrounded by soft marshmallow clouds. Deryck sat on the bed next to her, his pupils dilating as he touched his stone again. He leaned over and kissed her softly, one hand caressing the unbroken side of her face. He lifted his head and looked at their father, who seemed to be considering something.

'But Father, she doesn't have red hair,' Deryck said, his voice slightly slurred, whether from his stone or hers, she wasn't sure. Underneath it all she was screaming, her voice echoing around in her brain, but she found that if she didn't focus on it too much, the screaming faded away.

'I'll wait for Alma to come back to me,' Deryck said as he stood up.

After a long moment where she floated in and out of consciousness, her father nodded his acquiescence. She knew she should be relieved about something, but couldn't quite figure out what. She waved at Deryck as he left the room, giggling at the shapes her hand made in the shimmering air. Her father came to stand next to her, looking down. For a moment he seemed tired, then he smiled, his handsome face lighting up. She smiled back. He was so beautiful.

'Rest now, Ellery,' he said. 'You'll be staying in here for a little while, just until you get used to your stone. Hilde will come and see you later, help you wash your face.' He touched her hair once more and she turned her face to his hand as he trailed his fingers along her cheek. He turned and left, closing the door behind him. The lock clicked and Ellery felt sad that he was gone. Then she heard the soft voice again, though it was very faint. 'Roll onto your side, my lovely girl,' the voice kept saying, becoming more insistent, and so she did, finally. 'Now sleep.' She did as she was told, closing her eyes and drifting away.

CHAPTER 13
SINCE WE MET

Alma and Ethan stood on a bridge over a small ornamental lake. Ethan scrolled through his phone as Alma leaned on the balustrade, looking down into the swirling blue water. The sunny autumn air still held the warmth of summer, the leaves turning to gold in a last glorious burst before winter's arrival. Across the park, the twin crowns of the Oak Gate loomed.

'So, do you want to get this over with?' Alma nudged Ethan. As she did so the clasp on her talaith bracelet caught on a nail sticking out from the handrail and came undone. 'No!' She tried in vain to catch it but it slipped from her wrist and fell into the lake, with one last glimmer before it disappeared beneath the water. 'No, no!' She bent over the rail, reaching as though she could pull it back out of the water, tears starting in her eyes. To lose her talaith, her last tangible link with her father, was a blow beyond words.

Ethan kicked off his shoes, shrugged off his hoodie and started to climb the balustrade.

'Wait!' Alma grabbed his arm. 'What are you doing?'

He grinned at her, his dark hair falling forward over his blue eyes – he was utterly beautiful in that moment, with the sun shining on his hair, on the muscles in his arms. Alma was shocked into speechlessness.

'I'm getting your bracelet.'

He let go, landing with a splash, laughing. 'It's not that deep,' he called. 'See?' The water was up to his chest, though, and Alma had her hands to her mouth as he disappeared beneath it. He reappeared a moment later, drenched and breathless but empty-handed.

'Ethan, no,' she called. 'You've tried, don't worry about it.'

He looked up at her, brushing his wet hair out of his eyes. 'Really? Do you think I'm getting wet for nothing?' Once more he dived, his denim-clad legs flailing. He was down there for a while. Alma was about to go in after him when he emerged, gasping and staggering, with her bracelet in his hand.

Alma shrieked with joy, running down from the bridge to the edge of the little lake, getting her legs wet as she helped Ethan out of the water. They collapsed on the grassy bank. Ethan lay on his back, his wet clothes clinging to him.

'Oh Ethan, you didn't have to do that. Are you all right? How can I ever thank you? Oh—!'

Ethan rolled onto his side and kissed her, his lips cool and damp on hers. His hand found hers and put the bracelet in it. After her initial surprise, Alma didn't want to stop kissing him. Her arms went around his neck and his wet body pressed against hers as she lay back, giving in to the embrace. She could feel his energy and her own rising to meet it, twirling together as the talaith warmed her hand, like the heat of the summer sun on her back or a warm fire on a cold day. Finally, the kiss ended.

Ethan raised his head, a smile in his eyes. 'I've been wanting to do that since we met,' he murmured, his mouth still close to hers, his breath warm on her face.

'I have, too,' replied Alma, breathless, realising it was true. She felt him shiver against her. 'But you're cold.'

'I don't care,' said Ethan, kissing her again. 'It was worth it.'

He shivered again, though, and Alma gently pushed him away. 'Come on,' she said, sitting up. 'Come to my house and you can get dried off, at least.'

'My house is closer,' said Ethan. 'Why don't you come with me? You can meet my mother.'

'I'd like that.' Alma got up and offered her hand to help him to his feet. He stole another kiss before making his way to the bridge, where he put on his shoes and hoodie. Alma followed him, her heart pounding, hardly able to believe what had happened. Her hand was hot and she realised she was still holding her talaith. She put it on her wrist, making sure the clasp was secure. Ethan put his arm around her, pulling her close as they made their way from the park out onto the main road. There were houses here, Alma knew, though they were all huge, hidden behind hedges at the end of long driveways. Surely he didn't live in one of those places. Huh. She knew so little about him. Not that it mattered.

They reached the entrance to a long gravel driveway, separated from the road by a line of brickwork. Ethan turned down it, pulling Alma along with him. Soaring oak trees lined both sides of the drive, with dark holly bushes clustered between them. After a minute they could no longer hear the road, as though they were in a wood.

'This is amazing!' It was like stepping into another world.

'It is, isn't it?' He pulled her to him for another kiss.

'Come on,' she murmured against his mouth. 'You need to get dry.' She felt him smile, then one final kiss before he let her go, taking her hand again. They reached the last curve of the drive, which opened out to a large garden in the middle of which stood a small cottage. Alma's jaw dropped.

The cottage was very old, with ancient red brickwork and dark timber frames, white plaster in between. The tiled roof was humped and hollowed, curving above tiny dormer windows. The garden was edged with more tall trees and Alma realised it backed on to the park, though it was hidden beyond the high hedge. A couple of apple trees stood in the centre of the lawn, fruit still clinging to them, while a small greenhouse and vegetable garden were just visible to the rear of the cottage.

'This is your house?' Alma looked at Ethan in amazement.

'Yeah. You like it?' He grinned, leading her to the front door.

'I love it! I mean, I had no idea it was here. It's so old, not like the other houses along here.'

'I think it was part of the old estate, you know, that the park originally belonged to.' Thick beams held up a tiny curved porch above the old timber door. A small bench was tucked in the side, a pair of wellies beneath it. Ethan turned the round handle and opened the door. They stepped into a narrow hallway scented with lavender and beeswax polish, the floorboards glowing with a mellow sheen.

'Ethan, is that you?' A tall, slender woman came into the hallway. Long dark hair fell halfway down her back, with streaks of grey at the temples. Her blue eyes opened wide, her pale smooth skin marred only by the line between her brows. She was so beautiful Alma stared at her in wonder. It was like finding a fairy-tale princess hidden away in the little cottage.

'Mum, this is Alma,' said Ethan, taking Alma's hand and bringing her forward. 'Alma, this is my mother.'

'Pleased to meet you,' said Alma, smiling at her. Ethan's mother smiled back, though there was something somehow vague about her, as though she were slightly out of focus.

'Hello dear,' she said. 'Please call me Dana.' Then she took in Ethan's state and her beautiful face creased with worry.

'Oh Ethan, come here.' She started to fuss around, her hands flapping as she opened a cupboard, pulling out a towel for him.

'Alma, I'm just going to change. I'll be quick, I promise.' He kissed her on the cheek and disappeared down the hall, leaving Alma stunned.

'It's all right, I'll look after you,' said Dana. 'We're safe here.'

Alma blinked. 'Would you like a cup of tea? I think Ethan will have one, and so will I if you do.'

'Oh, yes please, tea would be lovely.' Alma wasn't soaked but her clothes were damp and she was feeling chilly, even though the cottage was deliciously warm. She followed Dana through to a small kitchen with painted wooden cupboards. Bunches of dried herbs and garlic hung from hooks in the wall, scenting the air. What had Dana meant by that comment, 'We're safe here'? Alma shook her head. Curiouser and curiouser, she thought, as she perched herself on a stool next to the breakfast bar. Dana put the kettle on to boil and took three mugs from a high cupboard. She was entrancing; her delicate movements made it almost like a dance. Alma could see how she would have beguiled someone like Cedran.

'So you're Ethan's... friend?' asked Dana, looking over her shoulder with a smile. Alma blushed. Well, Ethan had just kissed her, so she guessed it was pretty obvious.

'Um, well, that is, I guess we are... sort of dating?' Her voice went up at the end of the sentence. 'That is, we haven't actually been on a date, but, um—'

Dana laughed, an attractive sound. 'Ethan has mentioned you to me already. I figured I'd get to meet you eventually.' She poured hot water into the mugs. 'Sugar?'

'Sorry, what?' Alma shook her head, confused, before she realised what Dana meant. 'Oh, yes, one please. This is a great kitchen,' she said, to change the subject. She meant it, though, taking in the small paned window over the sink, the heavy ceiling beams festooned with fairy lights. 'In fact your whole house is beautiful. I love it. I never even knew it was here.'

'Thank you. It's been here a long time, of course, but I've only lived here since just before Ethan was born.'

Ethan appeared, his hair still damp but the rest of him in dry clothes. 'Tea – you read my mind, Mum.' He kissed Dana on the cheek, taking two of the mugs and bringing one to Alma.

'Um, thanks,' she said as he handed it to her, lost for a moment in his eyes, his smile.

'So, Ethan, Alma was was telling me you haven't been on a date yet? Are you going to change that soon?'

'Dana!' Alma hid her hot cheeks in her tea, taking a long sip.

Ethan just laughed. 'You bet,' he said, sliding his arm around Alma's shoulders. 'Maybe we can do something this weekend?'

'Sounds good.'

Ethan stole a quick kiss and she blushed even more. Dana smiled at them.

'Um, Mum, there is something you need to know, though.' His voice had changed. Alma could feel tension in him that hadn't been there before.

'What's that?' Dana's eyes widened, her hands tightening around her mug.

'Well, Alma, she er...'

What was going on?

'She knows about Ambeth. And she knows... Dad.'

Dana went white. Ethan darted forward, taking her mug before it fell out of her slack fingers.

'Oh,' Dana gasped, one hand to her mouth and her eyes fixed on Alma. 'Oh, oh.'

'Mum, it's all right. Alma's like me. Her father was Galen, of the Light.' Ethan had one hand on his mother's shoulder, the other smoothing her hair. 'Come on, Mum, it's okay.'

Alma got up from her stool. She could see the energy running through the other woman, the swirls and jagged lines of her agitation glowing. 'May I?' She took Dana's hand, rubbing her fingers on the cool smooth skin, trying to access her power. Dana stared at her.

'What are you doing?' But she sounded more curious than afraid, so Alma kept going, her hands warming on Dana's skin. The glow of the other woman's energy became less ragged and the colour returned to her face. Dana let out a sigh.

Alma released her hand. 'Thank you for letting me do that.'

Dana looked at her for a long moment, her beautiful face thoughtful. 'Alma, I think we should talk, if you'd like.'

'I, er, might go outside, give you both a minute. I'll see you in a bit, hey?'

'Ethan, you don't have to go.' Dana reached out to him but he shook his head, then slid his arm around Alma's waist and kissed her on the cheek. 'Thank you,' he whispered. Then he was gone, the door swinging closed behind him, letting in a swirl of autumn air.

Alma sat back on her stool, and Dana brought two fresh mugs of tea over. Alma sipped hers while she waited for Dana to speak, trying not to stare at her too much. Dana picked up her own mug, then smiled at Alma.

'Will you let me tell you? About Cedran?'

Alma's eyes widened. 'Oh, um, of course,' she said.

Dana frowned. 'Oh, I won't, not if it will upset you. It's just, I can't talk to anyone about it. And after what you just did...'

'It's fine,' said Alma. 'Of course you can. Please...'

Dana nodded, her hands curving around her mug as though to take comfort from the warmth. Her eyes fixed on Alma. They were beautiful, fringed with dark lashes, and almost violet like periwinkles.

'I met Ethan's father when I was quite young,' she started. 'I was working in a boutique in town, just a few years out of school. I was saving to go to university.'

'To do what?'

'Oh! Well, I wanted to be a lawyer.' Dana smiled, her expression becoming distant. Then she focused on Alma again and her smile slid away. 'But meeting Cedran changed all that and here I am, in my cottage with Ethan. It's fine,' she went on. 'I wouldn't change things, even though it's been hard. Ethan is everything to me. And his father...' She looked away for a moment, taking in a breath. 'I met him by chance, sitting in the park one day, having my lunch.'

'The park.' Alma made a face and Dana nodded.

'Indeed. I was at one of the cafes. The sun was shining and he came up to me. I remember it so clearly, the first time I saw him. I'd never seen anyone so beautiful in my life.' Alma nodded. 'And the marvellous thing was, he seemed to feel the same way about me. He introduced himself and sat down, and we started talking. I was an hour late back to work and almost lost my job, but it didn't matter.'

'Because you were in love already.' Alma was already caught in the story, in the romance of it. Dana nodded again, her eyes suspiciously bright.

'It wasn't until I was pregnant that I found out who he was, what he was.'

'What, you mean he didn't tell you? I-I don't understand…?'

'I only ever saw him here. This cottage was his, hidden away in the trees so he could come and go as he pleased. There used to be a way through to the park from the garden, but I had it blocked off, after…' Her mouth twisted, and she set her mug down on the table. 'You have to understand, by the time I found out it was too late for me. I loved him desperately, and I was carrying his child.'

'But…what happened?' Alma whispered. The air in the little kitchen was heavy with memory.

'I couldn't deal with it, I suppose. I can't… do that kind of thing.' Dana shook her head, her dark hair flying around her face as she lifted her hands, spreading them as if to ward off a blow. 'Magical lands, dark forces. No.' She was frowning now. 'It terrified me, if I'm honest. And the fact that he was some sort of Dark Prince. It was too much for me.'

'S-so, what did you do?'

'What could I do? I loved him, but I couldn't deal with who he was. I was frightened of what it might mean for our child and, even though he told me he loved me like no other, that he wanted me to come and live with him in... Ambeth, I couldn't do it. Even though it broke my heart.'

'Oh, Dana, I'm so sorry.'

The other woman shook her head, a half-smile on her face. 'It's fine, Alma. It was a long time ago. And he was good to me, still is. I haven't seen him since Ethan was small, but I know he cares for our son.'

But Alma wasn't fooled. From the way Dana's lips were trembling and the tears pooling in her blue eyes, it was plain that the hurt was still raw.

'Ethan told me that his father showed him how to use the Gates, that he wants him to be able to choose where he lives. Have you never thought of—'

'Crossing over? No. I can't do it, Alma, no matter how much I may wish to see – huh. Well, it doesn't matter. Will you have more tea?'

Dana rose with a swish of skirts and went to the sink, rinsing her mug. Alma sat still, stunned by the story. Poor Dana.

'So, does it bother you that I'm from, well, that my father...?' She trailed off.

Dana turned to her, shaking her head. 'You make Ethan happy, that's obvious. And in some ways it's better that you know, that you're like him. So, no, it doesn't bother me at all. And I understand why he had to tell me.'

Alma swallowed, then let out a breath. 'My father died, before I was born. My mother knew about him, and she loved him so much as well. It's when a lot of things changed, I think, in Ambeth.'

'I'm sorry to hear that. Perhaps... I could talk to her one day?'

'I think she'd like that. She hasn't anyone either, well, other than me, to talk to about it all.'

Dana nodded, returning to the table with a fresh pot of tea. 'So... you've met him?'

Alma looked at her nonplussed for a moment, then realised what she meant. 'Oh! Lord Cedran? Well, yes, I have.'

'And?'

'Um, well, he kind of frightened me at first.'

'Really?' Dana sounded amused.

'Well, it was quite different, you know, for me. He was all in armour, and I was there for the Light and he was from the Dark, plus he was with another lord who, um, I guess, doesn't like me so much.' It was garbled, Alma knew, but she couldn't tell Dana about the Prophecy. She didn't want to worry her; it was obvious how fragile she was and really, it was up to Ethan if he wanted to tell her any more.

'Why doesn't he like you?'

Oh. Right. How to explain this one? 'Um, well, I was dating his son for a while.' Her eyes filled with tears and she wiped them away, annoyed with herself. 'Anyway, it didn't work out, it's over now. I'm, um, really happy with Ethan.' She blushed, hiding her hot cheeks with her hair. Where had that come from?

'It's obvious he's happy with you, too.' Dana smiled. 'So why don't you go and get him? I can make us all something to eat, if you like.'

'That sounds great.' Alma stood up. 'And, thanks, for telling me. You always can talk to me, whenever you want.' It was awkward, but Dana seemed pleased. Her beautiful face lit up in another smile, the vagueness gone.

'Thank you.'

OUTSIDE THE SKY WAS FADING TO DARK, THE AIR SCENTED WITH smoke and leaf mould. Leaves crunched underfoot as Alma walked over to Ethan, who was under one of the apple trees. He slid his arms around her waist as she kissed him.

'Hmmm, that's nice,' he said. Alma grinned, playing with the hair at the nape of his neck. 'Is Mum all right?'

'She's fine – she sent me to come and get you, she's making soup or something,' said Alma. 'I really like her.'

'So, what did you do in there? Was that, like, your Channelling thing?'

'Um, yeah, I guess. I could see your mum's energy and, well, I just wanted to fix it.'

'Well, whatever you did, it was amazing!' His eyes were wide. 'I mean, I've never seen anything like—'

'Don't.'

'Don't what?'

'It's just, I just wanted to help, that's all.' Her mouth twisted. 'I don't want it to make things weird between us.'

Ethan kissed her again, lingering, his mouth moving to her cheek, her eyelashes, his breath warm on her face.

'Nothing weird here,' he murmured. Alma found his mouth with hers, and a few moments passed before they could talk again.

'So, did she tell you about Dad?'

Alma nodded. 'It's kind of a sad story, hey?' she said. 'Your mum is so lovely... You know, it seems they come over here from Ambeth and it's like they cast a spell or something. My mother still loves my father as well.'

'It's our special magnetism,' said Ethan, squeezing her waist so she squealed.

'Well, if you have it, I have it, too,' she retorted.

'Oh, you have it,' he murmured, bending to kiss her again.

Alma laughed against him, taken by the moment, once again getting the sense of their energies merging, a connection deeper than any she'd felt before. She rested her head on Ethan's shoulder, enjoying the feel of him, his warmth, his hands on her back.

'So that energy thing you do, can you do it to me?'

Alma lifted her head. 'Um, I suppose. I mean, I already feel connected with you.' She hadn't meant to let that slip. But he was so close, his arms around her felt so good, so warm.

'You do?'

'Well, yeah. Um, it's like, when we're close, or when you touch me, or I touch you–' her hand came up to rest on the bare skin at the neck of his hoody, her fingers curving over his collarbone, and she closed her eyes '–I can feel you, feel your energy, and it's, um...' She bent her head, feeling silly, but his hand came up to cover hers.

'Tell me.' His voice was a whisper.

'It's like nothing I've ever felt,' she said finally, lifting her head. 'Like we match. Like I'm home.'

It was unbearably intimate, and she couldn't believe what she was saying. At the same time she knew it was true, every word of it. His face lit up in the fading light.

'Really?'

She nodded, her cheeks turning pink. His hand came up to her face.

'It's the same for me,' he said, his eyes intent on hers. 'I don't have your talents, I know that. But it feels the same. Like I'm home. And I never want to leave.'

CHAPTER 14
PERSISTENCE

Ellery woke suddenly, a noise shaking her from sleep. She sat up, groaning at the pain in her shoulder, tasting blood as the split on her lip opened again. Her face was throbbing and one eye wasn't opening properly. The noise came again, a rattle at the door. She froze. Was it her father? The beating had been bad enough, but she had a feeling there had been something after, something that might have been worse. The door opened and she shrank back, but it was only Hilde, one of her father's maids. The old woman was pushing a small trolley laden with a bowl of steaming water and some soft towels. Coming into the room she couldn't hide her shock. Her lined face stretched in horror as she saw Ellery.

'Oh, my child,' she breathed. There was a sound in the hall and Ellery heard, distantly, her father's voice. Hilde's face became blank once more. Rolling the trolley to the side of Ellery's bed, she bobbed a small curtsey.

'Hilde—' Ellery stopped, tears forming in her eyes. She'd known the old woman her whole life and felt ashamed that she should see her like this.

'Your father will be here soon, my lady. He sent me to help you, to make you presentable for his arrival.' Hilde held Ellery's gaze a moment longer than necessary, a warning in her faded blue eyes. Ellery nodded. Hilde curtseyed again, then went over to the fireplace.

'Let me set the fire first, my lady. It's cold in here.' Hilde busied herself with the kindling, blowing on the embers and coaxing them into a crackling blaze, which she supplemented with several small logs from the basket on the hearth. Immediately the room was cheered, filled with golden light and warmth. Hilde came back to Ellery.

'If you please, my lady, I will help you into a fresh gown as well.'

Ellery looked down at her dress – it was creased, blood spattered down the bodice. She supposed it was her own. One sleeve was torn. Again she felt ashamed, hanging her head.

'Come on, my child,' whispered Hilde, sharp and fast. 'This was not your fault. Come, let me help you before he arrives.'

Ellery looked up in surprise, but let Hilde help her from the bed, breathing hard at the effort. Her legs were like rubber and she struggled to stay upright as Hilde unlaced the back of her dress, slipping it gently from her shoulders. She gasped in pain – her left shoulder felt strange, as though wadded in fabric, and she couldn't move her arm properly. Her dress fell to her feet and she stood in her slip as Hilde dipped a sponge in the steaming water and wrung it out, releasing the sweet scent of roses. She started to dab at Ellery's face, wiping it gently, then across her shoulders and chest. *Her chest.* Ellery went rigid with horror.

'What is it, my lady? Am I hurting you?'

'Hilde.' Ellery's voice was a whisper. 'Where's my necklace?'

The old woman put the cloth down and looked around. 'Not to worry, my lady. It is on your bed. Shall I get it for you?' She went over to the bed.

'Don't touch it!' The words came out hard and fast. Hilde started in surprise, her hand hovering over the chain. She turned, her brow furrowed.

'I'm sorry, Hilde,' said Ellery. 'It's just, I don't want you to be hurt.'

Understanding dawned on the woman's face and she recoiled, returning to her task. Gently she washed and dried Ellery, brushing her long dark hair till it was smooth again, dabbing salve on the wounds on her face. Tears threatened again but Ellery held them in, not wanting to distress Hilde any more. She held up a soft woollen dress but Ellery couldn't get her arm to bend into the sleeve, crying out in pain when she tried. Hilde tutted and made her sit on the side of the bed. She took a little pot of ointment from the trolley and opened it, the room filling with the strong smell of eucalyptus. Scooping a dollop with her fingertips, she rubbed it gently into Ellery's shoulder. Ellery gritted her teeth. The ointment burned her skin at first, but then she could feel warmth in her tortured muscles, releasing them enough that she could move her arm a little more. Once she'd finished rubbing in the ointment Hilde produced a length of bandage that she wound expertly around Ellery's arm and across her shoulder, tucking the ends in.

'There, that should help, and it will be covered by your dress.'

'Thank you,' said Ellery, her voice low. She was hungry now and thirsty, but mostly she was just afraid of what her father would do when he came to her. Managing to get her arm into the dress, she waited as Hilde laced it up, then reached for the necklace. It looked as though the clasp had come undone while she was sleeping. She frowned, turning it over in her fingers, wondering how it had happened. There was a knock at the door.

'Come in,' tried Ellery, but her voice was weak. Still, she knew it wasn't her father – he would have already come in. 'Come in,' she managed, more loudly, and the door opened to reveal a maid with a tray. She brought it in and set it on the small table – it held a jug of water and goblet, a teapot and a mug, plus a covered dish. The smell of food made Ellery's stomach growl.

'Lady Ellery,' said the maid, curtseying. 'Your father sends refreshment for you. You are instructed to eat and drink, then he'll be with you. You're to have all your meals in here for the next while.'

Ellery glared at the maid.

'That's enough, Marte!' snapped Hilde. The little maid jumped, losing her smug expression. 'On your way, or the master will hear of it.' Marte made a face but turned on her heel and left. Hilde huffed, gathering up the towels and Ellery's torn and stained dress.

'She's well above herself, that one. Ideas above her station, that's for sure, and all because of— Well.' She pursed her lips, her face tight with disapproval.

'Let me guess,' Ellery said. 'My brother has had his way with her. Or was it my father?' Not that she cared, either way.

She went to the table and took the cover from the dish, revealing fresh bread, scrambled eggs and mushrooms, all steaming hot, and sausages still sizzling in their own little tray. Her face felt less painful, Hilde's salve working. She carefully sat down, discovering another bruise on her hip as she did so.

'Well, my lady, I'm sorry, but these things do happen. Forgive me, I shouldn't have mentioned it.'

Ellery shook her head, her mouth already full. 'No, it's fine,' she managed, her voice muffled. 'I'm sure it was Deryck, and recently, am I right?'

Hilde said nothing. Ellery returned to her meal, washing it down with the hot sweet tea. All was silent for a few minutes.

'Daughter.'

Ellery looked up, the food turning to ashes in her mouth. Hilde hastily piled the things onto the trolley and pushed it towards the door, her head bowed.

'Thank you, Hilde,' he said, coming into the room. 'I see

you're looking better already, Ellery. How do you feel?'

Ellery stared at her father. His face was amiable, his tone mild. There was no indication of his earlier violence, or any guilt at what he'd done. The hurt inside her was almost unbearable.

'Well?' Denoris came closer, his eyes narrowing.

'Um, I'm better than I was,' she said, her voice low. It wasn't a lie.

'You'll feel better still when you use your stone,' he said. 'Come, now. I'll sit with you a while, just to make sure you're all right.'

The false concern in his voice broke Ellery again. Tears started in her eyes. She was sure he didn't care whether or not she was all right. But he did want to make sure she was using the stone.

'Come on,' he said, anger creeping into his tone. 'Lie down on your bed. Would you like me to help you?'

'No!' Ellery's eyes widened and she shrank away from her father's outstretched arm. She went to her bed and sat down, then lay back, her arms crossed over her body. Her father pulled a chair up beside the bed, sitting down. He took a book from his pocket, opening it. Then he stopped, looking at her.

'Ellery, use the stone.' It was not a request. Tears leaking from her eyes Ellery reached for her necklace, moving the stone so it sat on her skin. Then she was gone.

'LORD DENORIS.' TOMAS BOWED DEEPLY, SURPRISED THAT THE Dark Lord had answered the door and not a little nervous. Ellery's father had a well-deserved reputation and Tomas didn't want to get on his wrong side for a lot of reasons. Denoris was frowning. Tomas swallowed, bracing himself against the famous green glare.

'Yes?' The Dark Lord's tone was curt. It took Tomas a moment to answer. But he wouldn't leave, not without seeing her.

'I was wondering if the Lady Ellery is free this evening, my Lord? I have a gift for her, and perhaps I could escort her to supper in the Hall, if that's all right with you.'

He took a breath and stood straight, shoulders back. He thought he saw, for a moment, a flicker of respect in the green eyes, but then it was gone.

'Ellery is not free at the moment. Nor will she be,' said Denoris. 'So if you please, I have work to do—'

'Is she all right?' The words tumbled out, his fear for her growing, trumping any concerns he might have for his own safety.

The Dark Lord frowned. 'She's fine.' He stepped back and went to close the door, but Tomas put his hand on it. Denoris stopped, his stare incredulous.

Tomas knew he was pushing it, but he wasn't ready to give up, not yet. 'Can I, would you, er, I would like to leave this gift for her.' He held out the small silk-wrapped parcel. Denoris looked at it as though it were a dead mouse. But Tomas persisted, trying to see over the Dark Lord's shoulder into the hallway. Denoris pushed him back, though not hard. His emerald eyes narrowed, though once again Tomas thought he caught a flicker of respect.

'Tomas, isn't it?'

'Yes, my Lord.'

'Well, Tomas, let me make this very clear. My daughter—' Denoris stressed the possessive, '—is not free to meet with you now, or ever. Nor do I wish for her to have your gifts. Be assured she is taken care of.'

'But my Lord—'

Denoris shook his head slightly, his hand tightening on Tomas's shoulder. 'I don't wish to make this unpleasant. However, if you don't leave, I will have no choice but to do so.' He leaned closer, his jaw tight. Fear flickered through Tomas, but it was nothing compared to his worry for Ellery. His instincts screamed that something was wrong. He opened his mouth to protest again.

'Take this chance, and go now,' said Denoris, before he could speak. 'And be glad of it. I do so only because of your father. Go, and do not come for Ellery again.' He shoved Tomas back and closed the door firmly in his face.

Tomas swallowed, shaken to his core. He thought for a moment of banging on the door, of demanding to see her. But he knew where that would lead. Chewing his lip, he looked around the darkened gardens, as though they might hold some solution. Maybe he should try to find Deryck – perhaps her brother could shed some light on what was happening. But he was loath to give up, to just leave her to whatever her father was doing. The memory of the bruises on her arm, the fear in her face, tore at his heart. Tucking his gift into his tunic pocket, Tomas walked around to where he thought Ellery's window might be, but the shutters were closed, a faint flickering line of light the only indication that someone might be in there. He knocked lightly on the wood, wondering if she could hear him. There was no answer. He waited, then tried again, harder this time. Nothing. Heart sore, he finally left, heading for the Hall in the hope that Deryck would be there.

DENORIS RAISED HIS HEAD, SHAKING IT IN DISBELIEF AS Ellery's shutters rattled. The boy was persistent, he gave him that. And his lineage was respectable, a good Dark family, though not as impressive as that of Denoris. Still, he would not do, not for his half-blood daughter, for what he had in mind for her. He looked down at Ellery. Her dark hair was spread across the pillows, her green eyes half closed. She sighed, her lips parting in ecstasy as the stone lay on her skin. He'd never seen anything like the effect the tallus was having on her. He ran his fingers through the dark silk of her hair, gleaming in the firelight. She turned her face to the warmth of his hand as it trailed across her cheek, caressing the soft skin. Then he bent his head once more.

CHAPTER 15
A LOVE TOKEN

Denoris stumbled as he came through the Gate into the Garden of Shadows, his hand going to his tallus stone. He took a moment to catch his breath, then turned to close the doorway, the little pool of dark energy gleaming in the morning light. He made his way to one of the benches set into the wall and sat down heavily, wiping sweat from his brow.

He needed the girl, dammit! Since the return of the Cup and Sword it had become more difficult to send out Dark energy, and he was doing it more often than he used to, sending it further than before to try and counter the effects. He wouldn't be able to sustain this pace for much longer, though he needed to, if his plans were to succeed.

The energy from his tallus flowed through him, restoring him, his breath returning to normal. He was still tired, but there were things to do. With a sigh he got to his feet, leaving the Garden and heading for the stables.

Soon he was out in the hills, riding hard towards his country house. Birds wheeled overhead, the sea glinting in the distance. As he drew closer, there was no sign of the Watchers he'd sent from Etras' stronghold. He frowned as he rode into the stable yard, his mount's hooves clattering on the stone cobbles. Where in Darkness were they?

Dismounting, he handed the reins to a cowering groom and stalked inside, not bothering to wipe his boots. 'Aeres,' he called. 'Where are you, my dove?' He opened one door after another. Where was his wife? The double doors at the end of the hallway opened and she stood there, silhouetted against the morning light.

'Denoris.' She half gasped the word, the emerald on her finger glinting as she put her hand to her chest.

'My dear.' He went to her, taking her hand in his and kissing it, once again surprised at her beauty, forgotten in the hills. Gwenene held his heart, there was no doubt of that, but his wife, all slumberous eyes and red-gold curls, was a temptation he could never resist. His kisses lingered, until she pulled her hand back, folding her arms.

'What,' she began, her eyes narrowing, 'is the meaning of those *creatures* who have taken roost in the second-best bedroom? For I tell you,' she went on, 'if this is another one of your schemes, I will—'

'You'll what?' Denoris took a step towards her. She took one back. Beautiful, she was, but challenging, too. Her fire was what had drawn him to her in the first place. That, and the promise of a son who would bring about change. He still recalled the smoky scent of the Seer's island, the burning piles of sacred wood, the creature that guarded the way. He'd had no power there, had been made to kneel like all the others in a place of candles and stone, as he made his offering and learned his fate.

The promised son had eventually been born, despite the fact that his wife had turned from him soon after they were married, preferring the solitude of the hills to his company.

'Get rid of them!' Her voice jarred him from his thoughts. She seemed angrier than usual, more willing to fight him than she had been in a long time. Her hand went to her head, her eyelids fluttering. 'Can't you hear them?' Her lips drew back from her teeth. 'They're in my head, I swear.'

Ah. That explained her agitation. He wondered, though – the creatures were tuned to his mind, not hers. But then she'd always been unusually sensitive – probably where the boy got it from.

'Now why would I get rid of them?' he said, taking her hand again, his lips moving across her knuckles. He felt his passion rise as she pulled back from him, her gaze defiant. 'When I was the one who sent them here.' He reached out, pulling her hard against him, ignoring her protests about the mud on his breeches.

'You sent them?' She turned her head away, leaning back. 'What for? A love token? I would rather another ring. Or perhaps an invitation to join you at the apartment, to go dancing in the Great Hall once more...' She put her hand to her head again. 'I do miss dancing with you,' she murmured, her eyelids half-closed.

'We can dance here, my lady,' he said, twirling her around. She laughed, falling against him, her tumbling hair releasing the scent of lavender and roses. Yes, a temptation indeed, especially when her hands were on him as they were now.

'There will be time for that, my lady,' he said. He set her back from him, but gently. He wasn't going to let the opportunity pass, of course he wasn't; it was so rare that she was receptive to his overtures. But first he had something to do.

'Let me sort out your problem,' he went on, as she pouted. 'And then...' He raised an eyebrow.

'Fine,' she said, moving away from him, once more the elegant lady. 'But be careful.' Her jewel-like eyes gleamed. 'They have already taken one of the servants. I had to have the door barred.' She drifted back into the room from whence she'd came, taking a seat by the window and looking out to sea.

Denoris shook his head, blinking. His wife had always been, and remained, a puzzle to him. Perhaps that was why he found it easier to leave her to her own devices. He ran a hand through his hair, then turned, heading for the stairs.

Upstairs, the long hallways were deserted. He headed into the wing where the guest quarters were, remembering days when they were full, the house busy with guests. Strange how things changed, almost without realising; the years sliding by, taking friends and lovers and children with them. He stopped, rubbing a hand across his face, reaching once more for his tallus.

The door at the end of the doorway was indeed barred, as Aeres had said, with lengths of timber nailed across it. The door itself was scarred; several holes were punched through it. He put his eye to one, and laughed out loud.

The creatures were there, sure enough. A nest had been made on the bed and several others on the silk carpet, which was soiled with mess and feathers, the furniture in the room broken and tumbled. He spotted the gleam of bone, and tattered rags of clothing – probably the remains of the unfortunate servant. He reached out with his mind, testing the connection. The creatures all turned their heads as one, staring at the door. Good. The connection held. Now all he had to do was figure out how to get in there.

He couldn't risk opening the door and letting the creatures out to further ravage his home and servants. He stood back from the door, his hand rubbing his chin, as he considered the problem.

Then he looked through the hole in the door again, a glimmer of an idea coming to him. There were two large windows in the room, one either side of the large bed. Both were shattered, the frames and glass gone.

His decision made, he opened the next door along the hallway. It was another guest room, with the same large windows as the one the creatures were in. The walls were stone, so there was no way the creatures could break through. Denoris went to the window, opening it wide. There was a narrow ridge of stone running above and one below the window, just wide enough for a foot to balance on. Swinging himself out, Denoris clung to the ridge above, his toes on the ridge below. He reached out with his mind again, holding the creatures still, as he inched along, his muscles straining, until he reached the first of the broken windows and swung himself inside.

The creatures were watching him, their great leathery wings folded back. Denoris held them with his strength of will, mentally cursing himself for not having his sword. Any slip, any error, would be fatal. But he was stronger than they were. He stepped carefully over the mess and feathers, grabbing the closest Watcher by the neck, forcing his gaze onto the red staring eyes, melding with the hive mind.

'Go,' he sent. Images flowed from his mind to theirs. *Find this girl, and the boy, and report back to me. Scare them a little, but do not harm her. Oh, and when you return, the barn will be a more comfortable place to rest.'*

A small favour to Aeres, he thought, as he pressed himself against the wall. The creatures flew out en masse, their wings displacing great draughts of air as they squeezed through the windows. Their cries echoed, fading away, as they winged their way from one world to another, leaving Denoris alone in the room.

Not quite alone, as it turned out. There were three babies in one of the nests, small feathered creatures who snapped and hissed when he came near. He took a blanket from the fouled bed and threw it over them. He would send servants to unbar the door and block the windows, moving the nests to the barn before the creatures returned. After all, once his plans came to fruition, the house would be full again, when his influence stretched across the worlds.

He left the room via the window once more, swinging himself back into the room next door. He paused, panting, wiping his hands down his already filthy breeches. He peeled his shirt off as he went down the hallway towards the master bedroom, calling for a servant to run him a bath, and to send in the Lady Aeres. She would no doubt be pleased when he told her the creatures were gone, and he planned to take full advantage. He needed a lie down, anyway.

~

'I LIKE ETHAN.' SARA LINKED HER ARM WITH ALMA'S AS THEY walked along, Josh and Ethan behind them. They were heading for a funfair that had set up in the park. Music pumped and lights flashed from up ahead, the smells of fried food and candy floss mingling in the dusky air.

'Thanks.' Alma grinned. 'I like him, too.'

'Duh, really?' Sara laughed. 'So, are you guys, uh, you know?' She waggled her eyebrows and Alma blushed, glancing back at Ethan.

'Shhh. No, not yet, but, you know, ha, one day, probably?' She giggled. It had only been a few days since their first kiss, but she already knew how she felt about Ethan. And how he made her feel. 'So how about you and Josh? Are things still...?'

'Oh, yeah, they're great.' Sara smiled. She squeezed Alma's arm, leaning into her. 'I'm just happy you're happy again, you know? After the whole David thing, and how I never met him.' Her brown eyes were concerned.

'I'm so sorry,' said Alma, emotion welling up as she realised anew how her life in Ambeth had almost taken over, putting their friendship in jeopardy. 'For all of that. I'm just so glad we're still friends. I couldn't have made it through... everything, without you.'

'Anytime, bestie,' said Sara.

Shouting erupted up ahead and both girls looked up. A group of young men, yelling and pushing each other, had turned on the crowd, jeering and laughing as one flicked the cap from another boy's head, while another pushed a teenage girl so hard she fell into a stall, banging her arm and starting to cry. Her boyfriend fronted up to the boys but was swiftly beaten down by two of them, while the others tipped all the condiments from a food van on the floor, squirting the front of the van and the furious proprietor with sauce bottles, laughing uproariously. Josh already had his arm around Sara, steering her away. Alma felt Ethan take her hand, pulling her. But she didn't move. Something wasn't right. There was a curious feel to the air, a heaviness that prickled against her skin. She looked around, trying to figure out what was going on, why everything felt so wrong. Then energy pulsed through her feet, so strong it almost knocked her over. Her eyes widened. She turned to Ethan.

'Can you see it?'

ETHAN HAD BEEN ENJOYING THE FAIR. WELL, HE WAS ENJOYING being with Alma – he really didn't care where they were as long as they were together. Though he would have preferred just to be with her alone, he didn't mind being on a double date – there would be time enough to spend together later, in Ambeth. Then the shouting started. He moved forward quickly, his protective instincts taking over as he grabbed Alma's hand and tried to move her away from the hooded youths, their heads darting like predators seeking prey as they looked for their next target. But she wouldn't move. And then he felt it, the pulse of light coming from her so strong it made him jump.

'Can you see it?' As she touched him, it was as though he could see what she could, that they were connected somehow. A cloud of darkness surrounded the young men, roiling and shadowy, tendrils reaching like black fingers through their eyes, their noses, their mouths, worming their way inside. As the angry crowd grew larger the darkness expanded, twisting around and through them, as though feeding on their rage. Out of the corner of his eye he saw Sara trying to hold Josh back, the group of young men homing in on Alma. All this happened in a split second, yet it was as though time stretched into a bubble around them and he could see everything.

'I see it.' He pulled on her hand again as the darkness rolled towards them. He could feel a response to it inside him, a slight tugging. He didn't want to think about what that meant. 'What the hell is it?'

'It's Dark.' She turned to him and his eyes widened.

Alma was *glowing*.

CHAPTER 16
SPARKS FLY UPWARDS

Alma's eyes shone brilliant blue against her pale skin, dark red strands of hair snapping around her face as though alive.

'We need to go,' Ethan said, trying to keep control of himself, so they didn't expose themselves for what they were any more than they already had. Alma reached out her other hand and he could see the stone of her talaith burning golden through the sleeve of her top, sparks starting from her fingertips. The whole world was moving so very slowly. He tried again.

'Come *on*. I know you're tough, but we can't fight all of them.' But he was too late. She released his hand and he recoiled, staggering.

'What're you lookin' at?' One of the young men had reached Alma, getting in her face. His friends closed in. But before Ethan could move she touched the boy on his arm, her hand pale against his dark top. There was a split second flare of light, bright gold against the dark and sparkle of the fairground, and the black cloud was gone, drifting apart and dissolving like mist.

'What the hell was that?' Josh looked dazed, as did most of the other people in the crowd. The young men shook their heads and looked around, frowning as though they didn't know where they were. The one Alma was touching stepped back, his hands up, blinking like he'd just woken up.

'No problem, man,' he said, seeing Ethan approaching. 'It's cool, I wasn't touching her.'

'It's fine,' he said, putting his arms around Alma, relieved that she and her bracelet were no longer glowing. She clung to him, shaking, and he hugged her tight, kissing her hair, realising anew how much she meant to him. 'It's gone,' he murmured between kisses. 'It's all right.'

'I know,' she said.

There was more shouting and they both turned, Ethan moving in front of Alma. But this time it was the stall owner, gesturing angrily as he led a group of three security guards towards them.

'Just look at my stall,' he shouted, pointing at the piles of napkins and dripping sauces, drinks and chairs overturned. The boys looked at each other.

'Did we do that?' said one of them. Then the guards were on them. The group moved to the side of the stall, where the owner, red in the face, was obviously lecturing them.

'Are you insane?' Sara had Alma by the arm, her breath coming fast, her brown hair rumpled. 'What were you thinking? Are you all right? Is she all right?'

'It's all right,' he said, though he had no idea how to explain what she, what everyone would have just seen.

'I'm fine,' said Alma again, almost at the same time. 'It's okay.'

'But they, like, lit a flare or something! Like it was right next to you? Oh my god!'

'Um, yeah, the flare. Um, well, it wasn't as close as it looked, honestly. I mean, it just looked like it was.' Alma darted a guilty glance at Ethan.

He tried to smile, but he was still shaken. So that was what Channelling looked like. Huh. Perhaps it was time to go back to Ambeth, to see Thorion. And his father. No wonder the Dark wanted her. Sara still had Alma by the arm, was still talking furiously. Alma touched her, gently, just for a moment, and Sara calmed down.

And then there was his reaction to... whatever that had just been. It was Dark, that was certain, he had felt it calling him. Sighing, he shoved his hands in his pockets and went to talk to Josh.

～

LATER, ALMA WALKED WITH ETHAN THROUGH THE PARK, leaving the lights of the fairground behind. The strange events of the evening had put a dampener on the date. Sara and Josh had left to get food, saying they'd catch up with them later. Sara had hugged Alma before they'd parted, telling her to take care of herself, to not do anything else silly. She'd almost laughed. If only she knew.

They crossed the playing fields. The starlight turned everything to grey and black, the War Memorial like a pale finger above the huddled trees. Ethan was quiet, his hands in his pockets, his head down.

'Come on,' said Alma, as they passed the playground, the castle-shaped climbing frame a darker silhouette against the dusk. 'Come and sit for a sec.'

She went over to the swings and sat on one, her heels dragging in the dust. Ethan took the one next to her, twisting the chains so he spiralled around.

'Are you... is everything okay?'

He looked up. 'So that was Channelling, hey?'

Alma bit her lip and nodded. Was he... had she *scared* him? Her heart hurt at the thought. 'Yeah. I mean, it's all still pretty new to me, but, um, I think so. I just wanted the darkness to go away.'

Ethan was silent, his head dropping once more.

She frowned as realisation washed over her. 'Oh, Ethan, I don't mean—'

'No, it's okay,' he said.

'Ethan, I—'

'It's just, is that the Dark? Is that what I come from?' He sounded so troubled she reached out to him, taking his hand.

'Your father is Dark, but it doesn't mean you are,' she said. 'And that thing, what we saw tonight, was Dark energy, pure and elemental. Plus, you're half human, which means you get to choose.'

'To choose?' He glanced at her, light catching his eyes.

'Yes, like my friend Merewyn—' She broke off. A shape moved on top of the nearby climbing frame, like a shred torn from the night sky, black wings flapping like a bat. 'Ethan, what the hell is that?'

He followed her gaze and his eyes widened.

'It's a Watcher.'

CHAPTER 17

FEATHERS AND SHADOWS

Ethan grabbed Alma's arm and pulled her to her feet. They ran, pounding along the pathway leading to the edge of the park. Street lamps stood at intervals along it, casting pools of light.

'Stop, stop!' Alma's shoelace had come undone and her trainer was sliding on her foot. She bent over, gasping, and tied the lace. Ethan doubled back to her. She straightened up, squinting and peering back along the pathway, but couldn't see anything coming. The black shape was still on top of the climbing frame, flapping away. She suddenly realised what it was. She laughed.

'It's fine, Ethan,' she said, pointing. 'It's just a plastic bag, look. Someone must have left it there.'

He shook his head. 'It wasn't a bag. We need to—'

There was a shriek and something crashed through the nearby treetops. There was a scent of rotting meat and a dark shape plunged down. Alma screamed, throwing her hands up. Then Ethan had her, spinning her away from the creature's snapping jaw, pulling her deeper into the shelter of the trees.

She gasped as she hit a tree trunk, hard. Ethan came up

against her, an arm either side of her braced against the tree trunk.

'What's happening?' she said.

'Shhh. Don't let them hear you.' He closed his eyes and took a deep breath, the faint light from the pathway carving his face into angles so he looked like his father. She gasped again, she couldn't help it, as dark wings rose up from his shoulders, wrapping around them both to block out the twisting black shapes of the Watchers. She reached up a trembling hand to the billowing darkness surrounding her and felt the softness of feathers. Then Ethan's gentle mouth was on hers and, despite the terror of the night, she began to relax.

'They can't see us in here,' he whispered, his mouth still close to hers. 'Just wait a moment, I'll know when they're gone.'

'But... but how?'

'Because I'm Dark, Alma, and so are they.' She could feel his smile against her cheek, his warm breath, the tickle of his eyelashes. They stayed that way for a while, Alma straining to listen, the trees creaking and rustling as the Watchers whooped and squealed. She was increasingly aware of Ethan so close to her, the heat of his body. Her arms were curled up between them, her hands resting on his chest, feeling the smooth muscles under his sweatshirt. So what if he was Dark? It changed nothing about how he made her feel, how safe she felt with him. It was different to the madness of her time with Deryck, more like how things had been with Caleb, though with Ethan there was more, an attraction that made her burn like fire. She ran a gentle finger across his lips, feeling his kiss on her hand. He leaned in closer and she took a breath, sure he was going to kiss her again. But instead he whispered, 'They're gone,' his wings dissolving like mist.

Alma blinked. The half-light seemed bright after the darkness. Ethan smiled. 'Are you all right?' She caught the gleam of his eyes as he bent his head, kissing her with more heat this time, his arms tightening around her.

'We need to go,' he said eventually, pulling back. 'They'll be back.'

'But where can we go?' This was all very nice and distracting, but she doubted the creatures of the Dark would be gone for long. She was desperate to be indoors, but the nearby café was closed, and they were on the wrong side of the park from her house.

'My house,' said Ethan. 'My father has it well protected. They won't be able to get us there. Come on.'

Taking her hand, he led her between the trees. Alma glanced up nervously. But there were no shrieks, no flapping wings, no churning sense of wrongness. Maybe they'd gone, after all.

They'd left the park by now, heading along the main road. Ethan put his arm around her and she leaned into him, looking forward to getting to his house. Then her stomach dropped. At the same moment Ethan tensed.

'Run!'

And the night changed. Dark shadows swooped from the trees to tug at Alma's hair, claws scratched her shoulders as she ducked and screamed. Ethan pulled her ahead of him. 'Go!' he said, picking up a tree branch and turning to face the approaching Watchers. 'It's the next driveway, you'll be safe there.'

Tears running down her cheeks, not wanting to leave him, Alma put her head down and made for the line of bricks that marked the edge of the driveway. The Watchers were calling to each other, whooping and shrieking, and Ethan was shouting. She turned to see him running, a stream of dark shapes with red eyes swooping down from the trees above.

'Ethan!' she screamed. He caught up to her, slamming into her and nearly knocking the breath out of her.

'Come on.' He grabbed her around the waist and dragged her the last couple of metres to his driveway, where he threw himself over the line of stones, taking Alma with him and twisting his body so he landed on his back, cushioning her landing. He grunted as they hit the ground, Alma's hair flying around them as they collapsed onto the grass and pebbles. The whooping and shrieks rose to a crescendo and, as she looked back, Alma could see the Watchers battering themselves against an invisible barrier. She rolled off Ethan, touching his face, tears falling. He wasn't moving.

'Ethan, oh, Ethan, are you all right.' She sobbed, reaction to the stress of the night hitting her hard.

Ethan groaned, his eyes coming open. 'I'm okay,' he managed, 'just a bit winded.'

Alma laid her head on his shoulder, her arm around his chest. He brought his hand up to clasp hers as they lay there, catching their breath.

'They're never going to stop, are they?' Tears ran down her face, warm on her skin.

Ethan squeezed her hand. 'The Dark?' His breath was still short, and her heart broke to hear it, the guilt carving through her.

'Yeah. Not until...'

'Until you find the Crown.'

'Or they get me, whatever happens first.'

'I won't let them touch you,' said Ethan, his lips on her brow. 'But I think, perhaps, we might need to speak to Thorion about this, hey?'

Alma nodded. Still sniffling, she got to her feet, holding her hand out to Ethan. They were both covered with mud and leaves. Ethan limped a little as he took Alma's hand and they started down the drive. Behind them the Watchers swooped and squealed, still trying to get through the wards.

They finally reached the cottage, standing serene in the dusk, the garden a shadowy calm oasis after the wild terror of their journey. There was a light in the small wooden porch, a large candle in a hurricane glass sitting on a shelf set into the thick wall. Ethan turned the round handle and the front door swung open. Alma was glad to be inside. They headed for the sitting room, where a gentle glow of light indicated the room was occupied.

'Hi, Mum,' said Ethan, sticking his head around the door.

'Oh hello Ethan. Alma, come in,' said Dana, looking up from her embroidery. Her lovely face filled with concern as she took in their state, the dishevelled clothing and Alma's tear-stained face. 'What's happened?' She put her embroidery to one side, getting to her feet and coming over.

'It's okay, Mum, we're all right,' said Ethan. 'Nothing to worry about.' He held her hand for a moment.

'Really, Dana, we're fine,' added Alma, her voice still rough with emotion. 'Um, it was just, well...'

'It's fine,' said Ethan. 'Just a spot of trouble, over now. I think we might go upstairs and freshen up.'

'All right,' said Dana. 'Why don't I make you both some tea?' Her voice had become vague, her gaze sliding away, as though she didn't want to know.

'That would be great, thanks,' said Alma, managing a smile, though her legs were still shaking.

'It'll be ready in a minute,' said Dana, heading towards the kitchen. 'There are towels in the airing cupboard,' she went on, 'so help yourselves.'

Ethan jerked his head towards the narrow twisty stairs. 'Come on.'

Alma followed him up the dark-beamed stairs, stopping on the landing to peer through the tiny mullioned window. Outside everything seemed still, no shapes lurking in the darkness. All she could see was the peaceful garden, the old apple tree, though she could still faintly hear the Watchers shrieking somewhere beyond the borders.

'They're still out there,' she said.

Ethan put his arm around her. 'We're safe in here.' He paused.

'What did you mean before, when you were talking about your friend?'

The question took her by surprise. 'Merewyn?'

'Yeah. You were trying to tell me something, when we were on the swings.'

'Uh, yeah.' Alma thought for a second. 'Right. Well, Merewyn is half Dark, half Light. So she gets to choose. And so do you. Besides, what I really wanted to tell you—' she leaned on him '—is that it doesn't matter anyway.'

'What?'

'About us, about how I feel about you. The fact that you're half Dark changes nothing. Because I can feel you, your energy, and it's nothing like what we saw back there.'

'Really?'

'Really.'

He turned to face her and put his around her. 'Good,' he said, 'because I don't want it to change – you and me, I mean.' Then he kissed her.

'I do need to ask about something, though,' she said, when he lifted his head. 'So, um, you have wings?'

'Yeah.' He huffed out a laugh.

'But... how?'

'You have powers from your father, right?' he said. 'Well, that's what I have from mine. A sense for danger, and the wings to protect me, or us, in this case.'

'Wow,' said Alma. 'That's... pretty amazing. I mean, do they work? Can you fly?'

'No, they don't have enough substance for that. I tried it, once, when I was younger. Luckily I was staying with my father at the time and he caught me just as I was going to jump off the roof of the Great Hall.' Alma's mouth dropped open. 'Yeah, well, he wasn't too pleased,' Ethan went on, laughing a bit. 'But at the same time I think he was kind of proud of me, that I had that power. We have an... unusual relationship, as you know.'

Alma nodded. Ethan took a leaf from her hair. 'Come on,' he said. 'Let's get changed.'

She followed him up the last few steps into a narrow hallway with heavy dark beams in the walls and ceiling, the plaster between painted white. A small niche held another candle inside a glass lantern, already lit, the warm glow lighting the space. Alma followed Ethan past two doors; one stood ajar and she glimpsed an iron bedstead with lacy covers, an old chair against a pale wall. The last door in the hall was made of heavy wood and had a metal latch. Ethan lifted it and the door swung open.

'My room.'

Alma went inside. So this was his private space. 'This is nice,' she said, looking around. The same heavy beams and light plaster as the hall hinted at the age of the house, as did the sloping ceiling and wide-beamed floor. He went to the bed and switched on the lamp on the small table next to it. The rest of the furnishings were simple – a scrubbed pine chest of drawers and an assortment of shelves holding books and other items. There was a large poster on one wall, a photograph of a green forest with the sun shining through the leaves. Alma went over for a closer look. It was actually a canvas, the photo stretched over a wooden frame.

'This looks like—'

'Ambeth? It is, actually. I took a photo on one of my visits there, and I liked it so much I had it done as a canvas.'

Alma's eyes widened. She looked again and recognised the path leading through the woods. It was a beautiful image that tugged at her heart. She realised how much she loved Ambeth, loved the magic it had brought into her life.

She turned around just as Ethan was pulling off his shirt. He dropped it on the floor as he rummaged in the drawer for a clean one, his muscles moving under his smooth skin. Then he turned around and caught her watching. Her face flared bright red.

'Sorry,' she mumbled. He laughed, shrugging on a T-shirt as he moved towards her, another shirt in his hand. She bit her lip as the dark fabric covered his stomach muscles.

'Here's one for you,' he said, holding out the other shirt. 'If you want. I won't look.'

Alma giggled. She didn't mind if he looked. 'Thanks.' She took the T-shirt from him; it was blue, the fabric soft in her hands. Ethan grinned and put his hands over his eyes. She turned her back, peeling off her dirty hoodie and dropping it on the floor. Hearing the floorboards creak she looked over her shoulder. Ethan was leaning against the chest of drawers, arms folded as he eyed her appreciatively.

'Hey!' she said, pulling on the shirt. It smelled like him, warm and clean. 'You said you wouldn't look.'

'I know,' he said, coming over to slide his arms around her waist, laughter in his eyes, 'but I just couldn't resist.'

'And?' said Alma, looking at him through her lashes.

'And,' he murmured, kissing her. 'I'm glad I looked.'

'Oh,' said Alma. She pressed herself against him, her hands in his hair, kissing him back as they moved towards the bed. She lay on her back, Ethan half on her, half next to her, one of his hands sliding up under her blue t-shirt, warm on her stomach.

'Beautiful Alma,' he murmured. She arched against him, pulling him so he was on top of her completely, her hands around his back under his shirt. Things were getting heated when they heard Dana calling up the stairs. Their tea was ready.

'Ignore her,' gasped Alma. Dana called again, her voice sounding closer as the stairs creaked.

'No, we can't.' Ethan groaned, rolling off her to sit up, panting. 'She'll come in here in a moment if we don't answer. She worries, you know?'

Alma sat up as well, pulling her shirt down, running her hands through her hair. 'Yeah, I know.'

There was a knock at the door and it opened to reveal Dana, a line between her dark brows, which smoothed out when she saw Alma and Ethan.

'Oh,' she said. 'Oh, you're all right. Your tea's ready, if you'd like to come down.'

'Um, thanks, Dana,' said Alma, blushing.

'Thanks, Mum,' said Ethan. 'We'll be down in a sec, okay?'

'Don't be too long,' she said, smiling, though the line between her brows had returned. 'It will get cold.' She withdrew, closing the door.

'Well,' said Ethan, taking Alma's hand. 'Guess we'd better go.'

'Yes,' she said, but she didn't move, leaning her head on his shoulder. Ethan put his arm around her. 'You know,' she said.

'What?' said Ethan, his breathing almost back to normal.

'When we go through the Gate next time, um, you know they have music in the Hall most nights, and then...' She lifted her head.

Ethan was smiling at her. 'And then what?'

'Well, you know I have that nice room there. With a locking door.'

Ethan's smile grew broader. 'Sounds like just what we need.'

CHAPTER 18
HUNTED

'Have you seen Rozelle, of late?'

The young man's eyes widened and he stood up abruptly, the wooden legs of his chair scraping the floor. Denoris suppressed a grin.

'I have not, my Lord. She hasn't been around for some while. I heard she'd gone to visit her family, in the hills.'

He was trembling slightly, his pale cheeks flushed. Denoris held his gaze, keeping his expression neutral. The young man dropped his eyes first.

'Thank you. Now, leave.'

'My Lord?'

'Get. Out.'

The young man's mouth dropped open. He bent to gather his notes, the pen rattling against the table. Clutching his papers, he bowed and headed for the door.

Denoris looked around the room. There were only two other people in the library of the Dark – a man and a woman, seated together in one of the window seats, the sunset sky behind them. The woman was holding a book, the red cover vibrant against the dark skin of her hands. Both of them were staring at Denoris, their mouths half open. He glared at them, half snarling, his fists clenched. By the Dark, he'd had enough of this! The man touched his companion's arm and she put her book down, both of them getting to their feet. As they moved past him to leave the library, the woman glanced at him and frowned. He held himself back, just, though his snarl deepened.

When the door closed behind them he sealed it with a charm and went to the carved bookcase. Pressing on one of the leaves, he waited for the hidden drawer to slide out. Avernath. Stolen by him, so long ago. When the Dark had moved away from reading the skylore only he had seen the folly of doing so. And now they looked to him once more, to reclaim the old ways and make them anew. It was difficult, without the Shield Stone, but not impossible. Besides, that would be his, soon enough. Thorion would beg him to take it.

'YOU READY, PRETTY BOY?' FLORIA, HER LONG DARK HAIR braided back from her face, brought her horse around next to Deryck's. Both mounts were snorting, chomping at the bit. Hounds weaved around everyone's legs, already squeaking and whining in anticipation of the chase. Deryck wasn't riding Thetis, not wanting to risk her on the Hunt. Instead, he'd borrowed a black stallion from his father's stables. The animal was all heat and smooth muscle, strong beneath him.

'He'd better be. We don't babysit.' Simeon, the red jewels on his black armour catching the last of the light, came around their other side. He nodded at Deryck, his dark eyes fierce. Deryck nodded back, keeping his expression smooth. He could play this game, even though he was shaking inside. He fought to control himself – he was more than capable, a fierce rider and strong fighter. This was not his first hunt.

But it was the first time he'd hunted a human.

The call had gone up a short while before. The prey had been spotted in the fields beyond the Palace, running for the hills. Deryck didn't know who it was, only that they'd been marked by the Hunt for some transgression or another. He was already half drunk, playing drinking games with Floria in the Hall, when Simeon arrived and summoned them all to the stables.

But he was well and truly sober now. Adrenaline and his stone sharpened every edge, every noise, every shadow. The rest of the Hunt were assembled, their fierce hawk-like faces above blackened armour, red jewels glinting like blood as their horses pranced and snorted, tossing their manes. The stables were deserted; the grooms had all run to hide. Feathered purple clouds streaked the sky, the first stars peeping through. Night was coming. It was time to ride.

Simeon wheeled his horse around, placing a horn to his lips. He blew, and it was the sound of the wind shrieking around distant crags, of crashing waves and the screams of hunting birds. Howling, whooping, the Hunt surged forward into the night.

Deryck bent low over the reins, keeping up easily. Floria, next to him, laughed up at the darkening sky. He'd thought he would be excited, that the Hunt would bring him out of himself, something new to fill his time. But instead all he could think of was Alma at her tower window, her skin ivory in the moonlight, watching the Hunt stream past before returning to bed and to his arms. Or, worse still, the sight of her running that awful day at the tournament, her bright dress standing out against green fields as the Hunt rode her down.

Tears streaked his cheeks. He touched his stone, baring his teeth and shrieking. But it was pain, not excitement, that drove him. He spurred his horse onwards, faster and faster, the creature responding, taking him past the other riders to the head of the Hunt. Simeon raised his arm, screaming his eerie battle cry, speeding up to keep pace with him as they flashed across the fields, the land rising. The hounds were in full cry, racing ahead, and Deryck tried not to think how it must have been for Alma, alone in the woods, to hear them coming for her.

A cry went up, and Deryck saw a pale figure moving on the slopes ahead. His father's estate was a dark shadow in the distance. He thought briefly of peeling away and riding there, seeking the wine-soaked oblivion of his mother's cellars, her vague ministrations.

But he dismissed the idea. He'd made a vow, and he had to honour it. Floria was on his other side now, howling, one arm raised as she urged the Hunt forward. The pale figure was closer – Deryck saw it turn, then speed up, scrambling with hands and feet up the hillside. There was no refuge there, Deryck knew. He was familiar with the landscape since childhood. Unless they made it to one of the passes, and there was no chance of that, not at the speed they were moving.

He drew close enough to see that the figure was male, dressed in a tunic and breeches, his feet bare, his blond hair pale against the darkened hillside. More flashbacks, this time of Caleb, his eyes wide as Deryck stabbed down, of Alma screaming in the stands. Unable to take any more, he pulled his horse up and back. The animal reared and several of the riders cursed as they swerved around him.

But the first of the hounds had caught up to the figure now, leaping smoke pale against the hillside to take him down. Several more joined in, pulling him by the leg so he fell. Simeon drew his sword, flashing a snarling smile as he sped forward. The hounds scattered as he rode through their midst, pulling to a stop at the struggling figure.

Then he turned, sword held high.

'Son of Denoris! The kill is yours.'

～

'THEY SEEM WELL SUITED.' ADARA SMILED, THE FADING SUN reflecting in her golden eyes. To the uninitiated, it would seem as though she stood on the flat top of a tower, open to the sky. Below her Ambeth unfurled like a beautiful carpet, the woodland and gardens, the shimmering sea painted with the last colours of sunset, the purpling mountains stretching to the distance, faint gleams of light among their folds. And above, the great dome of sky was darkening, the first stars starting to appear. It was almost time. But not quite.

'Ethan and Alma?' Thorion came to her, dropping a kiss on her hair. 'You're such a romantic.'

'And you love it.' She turned, reaching up for another kiss.

He laughed. 'I do,' he said, 'along with everything else about you.' He still couldn't believe his good fortune, to have found love again – and with his best friend. Such a long and painful road it had been, yet they had found each other at the end of it, in part thanks to Alma.

'It will be nice to see her happy again, and he seems very taken with her.'

'For all that he denies it.' Thorion laughed. 'Even Cedran could see it.'

'Well, they'll figure it out eventually. We did, after all.'

'And I'm forever grateful for that,' said Thorion.

A cacophony of noise rose up from below, howls and whooping, the squeal of hounds. Adara turned, as did Thorion, his smile fading, to see the Dark Hunt streaming by the base of the tower, heading for the hills. They both watched in silence as it passed, like a snake winding across the landscape, red and silver and black. They had no concerns about being seen – the magic of the Crystal Chamber only worked one way, the walls that were transparent from within appearing as solid stone from the outside.

'Deryck has joined them. I wonder what Denoris thinks about that.' Adara's eyes were shadowed, her mouth twisting.

'I cannot imagine he's pleased. Though I'm more worried for the boy, myself.'

'You are?' Adara's frown deepened.

'I saw him, that day at the Garden of Shadows. He hasn't had the time or support to move on from what happened.'

'And why should he?' Adara's voice was uncharacteristically sharp. Thorion raised his eyebrows. 'I know what it did to you,' she went on, her lovely face fierce. 'I saw how you suffered. It seems only right that he should also know pain for what he did. He nearly lost us Alma as well.'

'Peace, dear heart.' Thorion touched her cheek, then tucked a loose curl behind her ear. 'I am better, now.'

'But not fully! You still have nightmares, I know you do!'

'It's true, dear one, though they are not of Caleb these days. Now when I see him in my dreams I can talk to him and he knows me as his father. Those are not nightmares, beloved.'

'Really?' Her face softened. 'That is a wonder. I didn't realise...'

'It is only of late, since I've been with you,' said Thorion. He bent his head to hers, his arms around her, enjoying the moment.

There were footsteps and the sound of someone clearing their throat. They came apart to see Artos, smile wide and eyes twinkling with humour. Adara blushed, rose pink, and Thorion grinned.

'Oh, don't let me stop you,' said Artos, waving his hand. 'The stars will wait, surely?' He laughed and so did Thorion, releasing Adara to shake his hand.

There were more footsteps and several more Elders emerged from the staircase onto the top of the tower, Meredan among them, splendid in crimson armour. Thorion greeted the new arrivals, and they took their seats around the edge of the room. There were only a couple more to arrive and they could begin.

～

THE DOOR IN THE ANCIENT STONE WALL CREAKED OPEN. Torches flickered in their sconces. Several of the benches set into the curving wall were already occupied. Gwenene, moon-pale and razor sharp in blue silk and velvet, her eyes intent on Denoris, sat in one of them. Nevros was there as well, all red and gold glitter, and Ghislaine, wild-eyed and restless, still wearing her mud-streaked navy blue armour from the training yard. Denoris, standing at the centre of the Garden of Shadows, Avernath open on the table before him, narrowed his eyes briefly as they landed on her. She was one to watch, a wild card if ever there was one.

Cedran, clad in grey armour, closed the door in the wall, nodding to Denoris before taking a seat.

Another one to watch. Denoris reached for the tallus at his throat. It had not escaped his notice that Cedran was the last to arrive. And now there was the business of his son with the girl. If their plans were still aligned, as they had once been, he would have simply asked Cedran to bring her to him. But he knew the other lord, the closest thing he had to an equal in Ambeth, would never use his son in that way. He had seen the shock in his eyes during their recent conversation. But their plans had to change! What had started so simply, his son meant to capture a girl as she passed through a Gate, had become more complex than it ever needed to be.

Grasping the tallus in his hand, he let the dark energy run through him. Then he raised his eyes to the stars, seeking the patterns that lay there, the reassurance they held.

It was time to bring the Dark back into line, so they would be ready for what was to come.

'ANOTHER CLEAR NIGHT. SPRING IS HERE.' SEREN STARGAZER came to stand next to Thorion, her lavender robes whispering across the tiled floor. He smiled, half turning to her.

'It is,' he said. 'And with it, the return of hope to the land, the great cycle of the year turning once more.'

Adara's hand slipped into his, her skin warm and soft. Heat rose in him at the thought of her hands, of what they could do. His smile deepened, but he pushed his desire to one side. It was a clear night, as Seren said, and he needed to focus. The Crown was still missing, the Dark still moving, and Alma... His smile slid away. Despite her friendship with Ethan, Thorion knew how hard it was for her. Despite his need, despite the need for all the worlds, he didn't want to push her. The choice was still hers, if she wanted to help them. He wouldn't blame her if she didn't.

He released Adara's hand. She nodded, going to take her seat with the rest of the Elders on the embroidered chairs lining the edge of the room. Moving to the centre of the tiled floor, Thorion waited. Seren Stargazer extinguished the lone lantern in the room and stood to one side, waiting. Lamplight was replaced by starlight, the glory of the heavens revealed.

'Welcome,' said Thorion, slipping easily into the ritual. 'We are here to read the skylore, that we might know what is to come.'

'We are here,' the group replied, bowing their heads.

Thorion reached into his pocket, retrieving the Shield Stone. Holding it flat on the palm of his hand, he placed his other palm on top of it, feeling the buzz of power. He looked up, then lifted his top hand.

Shimmering rays shot up from the stone to create a glittering domed pattern, filling the room with light.

'It is done.'

DERYCK SWALLOWED, HIS MOUTH DRY. BUT HE KEPT HIS expression fierce, his brows lowered, as he moved his horse forward to where Simeon waited, his sword still held high. The rest of the Hunt were quiet, the only sound the snort and jangle of the horses, the squeak and rustle of the hounds.

Deryck touched the stone at his throat. Darkness pulsed through him, but not enough to completely cover his horror, to chase away the images coming thick and fast of Caleb and Alma, of love and death. He drew in a shaking breath, his mouth tight.

Simeon smiled. 'What are you waiting for?'

Floria was watching him, her eyes dark. The boy on the hillside was panting, lying on his back.

'What did he do?'

Simeon's smile slid away. 'Does it matter?'

'Yes. If he is to die, he should know what he did, shouldn't he?'

'Did Caleb know?'

'You go too far, Simeon!' said Floria, urging her horse forward between them.

Deryck recoiled, his eyes wide. He reached for his tallus again, letting the darkness in, letting it crystallise his emotions so he could control them. 'You dare,' he growled, his hand to his sword.

Simeon laughed, his head going back. 'Good,' he said. 'I was wondering where that fire was, when you would unleash it. Now, finish it.' He pointed his sword towards the boy. 'Let us see if you have what it takes to ride with us.'

Deryck could feel the eyes of the Hunt on him. He wondered what would happen if he refused, if he would then become prey, ridden into the hills until he could go no further, then dying beneath their swords. Part of him wanted it, wanted the release death would bring.

'Come on, pretty boy,' said Floria. But there was no teasing to her tone this time, more an urgency that reminded him, for some reason, of Alma. And with that came clarity that he needed to act, to stay alive for when she came back to him. He dismounted. The hounds twisted around his boots as he walked towards the young man cowering on the mountainside.

He drew his sword.

CHAPTER 19
STARGAZING

Seren Stargazer went to a small table at the side of the chamber. *Serennos*, one of the two ancient skylore books, lay there. She opened it, turning the pages. Thorion, holding his position at the centre of the room, knew she would be calculating dates and times, using her gift to find the precise page, so she could read the stars for them. She straightened up, turning to him.

'It is chosen.'

'And what do you read, Seren?'

The tall and slender Elder paced the room, her silver-gilt hair shimmering like a waterfall down her back. Her lavender eyes focused on the stars and the patterns projected by the Shield Stone. A line appeared between her pale brows.

'Things are improving,' she said, coming to a stop. 'But the Balance is still tipping. Do you see? Here, and here.' Her graceful arms moved like a dancer's as she pointed out jagged shapes in the crystalline patterns set against the stars. 'I cannot understand it. The return of the Sword and the Cup should have moved things closer to alignment, yet there is still uncertainty in the skies.'

She moved around the room once more, still looking at the

skies. 'Coralis has moved back into place, though,' she said. 'And, oh!' She stopped, her hand to her mouth.

'What is it, Seren?' The muscles in Thorion's arm were standing out.

She smiled, her eyes bright with unshed tears. 'The Sword has returned to the skies once more, as has the Cup. This has not been seen for centuries, not since the Light and Dark parted ways. See?' She traced the patterns with her fingers.

Thorion could see them, the sharp point of the Sword, the gleaming curve of the Cup. It was a sight unprecedented, and his eyes filled with tears. There were gasps in the room, the rustle of garments, as the others took it in. It was a wonder, but there was a dark space next to it where no star shone, the curving patterns of light from the Shield Stone absent. He knew what that meant, and he also knew what he needed to ask.

'And what of the Star of the Child?'

There was a silence, then, like a breath drawn in. All eyes went to the shimmering point of light that signified Alma and the hopes of their kind.

Seren tilted her head, studying the cluster of shimmering shapes like a perfect circle around the tiny star. 'She is surrounded... by love.' She smiled again. 'Her dark star has joined her now, and their paths will not diverge again.'

Sure enough, when Thorion looked, he could see the dark star, gleaming blue, next to Alma's. 'And where does their path go?' he asked.

'Their pathway leads through the tangle of Daearen, to land here.' She pointed to where the dark space was, next to the Sword and the Cup.

'To the Crown?'

'To the Crown.'

CEDRAN SETTLED BACK AGAINST THE STONE WALL, LETTING HIS thoughts drift to where they so often went. Dana. He still couldn't believe that she'd rejected him – perhaps he should have been honest with her from the start, but he'd seen no reason to be. However, once she was pregnant with his child and he knew he loved her like no other, he'd declared himself, expecting to be well received.

He hadn't been.

He still remembered her hysterical tears – he'd worried she would harm the child and herself – and knew he'd played the wrong hand. So he'd gone away, giving her the space she'd asked for, only to return and find the way from the park blocked and Dana a virtual recluse in the cottage. He'd forced his way in, determined to see his son and be part of his life. Dana had welcomed him into her arms and her bed that night, and he'd thought there might be a chance for them, but in the cold light of morning she'd turned to him, more beautiful than ever, telling him she could never be with him in Ambeth. So they'd come to an agreement. Cedran was unmoving on the matter of his son, wanting him to be able to choose where he lived, to know both worlds. Dana had given him this, in the end. He'd seen the heartbreak in her eyes, felt sorrow in his own heart as they'd parted, only to see each other when Cedran came for Ethan. Once the boy was old enough, Cedran had shown him how to cross over by himself, unable to bear the pain of seeing Dana any more. But he kept tabs on her, kept her well protected, and he would do so until she died. And if that put him at odds with Denoris, then so be it.

The Dark Lord had moved to the centre of the garden, his blond hair silvered by starlight. He clutched the tallus stone at his neck and Cedran saw him shudder as the darkness passed through him, his head going back. He suppressed a sigh. He wasn't old enough to remember the time when Light and Dark read the stars together, but he was sure it hadn't been this tangle of maybes and half-truths, all of them held hostage to whatever Denoris decided to tell them.

Ghislaine, on the next bench over, shifted in her seat, flashing her dark gaze at Cedran as though she could read his thoughts. Or perhaps she just shared his annoyance. 'Get on with it,' she said. 'Tell us of the change to come, of how the child will come back to you.'

Cedran raised an eyebrow. Ghislaine's tone had verged on scornful. Darkness knew she was an unparalleled fighter, but Denoris had ways of getting to a person that didn't always involve a sword.

'Give him a moment,' Gwenene hissed. 'Unless you think you can do it yourself?'

Ghislaine stared her down for a moment. Nevros, next to her, patted her thigh, giving her a warning glance. Cedran held his breath – she had gutted other men for less. But she remained silent, though her eyes were narrowed. Perhaps they were sleeping together. Cedran filed the idea away for later consideration, returning his attention to Denoris.

'The Balance is still tipping.' The Dark Lord's voice was strained, the tendons in his neck standing out. But his triumphant tone was unmistakeable. 'Despite the return of the Cup and the Sword, the Dark are still prevailing.'

'How is that possible?' said Nevros. 'Surely the Child has tipped the Balance back?'

'She would have done, were it not for one thing.' Denoris raised his arm, pointing. 'Do you see, next to the Star of the Child?'

'I see it,' said Nevros, his tone conciliatory. 'Another star. What is it?'

'It's a dark star. And its path is now forever linked with hers.'

'But who is it?' Nevros had his head back too, his wide eyes focused on the night sky.

'My son, of course. She will come back to him, and she will be ours.'

Cedran looked up, frowning. A blue star gleamed next to Alma's. It was a dark star, there was no mistaking it, and it was entwined with her path. But it wasn't Deryck. It couldn't be, not with what he now knew about the Prophecy.

It was Ethan.

~

'AVAGDU IS STILL MOVING OUT OF ALIGNMENT, THOUGH IT IS not as far gone as it was,' Seren continued, her slender fingers tracing patterns in the sky.

'That is hopeful,' said Thorion. 'Perhaps the Dark are finally beginning to see sense in all this, that the return of the Regalia benefits it all. And what of Daearen? The pattern looks to have changed again.'

'It is so,' said Seren. She moved across the tiled floor in a graceful arc, studying the tangle of crystalline light converging on Daearen, the star that signified the human realm. 'Hmm.' Her brows drew together.

Thorion's arm was beginning to ache with the strain, but he held his position.

'I would have expected this to have moved, to have lessened in intensity, since the return of the Cup. Daearen is still dimmed, but, and this is interesting, the *movement* of the pattern has changed.'

'What does it mean?'

'Well, before, it was as though the pattern was moving to cover Daearen, to dim its light. Now, it's as though the pattern itself is coming *from* Daearen. As though whatever comes is now based in the human world. Whatever is causing this imbalance is there, not here. And there is more.'

Thorion drew in a breath. 'Go on.' He kept his voice steady, though his emotions were in turmoil. He'd thought the stars would show the return of joy to the worlds, that things would have improved.

'Do you see this star?' Seren pointed to another bright point of light surrounded by jagged crystalline shapes, almost like lightning bolts. Her gaze came to meet Thorion's. 'It's not a star. It's a comet.'

'A comet?' He looked up again and saw the small tail, almost invisible. There were gasps around the room.

'Yes.' She went back to the table, leafing through the book. She turned to him again, and swallowed. 'It has not been seen in our skies for millennia. And it is heading towards Daearen.'

'What does it mean?' Thorion couldn't keep the tremor out of his voice. He could feel the tension in the room, like a held breath.

'Chaos. It is the Hunt.'

~

DERYCK RECOGNISED THE BOY. HE WAS ONE OF THE GROOMS from the stables, someone he knew worked hard. He frowned. The boy gasped, scuttling backwards, his heels sliding on the grass.

Simeon came to stand next to Deryck. 'Having fun yet?' he murmured.

Deryck glanced at him, his frown deepening. Simeon turned, raising his sword, shaking it and howling. The assembled Hunt did the same, the sound echoing off the darkened slopes, rising to meet the stars. The hairs on Deryck's neck lifted.

The boy had stopped moving now, like a creature in a trap who knows its time has come.

'Your turn,' Simeon said, giving Deryck a little shove. Deryck's throat was tight. He reached again for his tallus, wrapping his hand around the stone so the dark energy pulsed through him like electricity. He took it for as long as he could bear it, letting it push away his fear and sorrow and pity.

He raised his sword. Closing his eyes, he brought it down.

There was a clang of metal. Deryck opened his eyes.

'Well done,' said Simeon, one corner of his mouth curving up, his sword braced against Deryck's. 'I did wonder whether you had it in you.' His expression hardened. 'But the kill always belongs to the leader of the Hunt.'

Before Deryck could move, Simeon raised his sword again and slashed downwards. The boy cried out, then the night was still once more.

Simeon cleaned his sword on the boy's tunic, sheathing it, and walked away. Deryck thought he heard him laughing.

He felt like he was going to be sick. The boy had died with his hands up, his eyes wide. Again he flashed back to the tournament, to the waves of dark energy that had driven him to take a life, to do what he'd thought was best, to protect Alma. He reached for his tallus, the action automatic, and let it pulse through him, until it had washed everything away.

Later, he was unsure how he'd got back to the stables. The stars wheeled above in streaks of light, the Hunt flashing images, in and out, black and white and red like blood. He didn't know how he'd got home, either, or ended up in bed with Floria, who arched above him, her nails scraping across his chest as she cried out.

He wasn't sure about anything, any more.

～

'WE'VE HEARD THAT BEFORE, DENORIS, OVER AND OVER AGAIN. Yet the girl is not here.' Ghislaine had her arms folded, her chin high.

Gwenene half rose from her seat but Denoris motioned her back. 'True, she is not. Not yet.' His tone was mild, but Cedran could see murder in his green eyes. He wondered again at Ghislaine, at her nerve. But, truth be told, she was not the only one shifting in their seat or casting glances at their neighbour.

'But she will be,' said Nevros, his silky smooth tone cutting through the tension. 'I have faith. And so, it seems, do the stars.'

Cedran frowned. That was interesting. But he knew, as they all did, that the Light would be reading the skies tonight as well. He wondered whether they would see the same things. He also knew that, if it came down to it, he would protect the girl from Denoris.

'Thank you, Nevros.' Gwenene, all silk and steel, rose from her seat, nodding to him. She turned to face them all. 'So it seems the skies are telling us that we will still prevail. And we know the stars don't lie. The girl will come to us, thanks to Deryck, and the last piece of the puzzle will be in place. Let us be grateful now to Denoris, who has once again shown us that the Human Realm will be overcome, that the Dark will be in ascendancy once more.' The assembled group were rapt, even Ghislaine.

All except for Cedran. He saw Denoris stumble, bracing himself on the table with one hand as he released his grip on the tallus stone.

Interesting.

'THE HUNT? HEADING FOR THE HUMAN WORLD? IMPOSSIBLE. IT has been untold centuries since they were allowed to roam beyond the Gates.'

'And yet the skies do not lie, Thorion, you know this. You cannot take only that which pleases you from their movements.' There was a slight rebuke in her tone.

The corner of Thorion's mouth twitched. 'Indeed, Seren,' he said. 'So tell us, then, where do we stand?'

Seren nodded, her lips curving in a smile. 'As long as the Star of the Child keeps moving, as long as her dark star stays with her, there is hope, still, that we will prevail. Things are coming together now, do you see? The change is almost upon us.' She turned, her arms raised, fingers pointing out the patterns. 'The Hunt. The Child. The Dark Star. And the Crown. They are all converging on one single point.'

'Daearen?'

'Daearen.'

She made one more circuit of the chamber, the silver-starlight fall of her hair swaying. She came to a stop before Thorion. 'That is all,' she said. She placed her hand over his and the patterns from the Shield Stone disappeared, the room lit only by starlight once more.

'DENORIS, HAVE YOU A MOMENT?'

Denoris did not have a moment. All he wanted, apart from tearing apart most of those who'd attending the reading, was to return to his apartments and lie down, preferably with Gwenene. But he needed to hold on a little bit longer, to not give anything away. They would all bow to him, soon enough.

'Nevros.' He turned and managed a smile. The other Elder nodded, glitter on his cheekbones catching the flickering light.

'I wish to speak to you about your daughter. My son Rindor mentioned he saw her in the Hall recently.'

Denoris frowned. 'And?'

Nevros glanced to the side as one of the other Elders left and leaned in closer. 'Tell me, is she spoken for?'

Denoris raised an eyebrow. 'She is not,' he replied.

'Well, then, perhaps we might talk further, if you're amenable?'

Denoris waited a moment, long enough for Nevros to begin to squirm, for him to be cognisant of the honour when it was bestowed. For this would solve several problems, not that Nevros needed to know that. Judging the moment, he replied.

'I would.'

~

ARTOS ROSE FROM HIS CHAIR, HIS HEART LIGHT DESPITE THE mixed messages from the skies. Truth be told, all he could see in them was renewed hope. For him to have such a gift, his granddaughter back in his life! He'd had much sorrow in his long years, but Alma's arrival had shown him there was still joy to be found in the world.

'Will she be back soon?' Thorion came over, smiling, as though he knew what Artos was thinking.

'She will, I'm sure. It's been hard for her, being here, but I think, perhaps, that's about to change.'

'Ethan seems very nice,' said Adara, coming to join them.

Thorion glanced at her. 'And his father... Well, that's interesting. He even went so far as to warn me, the other day, against Denoris and his schemes.' Artos raised his eyebrows. Thorion nodded, his blue eyes changing to blue-grey. 'His main concern seems to be his son, that he is kept safe.'

'And his mother.'

'I heard about that,' said Adara. 'Well, I felt it, more than anything. His heart is full of sorrow.' Her brow creased.

'So what did you feel, with Alma and Ethan?' asked Artos. 'Though it's obvious, really.'

Adara laughed. 'Yes. They're already together, though they don't know it. I suppose he's the dark star.'

'I think there can be no doubt of it,' said Thorion. 'How do you feel about that, Artos?'

Artos took in a breath. How did he feel? He couldn't deny he was concerned. Despite all that Ethan had already done for Alma, he was cautious about any of the Dark near his granddaughter.

Thorion laughed. 'I suppose no one would be good enough for her.'

'Well, I suppose I just feel protective of her, where the Dark is concerned.' He stopped, considering. 'No, I think the boy to be a fine young man and I cannot doubt his motives are good, where she is concerned. And if they're meant to be together – well. As long as he makes her happy, that's all that matters.'

They made their way down the tiled stairs to the Foyer. The wall opened for them then closed; the secret of the passage through known only to the High King. Artos knew it, of course, though it had been many years since he'd held the throne.

He turned to Thorion and Adara. 'Well, my friends, I think I might—'

'Lord Artos.' The tone was nasal, slightly condescending. The three Elders turned to see a figure appear from behind the pillars, bowing slightly.

'Yes?' Artos frowned. He recognised the man as the steward who'd spoken down to him when he'd tried to visit Denoris. He must be doing his job well, to still be alive.

'I am here on behalf of Lord Denoris. He has asked me to invite you to join him, for wine, in the Great Hall.' The steward extended his arm towards the double doors, which were closed, guards standing either side of them as usual.

'Now? The hour is late.'

The steward raised an eyebrow. 'My master keeps late hours. If you do not feel able to meet with him, perhaps I can arrange some other—'

'You dare, do you? Lord Artos was once High King here, and deserves your respect!' Thorion strode forward, his dark brows lowered. Adara raised a delicate hand to her head, wincing. 'You tell your *master* that he needs to teach his servants better, if he wishes to deal with us!'

'Peace, Thorion.' Artos put his hand on the King's arm, feeling the muscles tense beneath the robes. The steward had turned pale. He stepped back, his supercilious air gone.

'M-my Lord. I am—'

'I would be pleased to join Denoris now,' Artos said.

'Thank you. I'll let him know.' The steward bowed, lower than before, and disappeared into the Hall.

Thorion called the guards over. 'Watch, and call me if there is need.' The two guards saluted and returned to their posts. Thorion turned to Artos.

'So. Things take another turn.'

'So it seems.' Artos kept his tone light but anger burned beneath it at Denoris and his endless scheming.

'Be careful,' Adara whispered, kissing him on the cheek.

'I will, dear one.' He smiled at her.

'What do you think he wants?'

'Oh, I know what he wants,' said Artos, glancing towards the closed doors. 'Alma.'

CHAPTER 20
THE DANCE BEGINS

'Thank you for coming, Artos.'

Denoris was leaning against one of the pillars in the Great Hall. The Dark Lord was armour-clad, wearing his sword, which was not unusual. The smile on his face, however, was. Artos returned the smile, though he was wary.

'Will you join me for a drink?' Denoris continued. 'I've arranged for wine to be served, one from my own personal cellars. An excellent vintage, if I say so myself.'

Artos raised his eyebrows but kept his smile, nodding in response. 'Thank you, I will. I've heard much about the quality of your cellar, and I appreciate the invitation.' *And I am ready for you*.

'Of course. If you please.' Denoris held out his hand. A steward in livery stood next to a table in one of the private alcoves, a bottle already opened next to two fine crystal goblets. Artos took the offered seat and accepted the goblet of wine, exclaiming over the first mouthful (no lie, it was excellent, with hints of mellow berry and sunshine). Once the proprieties had been observed, he set down his glass and waited for the dance to begin.

Denoris shifted in his seat, blowing out a long breath. 'Artos, I wish to make a formal petition for Alma's hand.'

'What?' Artos couldn't hold back the exclamation. It seemed the Dark Lord had lost none of his ability to surprise. He reached for his glass and took a sip. 'Forgive me,' he said. 'It's just, your lady wife...'

'No, not for me.' Denoris reached for his drink, his handsome mouth tightening. 'I ask for Deryck, my son, of course.'

'Of course.' Artos laughed, though he wanted to scream. 'Forgive me,' he said again. 'I wasn't thinking. But Denoris, this is not for me to decide.' He took another drink of the excellent wine, finding he needed it.

'But you're the head of her family, are you not? You stood and claimed her, in the Great Hall.' The Dark Lord's voice hardened.

Artos paused, the emotion of that eventful day rolling over him again. 'I did. But I cannot speak for her, not in this instance, nor am I sure she would be amenable to such a match. She's still young,' he said, wondering briefly if he was hallucinating the whole conversation. This was not the angle he had expected Denoris to take. But he couldn't give the Dark Lord any opening; centuries spent dealing with Denoris left him in no doubt as to where it would go if he did.

'But my son is a pure-blooded Prince! Can you not see the advantages of such a match? And he loves her, I can assure you of that.' Denoris shook his head.

'It wouldn't matter if Deryck were High King, Denoris! The choice is not mine to make, it's Alma's. And I cannot see her choosing him, not after what he did.' Artos held Denoris' gaze, wanting him to see that he was serious. The Dark Lord sat back, a muscle moving in his jaw. He took a drink from his goblet, then fixed Artos with an accusing gaze.

'Is this because of Cedran's son? You cannot be against a match with the Dark if you permit her to see him.'

'Ethan?' Artos smiled, though his mind was racing. By the

Light, Denoris' spies moved quickly! 'They're just friends. But he makes her happy, and that's all I could want for her. And I'm not convinced your son could do the same.'

'He did once – why could he not do so again?'

'I think things are too far gone for her to go back to him.' Artos kept his tone conciliatory, knowing he was on dangerous ground. What Denoris wanted, he usually got, and woe betide anyone who stood in his way. But Artos was not just anyone. 'I was uneasy at the time, but I did see it, how they loved each other. But...'

'I know, I know. Thorion's boy.'

Artos narrowed his eyes. 'So you knew about that?'

Denoris regarded him for a long moment, then quirked a half-smile. 'I'm not without resources. And it was not, perhaps, the secret he thought it was.'

How dare he talk of Caleb like that? The loss of his own sons, the pain as fresh as it had ever been, rolled across Artos once more.

'What?' Denoris spread his hands wide. 'Don't worry. I kept it to myself.'

'I'm sure,' replied Artos, not bothering to keep the disdain from his voice. By the Light, he was tired of these games, of Denoris' endless meddling. And now he thought to threaten Alma? His anger grew again, the fierce temper that ran in his family boiling in the pit of his stomach. Denoris must be mad to think he would even consider a match between Alma and his son.

'Tell me, Artos. Have you recovered fully from your injury?'

'My injury?'

'Yes, I heard you'd been injured. Out in the hills, wasn't it, near the Stone Gate?'

Artos almost laughed. He wasn't surprised, though. The healer who'd helped him after he'd been stabbed had been of the Dark – he didn't like to think what Denoris had done to the girl, to get her to tell him what she knew.

'I'm much improved,' he said.

'But what happened?'

Artos snorted. 'I'm sure you don't need me to tell you,' he said, draining his goblet and placing it on the table. The steward, standing to one side, stepped forward, but Denoris waved him back, picking up the wine himself and topping up Artos' goblet. Interesting. Artos nodded but offered no other thanks. He was starting to feel as though he had the upper hand. He was also tired. 'If that's all, the hour is late, and I must—'

'Tell me,' said Denoris, leaning forward, like a cobra above its prey. 'Did Alma have a nice time with her family this summer past? In Wales, wasn't it? Such a... nice place. I've not been there for a while, but perhaps I should visit again. Or maybe take a trip beyond the Oak Gate. Perhaps even take Deryck, now that his house arrest is over. She doesn't live far from there, does she?'

'You would defy the ban on crossing?' There was a sick feeling in the pit of Artos' stomach. His eyes narrowed. 'By the Light, I don't think I care for your threats.'

'Threats? I merely said that I, and my son, an Opener, as I think I've mentioned, might like to take a trip beyond the Gates. It's coincidence, that's all, that your granddaughter happens to live there too.'

'Coincidence? You mean like the coincidence of Etras, of all people, coming through the Stone Gate at the very same time as I did? Above the very town where she was staying?' His voice rose, his nostrils flaring.

'Etras?' The sneering tone had gone from the Dark Lord's tone. He swallowed, sitting back, and the dance shifted once more. 'Tell me, did he, was he—'

But Artos was done. He stood up. 'Denoris, let me be very clear. While I live, I will not suffer Alma to be handfasted to Deryck. You and your son cannot have her, and that is that!"

The Dark Lord looked up at him. 'What – even though it's written in the very stars?'

Artos became very still. Thorion had told him what Alma had said, about how Denoris had stolen *Avernath*, using it to read the skylore, using it against them all. 'And what stars would those be?'

Denoris smiled. 'Why, the ones above us. Do you think the Dark have moved so far from the old ways that we've forgotten the skylore?'

Artos did not smile back. 'No. Though I had thought you no longer held any interest in it, preferring to shape the future to suit yourselves.'

'Is that so bad?'

'It is when it's at the expense of all others!' Artos blew out a breath. He had to be careful. The game was still in play, after all. 'Perhaps it's better if we just agree to disagree, Denoris,' he said. 'Alma is not available to be handfasted to your son, whether the stars speak it or not. Let us leave it at that, for now.'

'That is a shame,' Denoris said, sighing. 'I had thought to do this through official channels. The boy is obsessed with her, you see. I cannot understand it myself.' He shook his head. Artos fought his temper once more. 'Well,' Denoris continued, getting to his feet. 'I will do what I can to dissuade him. But you know how it is, when you're set on having something. I still think it a good match.'

Artos was so angry he thought he might explode. 'Keep him away from her,' was all he said, before turning to leave the Hall. He didn't look back. As he entered the Foyer, the guards either side of the door bowed. They straightened up. One held his gaze a moment longer, and Artos nodded. 'It's fine,' he said. A lie, but there was nothing they could help with. They both stood to attention once more and Artos went towards the stairs to his chambers, looking forward to finally having some solitude, though sleep might be a while away yet.

But before he started up the stairs the double doors leading to the outside opened. A tall figure in grey armour, his cape swirling behind him, stepped through. And the game changed once more.

Lord Cedran.

Turning, Artos moved away from the stairs, towards Cedran. The Dark Lord seemed weary, rubbing a hand over his face. When he saw Artos he raised his hand.

'How goes the evening?' he said, coming over.

'It's been... interesting,' Artos said. Cedran raised an eyebrow. 'In fact,' Artos went on, 'I think we need to talk. About the children, and keeping them safe. Would you care to join me?'

Cedran's dark eyes narrowed briefly. Then one corner of his mouth lifted. 'An excellent thought,' he said. 'I've been of much the same mind.'

Together, the two Lords, Dark and Light, ascended the stairs.

DENORIS WATCHED ARTOS GO. ONCE THE DOORS HAD CLOSED, he turned to the table, to the wine and goblets, the red liquid catching the light. Roaring, he swept them to the floor. The crystal shattered, the wine pooling like blood on the mosaic tiles. 'You'd better clean that up,' he snarled at his steward.

'Yes, my Lord.'

Denoris left the Hall, rage coursing through him. His desires had been thwarted once again. And the *insult* – Artos turning down his only son for that half-breed granddaughter of his, when Deryck was a full-blooded Prince, heir to Denoris. It was unheard of. The Dark and Light had intermarried over the centuries, and what he'd proposed was perfectly reasonable. Why did Artos insist on her having free will? All that choice led to was mistakes, messes that needed to be cleaned up. If everyone would just do as he asked, it would be so much easier.

And Etras. If it hadn't been clear before who'd stabbed Artos, he knew now. Etras had no love for his former King. But how in darkness had Artos defeated him to escape back into Ambeth? His wound had been mortal, Denoris knew that from the healer who'd tended him, the girl breaking under his will. Yet somehow he'd survived it long enough to make it back into Ambeth, when Etras had not.

He strode through the darkened gardens towards the apartments, his thoughts swirling like his anger. A harsh cawing noise made him look up. Perched on one of the chimneys, its leathery wings gripping the red bricks, was a Watcher. When Denoris looked up it shrieked again, the sound echoing across the courtyard. He cursed. The last thing he needed was it drawing attention to his plans. Already shutters were opening and people were looking up at the roof. Denoris bent his will on the creature, and it rose into the air, dropping down behind the roof and disappearing into the trees. He changed course, heading into the darkness beneath their branches.

In a small clearing the creature waiting, red eyes gleaming. Denoris approached carefully, one hand to his sword, but the Watcher seemed docile enough, settling down on the grassy ground. He reached out, wrapping his hand around its neck. Then he closed his eyes.

He opened them a few moments later. His grip on his sword tightened, and he thought for a moment of striking off the creature's head. But he held back, just — they were useful creatures, and he had no idea how to get more of them. Instead, he sent it winging back to his house in the hills, to wait in the darkness of the barn for his next commands.

Then he strode back to the apartments. Just friends, were they? From what the creature had reported of Alma and Ethan, they seemed to be more than that. And that was a problem, because of who the boy's father was.

He still had something he could control, though. Inside, he hung up his cloak and headed for his daughter's room once more.

CHAPTER 21
WHAT ELSE IS THERE TO DO?

Someone was pulling at Ellery's eyelids. She frowned, swatting at them like she would an annoying fly. But they wouldn't stop trying to open her eyes.

'All right,' she mumbled. A hand was on her cheek and someone was talking to her. That was nice. Then she recognised the voice. It was her father.

'Ellery, wake up.' He patted her cheek. 'You need to focus, to learn how to use your stone or it's of no use to me.'

She felt a flare of annoyance. It jolted her out of her reverie. She frowned up at her father, the light hurting her eyes. She was cold, too, even though the fire was lit. She realised, as she turned her head, that her shutters had been opened, letting in the cool spring air and that for some reason she was dressed in only her slip.

'I'm cold,' she murmured.

'The cold air will help you to focus, then I'll get you something warmer to wear. Come now, you need to try and sit up. Can you do that?'

She just wanted to sink back into the stone. She was starting to get used to it, to look forward to the feeling of drifting in clouds. It had been this way for a while now, she wasn't sure how long. Her father would come to her, force her to touch the tallus and she would drift away, hardly aware of anything around her. Then he would leave and she would sleep and wake to find the necklace lying on the bed next to her with the clasp undone. Then the whole cycle would start again. She remembered bits and pieces here and there. Her brother had come in at one point, she was sure. Their father had asked him to do something and he'd refused, saying he didn't want to. How come he was so much stronger under the stone than she was? She remembered him sitting next to her on the bed, his hand on her waist, looking up at their father and shaking his head. She didn't know why but she was glad he'd said no, for she wouldn't have been able to resist him. She remembered somebody kissing her – she wasn't sure who, but that's all they did, kiss her. It had been nice and weird all at the same time. Then there was Deryck again, shouting about something, something about taking advantage. But she'd floated away, not caring, trying to find that sweet soft voice she heard sometimes, the one that told her to be strong, to stay alive, that she was important. She liked that, being important, even if it was only to a voice in her head. But now her father wanted her to do something so she had to try. She wanted to please him, to do as he said. She loved him so much, and she didn't want him to hit her again. Her face didn't hurt anymore, not really.

'Ellery!' Her father's voice was sharp now, his hand shaking her shoulder. She flinched. 'Come on, wake up!' She tried to do as he asked, focusing all her effort on regaining control of her limbs. She managed to wiggle her fingers, then move one arm, though it felt so very heavy.

'Good, good. The stone is much more powerful for you because of your human blood, so you need to keep trying. Come on, now your legs.'

She strained to move her legs. It was though stones were tied to her feet. She eventually managed to swing them over the edge of the bed, lying half on her side with her legs dangling.

'Here, let me help you to sit up.' Her father slid his arm under her shoulders. Part of her shrank back from him, she wasn't sure why. She loved him, didn't she? He lifted her to an upright sitting position, her feet coming to rest on the floor. Her head was spinning, lights flashing in her vision and she swayed. Her father crouched down, his face level with hers as he took her chin in his strong hand.

'Focus, Ellery.'

So she did, though her mind kept sliding in and out; one minute it was all clear and she could see the room and her father, then she was drifting away. The soft voice came into her head. 'Ellery, you can do this, my darling girl.' Oh, she loved the voice. It was so nice to her, nicer than anyone had ever been. For the voice she would try anything. So she took in a deep breath and really focused, working on holding herself in the room, even though all she wanted was to sink back down. If she kept breathing deep and didn't move too much, it was manageable.

'Good,' Denoris said. She wondered how long he'd been there, just watching her. What looked like the remains of lunch sat on the small table. She knew she hadn't eaten anything – her slip felt loose, as though she'd lost weight. So he must have been here for a while.

'I'm thirsty,' she managed to say, her mouth claggy from lack of use.

'Of course,' he said, getting up. He went to the table and poured her a cup from the flagon, handing it to her. She took a sip – it was water, pure and cold. It helped clear her head a bit more. Her father smiled at her.

'Good,' he said again. 'This is what I need you to do from now on. You've spent enough time lying around – you must learn to control the stone, rather than it controlling you.'

'So, can I leave my room?' she whispered, but he shook his

head. 'Not yet. But soon. I'll let you know when it's time. And until then you need to keep practising. I can't carry you around, can I?' There was laughter in his voice. Ellery nodded slightly, the movement setting everything rocking. She should be more annoyed but couldn't bring herself to care. Her father bent down to kiss her.

'I will leave you now. Hilde will be here later.'

'Thank you, Father,' she said. Then he was gone. She heard the key turn in the lock and she lay down again, staring at the ceiling. What else was there to do?

$\sim$

'I THINK I CAN DO THIS,' SAID ALMA

'What, go through the Gate?' Ethan grinned at her. They stood in front of the Oak Gate, hand in hand. Energy pulsed through Alma's feet. "Cause yeah, you can.'

Alma laughed. She felt lighter than she had in ages, and it was all because of Ethan. Forget the Dark, the Watchers and whatever other creatures they wanted to send. She'd made her decision – let them try to stop her. She'd proven them wrong twice before, evading their schemes to find the Sword, and then the Cup. Each time she'd had help, and it was no different now. Except, with Ethan, everything *was* different, wonderfully so.

'No, I mean, I can do this. I can go to Ambeth, we can find the Crown, and I won't let them st—'

Ethan let go of her hand and hugged her, picking her up and swinging her around. 'Really?' he said. 'Really? You'll look for it there?'

'We'll look for it,' she said, kissing him, joy coursing through her. 'So I think, maybe, the first thing we need to do is see Thorion, tell him about what we saw at the fair, and figure out what happens next.' The smile slid from her face and Ethan put her down, though he still held her close.

'What is it?'

'There's something else I need to do as well, something I need to face. Are you with me?'

'Always.'

CHAPTER 22
FOR ALL THE WORLDS

'I miss him so much.'

'So do I.' Thorion placed his hand on Alma's shoulder as they stared out to sea.

She swallowed, choked with emotion. Ethan, standing on her other side, squeezed her hand. Nearby, the small chapel shone in the morning light, its small stained-glass windows gleaming like jewels. The breeze off the ocean was fresh, blowing Alma's hair back from her face. The small bouquet of flowers she'd brought tossed on the waves as it made its way out to sea.

'It was such a waste.' She bowed her head, feeling anger in her heart at Deryck and what he'd done.

'It was,' said Thorion.

She lifted her head. The King was looking at her, his expression kind, though his eyes were changing to grey. Just like Caleb's eyes had used to. She still couldn't believe she hadn't realised, not until after he'd died, who his father was.

'Yet, had Deryck not done what he did,' Thorion continued, 'would you be standing here now, with Ethan?'

Alma's breath caught in her throat. She shook her head. 'It

changes nothing.' But the King's words made her cold inside. Where would she have been, if Deryck had let Caleb live at the tournament? Under the control of the Dark, and Denoris, most likely, despite the fact that Deryck had tried to keep her out of their clutches. She blinked back tears – this was even harder than she'd thought it was going to be.

She'd known she'd have to face it at some point, had hoped there would be a grave where she could at least sit with Caleb and talk to him, even though she'd dreaded the thought. But instead there were only waves on a whispering shore, and the image of a small boat, aflame, sent out into the night. And now this burden – that Caleb, perhaps, had died to save her from the Dark.

'I can't— I mean, I just—' Her voice was a whisper. 'I don't know.' She blinked, a tear rolling down her cheek.

'I'm sorry, dear one – I didn't mean to upset you. All I'm saying is that we must find whatever peace we can in order to move forward from tragedy. Caleb wasn't going to live forever – I would have lost him at some point, just as I did his mother. This is my burden to carry, dear heart, not yours.'

'His mother?' Ethan, who had been staring out to sea, turned to Thorion. 'Did you know her?'

Alma glanced at Thorion. She'd forgotten Ethan wouldn't have known, that hardly anyone did, about Caleb's parentage. It had been kept secret to protect him and his mother, though it had ended up leading to both their deaths.

Thorion's eyes widened briefly. Then he nodded, his mouth twisting. 'He was my son, Ethan. And his mother was human, as is yours, and Alma's.'

'Your son? But, why... I'm sorry, I don't wish to pry.' Ethan glanced at Alma, his brow furrowed.

'It's all right. I kept him a secret, thinking I was doing the right thing. I had my reasons, at the time. But... it was a mistake.' The King looked down for a moment. When he lifted his head, his eyes were changing back towards blue. 'But come,' he went on. 'It's a glorious day, and Caleb would not wish us to be sad. I know he thought of you as a friend, Ethan, and would be happy to see you with Alma, as am I.'

Alma leaned her head on Ethan's shoulder and he put his arm around her, his lips on her hair. She blushed, thinking of how it had been earlier, when they'd first arrived, going straight to her room. Ethan had been quite taken with it, especially the bed, and it had taken a lot of willpower to drag themselves away. But it had been important to her to do this, while she felt strong enough to face it. They would have time enough to be alone, later.

The breeze was picking up, whipping the waves into white foam, her flowers a distant spot of colour. She gazed out to sea, sending all the love she had to Caleb, wherever he might be, that he know she would never forget him, or what he'd done. She waited for a moment, but there was no soft kiss on her brow, no swirl of cool air around her hands. Instead, a feeling of warmth, like sunshine, spread through her.

'I'm going to find the Crown,' she said, as much to the waves and Caleb as to anyone else. Being there just reinforced her decision to finish the work she and Caleb had begun.

Thorion made a noise like a sob, his hand coming up to his face. When he lifted his head his eyes were fully blue again, and bright with tears. Alma went to him, kissing him on the cheek. 'For him, for all of us,' she whispered, as the King pulled her into a hug.

'For Ambeth and all the worlds,' he said in return, his voice rough. He released her, wiping his eyes, and then Ethan was there, holding her, his lips on hers.

'And I'll be there with you, all the way.'

LATER THEY SAT IN THORION'S COMFORTABLE CHAMBERS. MUGS of hot chocolate rested on the low table in front of the sofas.

'I know you'll want to see Artos and Cedran,' said Thorion, 'but I just wanted to go through what I've been working on with you.' He went to another table near the window that was piled high with papers and scrolls. Alma recognised the box that held the notes written by Llewellyn Davies, whose tragic story had led her to the Cup, and the knowledge that her family roots in Ambeth went back a lot further than her father.

'I've been doing an audit of the Gates,' Thorion went on, indicating a map marked with gold stars on the wall. 'I felt it necessary to do so, after you went and found one.' He grinned, shuffling his notes. 'I've also been reading through everything you and Caleb were looking at in the library, as well as anything else the Librarian has been able to find.'

'Did you find some clues about the Crown?' She got up and went over to the table. There was the scroll she and Caleb had found in the library so long ago, the images of the Sword and Cup and Crown drawn in fine pen and ink, the Prophecy in swirling letters about the three hearts. They knew who the first two were now: 'heart's love' had been Gwion, her uncle, lost in an effort to hide the Sword from the Dark, and 'heart betrayed' had been Llewellyn, who had loved Gwenene but in the end been betrayed by her, but not before stealing the Cup and hiding it away in an ancient castle. But the 'cold heart' still eluded her. She traced her finger along the delicate lines of the Crown, the curving ivy and jewelled berries seeming to move on the page.

'No. And that's the strange thing. There's a lot of references here to the Sword and the Cup, but almost nothing about the Crown, except for this scroll. It's almost as though it's been erased from existence, its power lost.'

'Its power?'

'Yes.' Thorion pushed his dark hair back, looking thoughtful. 'Each piece of the Regalia has its own properties, though they are designed to work best together. The Sword is a peacemaker, seeking justice and the fairest way. The Cup brings prosperity, fulfilment, to the lands. And the Crown magnifies power, Light and Dark, strengthening the Balance as it flows between the worlds.'

'That's right,' Alma said, her brows drawing together as she continued to trace the lines of the Crown on the page. There was something else she needed to tell Thorion, too. 'Dark energy comes from our world, doesn't it? Does it ever, like, get lost?'

'Get lost? What do you mean?'

'Well, Ethan and I, the other night...' She told Thorion about the strange events at the fair, and their terrifying run from the Watchers, Ethan interjecting with more details. Thorion sat down, his hand on his head, eyes widening as their story unfolded.

'Denoris,' he said, when they finished, the word heavy with menace.

'The Watchers? We did wonder,' said Ethan.

'Who else would it be?' Thorion shook his head. 'The nerve of him, though, sending them after you.'

'They were sent to frighten us,' said Alma. 'I mean, they did. But they could have killed us, if they wanted to. It was a message,' she said, realising as she spoke that it was true, remembering the way the creatures had tugged at her hair, taunting her.

'That he can get you, if he wants.' Ethan's voice had gone hard. 'Well, he won't while I'm around.'

Alma smiled at him, but she was cold again. Why did Denoris still want her? Surely it wasn't just for Deryck – the Dark Lord had never seemed the paternal type.

'And it was Dark energy you saw, you're sure of it?' Thorion blew out a breath.

'Well, I couldn't see it, at first,' said Ethan. 'It wasn't till Alma touched me. Then, well, I could *feel* it, you know?'

Thorion nodded, rubbing his hand over his face. He blinked and sat back in the chair. 'Your father and uncle were chasing something over there, you know,' he eventually said, looking at Alma.

'They were?'

'Yes. That's what they were doing when Galen met your mother. They had a base close to the Gate, in case they needed to get back in a hurry.'

'Their apartment? I think he and Mum lived there for a while, before, well...' Alma's mouth twisted. Her father's death, and the manner in which he'd died, were still hard to take. There were times when she wished more than anything she could have met him, but then Graham, the only father she'd ever known, wouldn't be in her life. Her heart was so twisted and torn by love she could hardly bear it.

'They did,' said Thorion. 'I remember.' He smiled, then it slid away, his gaze going to a painting on the wall of a posy of flowers. 'I met Caleb's mother when I went over to help them. And afterwards, Gwion and I were there, trying to keep going with the search.' He leaned forward. 'Alma. You have to understand. We tried. We wanted to see you, Gwion did, and Artos, but—'

'It's all right,' Alma replied, her chest tight. 'Mum told me. How she just turned her back on it all, wouldn't see anyone.' She blew out a breath. 'I get it, totally.'

'As did we.'

Alma bit her lip, her head down. 'So, did you find anything?' Sometimes being in Ambeth was too hard, the emotion too raw. She was committed now, to finding the Crown. But once that was done she wanted to forge her own path there, work out where she fit in.

'No. Hints here and there. But without your father, it was too difficult. And things were becoming worse in Ambeth, so we turned our focus back here. Until you arrived.'

'Yeah.' Alma huffed out a laugh. 'How is Ellery, anyway?'

. . .

'Why did you ask about Ellery?' Ethan asked Alma a little while later as they walked through the gardens, hand in hand.

Alma grinned. 'Because she pushed me through the Gate, the first time I came to Ambeth.' She stopped, leaning against him and kissing him before he could respond. 'Why did you insist on coming out here instead of going to find Artos and Cedran?'

'Hmmm.' Ethan grabbed her around the waist, pulling her through a wooden archway covered in ivy into a small walled garden, sweet with herbs. 'Don't you know?' Then his lips were on hers and Alma didn't care about Ellery or crowns or anything, lost in the sweetness of the moment.

They came apart a little while later, both panting. There were leaves in Ethan's dark hair and she picked them out, laughing, while he did the same for her.

'So, I guess we should go and find grandfather and your dad, hey?' Alma said. 'Though we might need to tidy ourselves up first. D'you want to come to my room and—'

'Alma, if we go to your room now I don't think I'll want to leave,' said Ethan. His breath was still uneven and she could feel his heart racing. Hers pounded in response. 'If you want to, go and I'll meet you. Though you look fine. Beautiful, in fact.'

'Thanks.' Her voice was croaky. She cleared her throat. 'You look very nice, too. Handsome.'

'Handsome, hey?' Ethan tightened his arms around her and kissed her again.

'Oh yes, very,' said Alma, when she was able to talk. He did, though she still felt shy to say it. He tucked her long hair behind her ear, kissing her neck as she tilted her head, then his lips found hers again and she could feel he was smiling. The kiss grew deeper, leaving them both breathless.

'Okay, we seriously need to go.'

'So the plan is, we find them, tell them, then...'

'Back to my room.'

He grinned, resting his forehead on hers. Then he got up, offering his hand to pull her to her feet. Trailing leaves, they wandered through the gardens towards the Palace.

The Foyer was busy, the scent of lunch drifting out through the open doors to the Great Hall.

'Come on,' said Ethan, tugging her hand. 'Let's go see my dad first.'

'Or we could tell both of them at once,' said Alma. 'Look.' She inclined her head towards the pillars lining one side of the Foyer. Standing close to them, deep in conversation, were Artos and Cedran. 'Grandfather,' she called, letting go of Ethan's hand and running over to him.

'Alma!' He caught her in a hug, kissing her cheek. 'Such a nice surprise to see you.'

'Hello, Alma.' Cedran took her hand, then leaned forward to kiss her lightly on the cheek. She suppressed her surprise, not wanting to offend him.

'Lord Cedran.' She smiled at him. Somehow he didn't seem as scary anymore.

'Just Cedran is fine.' He grinned. 'And I'm pleased to see you both together, finally.'

Alma's mouth dropped open. She shut it quickly, but not before Cedran caught the expression. His smile widened.

'Alma, it was obvious to me that this would happen. Your energies are matched perfectly.' She blinked. 'Oh yes,' Cedran went on. 'I have the ability to sense energy. Not like your father or your uncle, only really between people, and faintly at that. But enough to know as soon as I saw the two of you together.'

'Oh, um, well, that's great, Dad,' said Ethan, sounding as uncomfortable as Alma felt. Her cheeks were pink. She glanced at Ethan, only to catch him looking at her at exactly the same moment.

'See what I mean?' Cedran laughed, as did Artos.

'The Lady Adara saw it as well,' added Artos. 'And, truth be told, so did I.'

'And your mother?' Cedran turned his attention to Ethan. 'How is she?'

'Mum's fine, Dad. She's met Alma and she likes her.'

'I like her, too,' said Alma.

The Dark Lord's face softened from its usual stern lines. 'Really? I'm pleased to hear it. She's very... special.'

'So, shall we get lunch?' said Artos, inclining his head to the rapidly filling Hall. The scent of food drifting into the Foyer was making Alma's stomach growl.

Cedran nodded. 'In a moment. I wish to speak with Ethan first.' Ethan let go of Alma's hand, glancing at her. 'Just a small matter,' his father added.

'I'll see you soon,' Ethan said, kissing Alma on the cheek.

'Come, then.' Artos took her arm. She turned back to look at Ethan before they went through the double doors, the guards bowing. Then they were in the Great Hall. Alma swallowed. It was the first time she'd been in there since returning with the Cup and she'd fainted within moments of doing so. She needed a moment to take it all in. People were already starting to stare, whispering behind their hands, several smiling and waving. One person even bowed. Alma shook her head, blushing. She looked up at the huge lanterns, at the light coming in through the stained glass windows, painting colours across the mosaic floor, and remembered how it had been the first time she'd stepped in there, so long ago, it seemed, Thorion leading her through the crowd to an empty alcove, loss twisting in the air.

It was no longer empty. The Sword and Cup both lay there now, glowing and golden, beautiful as the moon. She felt calmer just looking at them.

'Alma!' She turned at the shout to see Meredan coming towards them, tall and muscled, crimson clad as always, a bright contrast to the darkness of his skin. Alma let go of her grandfather and ran to him.

'Meredan!'

He pulled her into a hug and swung her around, then set her down, studying her with his head tilted to one side.

'You are looking well, dear one.'

'And so are you,' said Alma. He was, handsome as always, his smile bright.

'More like your father every day,' he went on, winking.

She laughed. It must have been so hard for him, for anyone who'd known her father, to not tell her. But she understood why they hadn't, why the Light had wanted her to be free to choose.

Unlike the Dark.

'Drink?' Artos came up, goblets in hand, and Alma took one.

'Thanks.' She took a sip, pleased to find it was her favourite cordial. Her gaze was drawn again to the glowing alcove, the Prophecy engraved on the wall above. Now that she knew it wasn't just about her, that it was about Ethan as well, Alma didn't find it quite as daunting. Her focus drifted to the two empty thrones on their dais. She stared at them a moment, her brow creasing. Their emptiness felt wrong, somehow, like a skip in the perfectly balanced energies of the room.

'Something wrong?' Artos touched her lightly on the arm.

She turned to him. 'Oh! No. I mean, I was just wondering something.' Artos tilted his head. 'I've always noticed there were two thrones, and never knew why. Does, like, Thorion use one? And will Adara use the other one now? Ethan and I were talking about it the other day.'

But Artos shook his head. 'The thrones are very old, and aren't in use now.'

'They're not? How come?'

Artos smiled. 'It's a long story.'

Almost without realising, Alma began to move towards the thrones, as though they were pulling her. Her fingertips began to tingle, tiny sparks darting beneath her skin. She heard her grandfather gasp. He fell into step with her, Meredan joining on her other side, both of them shielding her from the room.

'Can you hold it, my dear?' Artos murmured.

Alma nodded, feeling for the reins of power in her mind, pulling them back so her fingers stopped glowing.

'You are strong,' said Meredan, his voice low. 'But then, so was your father.'

They came to a stop in front of the thrones. They were made of beautifully carved timber, inlaid with enamel and jewels, the seats padded velvet and silk in deep purple shades. At the top of each throne, etched into the timber frame, was a symbol. They were familiar. Alma realised they were the same as the symbols carved on the Gates, one for Dark and one for Light.

'What is it you feel?' said Artos.

Alma's brows drew together. 'Only that it's... wrong, somehow, that the thrones stay empty. It's like it's, I dunno, throwing off the balance of the room or something.'

Artos glanced at Meredan, one eyebrow raised. The other Elder nodded.

'Do you remember, Alma,' he said in his deep voice, 'when you did your lessons with us? And we told you of the division between Light and Dark?'

Alma nodded. She'd loved and hated the lessons, hated the pressure she'd felt and, later, the time they'd taken away from Deryck. But she'd loved learning about Ambeth, about the history.

'I remember. I mean, I think so. That Light and Dark used to rule together, once.'

'That's right. Artos placed one hand lightly on the carved arm of the throne. 'I remember those days, though I was little more than a child myself. But then the Balance shifted, the Dark moving away on their own agenda. A single High King or Queen took their place, the Light the only ones interested in maintaining things as they were.'

'So... the thrones stay empty, until you work together again?'

'It seems to be so. Interesting, though, that you can see it affecting the energy. This is the heart of our world, and it seems there has been a fracture here for quite some time.'

'It has been too long for us without a Channeller,' said Meredan. 'Your father and uncle worked in the human world, mostly. I wonder whether they ever noticed what was happening here.'

Artos seemed about to answer when Alma's stomach growled, loudly.

Meredan grinned. 'Another thing I remember about you, Alma, is your appetite.'

She laughed, the spell broken. 'Channelling is hungry work — what can I say?'

'Go on, get yourself something,' said Artos. 'I'll join you in a moment. I just need to speak with Meredan, first.'

'Oh! Okay, sure.' She kissed Artos on the cheek, smiling at Meredan, then headed over to the buffet.

'ARE YOU STILL WATCHING THE BOY?' ARTOS SPOKE CASUALLY, watching Alma cross the room. He kept his posture and tone relaxed, for all the world as though he and Meredan were discussing the weather.

'Yes. Thorion has bade me to do so until further notice. Though I think it as much for Deryck's own good as anything else.' Meredan shook his head, blowing out a breath. 'Our King has a good heart.'

'And a good sense of what is going on. He has his reasons, I'm sure.' Artos folded his arms. 'And what have you seen?'

'Deryck has joined the Dark Hunt.' Meredan's brows lowered.

'I'm concerned, not just for him, but also for their actions at the tournament. If they still consider Alma as prey...'

Artos took in a breath. He cursed himself – how could he have been so blind? 'Do you think they would? Alma escaped them, thanks to Ethan – surely that nullifies any contract called?'

'Even if so, Denoris would not stand for them taking her. But the fact that he's allowed his son to join them makes me wonder whether there's another plan in play. Perhaps you should warn her.'

'And scare her away from Ambeth again?' Artos shook his head. 'She's fragile enough, Meredan. I cannot lose her again. No, we'll all work to protect her as we always have.'

'I agree, she needs protecting. The Dark obviously still want her.'

'Denoris definitely does. For what, I don't know. Do you know he asked me for her hand, for Deryck?' Artos shook his head. 'Yet the Regalia is two-thirds restored; the Dark cannot possibly use it to tip the Balance now.'

'Yet it is still tipping! We saw it in the stars. There's something more afoot, and we need to keep our wits about us.'

'Agreed, my friend. Keep me posted about the boy, will you?'

Meredan nodded, then his eyes widened as he looked past Artos' shoulder.

Artos turned, and his stomach dropped.

THE BUFFET WAS ONE OF ALMA'S FAVOURITE THINGS ABOUT Ambeth. It appeared in the Hall every mealtime as though by magic, piled high with delicious food, open to any who wished to partake. Picking up a plate from the pile at the end, Alma moved along slowly, filling her plate. She was wrestling with a difficult set of tongs when her talaith stone began to burn. A warm golden hand covered hers, taking the tongs and picking up the small pastry, dropping it on her plate.

'May I?'

Alma's heart thudded in her chest. She turned to see Lord Denoris, smiling at her.

CHAPTER 23
DARK LORD

The Dark Lord was standing far closer to her than she liked. She stared, frozen for a moment. Then she pulled herself together. She was in a public place, there were people all around and there was no way he would try anything here. At least, she hoped not.

'Er, th-thank you,' she stammered, taking a step back. Denoris tilted his head, his green eyes warmer than she remembered.

'Are you well, Alma?'

'Wh-what?' Alma swallowed, her heart pounding. She could do this. Sure she could. 'Um, I'm fine, thanks. And you?'

'I'm fine, also,' replied Denoris. 'I would speak with you, if you have a moment.'

Alma blinked. Panic was causing her to lose her grip on the reins of power in her mind. Denoris flickered in and out, from person to energy pattern and back again. His energy was magnificent – an intricate coiled pattern of light and dark, the latter dominant, the colour of thunderclouds. He was extraordinarily powerful, but then she already knew that. Focusing on his face, she tried to listen to what he was saying, the lines fading away.

'It's about Deryck. I would like to apologise for his bad behaviour, and let you know he still cares about you.'

'What?' She took another step back, but he came closer. God, he really was beautiful, especially when he smiled. His grin widened, as though he could see the effect he was having. Maybe he could. She frowned.

'Alma, what's worrying you? I wish there to be no ill will between us. After all, I didn't get the chance to know you when you were with Deryck, something I regret almost as much as the fact you're no longer together.'

It was like a bizarre dream, standing in the Great Hall exchanging pleasantries with Denoris, the one who had killed her father and uncle. At this thought anger flared .

'Deryck is—'

'Alma! Have you had enough to eat yet?' A hand came down on her arm and she turned to see her grandfather. He was smiling, but she could see worry in his eyes.

ETHAN STOOD WITH HIS FATHER IN THE FOYER.

'I would like to mark Midwinter for your mother with a gift,' said Cedran, 'but I'm not sure what she would like. I also wondered if you were going to arrange something for Alma.'

'Um, well...' What would Dana like? For Cedran to release her? Ethan shook his head. He knew his mother still loved his father; he heard her crying at night when she thought he was asleep. He also knew Cedran frightened her. An impossible situation. His father was waiting, one eyebrow raised.

'Perhaps some jewellery? I know she liked the bracelet—' He broke off as Deryck came through the Foyer doors. Deryck's green eyes met his and narrowed. Ethan put his shoulders back, chin up, meeting Deryck's glare with one of his own. His father's hand came to rest on his shoulder. Then Ethan stiffened. Through the open doors leading into the Hall he saw Alma, standing by the buffet... with Denoris looming over her. And now Deryck was on his way in. He made to run, but his father held him back.

'No, Ethan,' he said. 'Don't worry. Look, Artos has her. He'll handle this.'

But Ethan couldn't relax, not with Deryck moving towards Alma. He knew what it would do to her, to see him again.

'Let me go!'

Cedran came around to face his son, blocking his path.

'Ethan, do you care for her?'

'What? Yes, of course I do!'

'And she cares for you?'

'Dad, let me go!' But Cedran was unmoving. Ethan sighed in resignation. 'Yes, she does.'

'Then for her sake and yours, do not create a scene. Both Artos and I are aware of the situation and are doing what we can to contain it. There's something going on here, something deeper, and we can't risk antagonising Denoris at this point. But believe me, we're doing our best to protect your interests.'

'So I just have to put up with Deryck hassling Alma?!' He threw off his father's restraining hand. 'How can you ask me to do that?'

'Grandfather!' Relief flooded through Alma. Meredan had also come to stand nearby, taking a plate and filling it methodically, though he kept glancing over at the three of them.

'Denoris, well met,' said Artos, extending his hand to the Elder. After a pause Denoris shook it, smiling.

'I was just speaking with Alma. Such a nice surprise, it must have been, to see her here again.'

Alma opened her mouth to protest. How dare he! But her grandfather gently squeezed her arm and she closed it again.

'It's a great joy to have her back in my life,' said Artos, his hand coming to Alma's waist. She put down her plate of food, not sure she wanted it any more.

Then, over Denoris' shoulder she saw Deryck enter the Hall. And he was coming in their direction.

She began to tremble in earnest. The Hall and everyone in it flickered in and out, lines and tangles of energy. Her talaith was burning her wrist, her fingertips buzzing with sparks. She hastily hid them behind her.

Artos glanced at her. 'Are you all right, my dear?' His face was coiled light, his mouth a dark hole.

'Er, I feel faint.' She wasn't lying. 'I think I need some air.'

'Perhaps a cool drink might help?' Denoris, all thunder and darkness, lifted a goblet. Alma managed to pull the power back again, digging her heels in, channelling it through her feet into the ground. She thought she heard a cracking noise, felt Artos flinch. But it worked. She blinked, as everyone and everything returned to normal.

'No thanks,' she said. 'I really think I need to go.' Her nerves were still screaming and it was all she could do to hold it together.

'I agree,' said Artos. 'Come, my dear. I know Ethan is waiting for you. If you'll excuse us, Denoris.'

'I understand.' Denoris reached out and took Alma's hand, raising it to his lips. 'But I hope we get the chance to speak again soon.'

She was going to faint, she was sure of it – only her grandfather's arm kept her upright. She nodded, unable to respond any other way. There were no words, really. Deryck was almost upon them. Artos whisked her past him, so close their shoulders almost touched. Deryck turned his head to her, his green eyes wide. She knew her expression was the same. She could barely breathe, but Artos kept hold of her, his grip strong, taking her towards the double doors.

~

'I'M NOT ASKING YOU TO DO THAT,' SAID CEDRAN. HIS FACE was tight. 'I'm asking only that you don't make a scene.'

Ethan glared at his father, his jaw tight. Was he serious? He stepped to one side, but Cedran moved with him.

'Dad!'

'Ethan, I won't ask you again.' Ethan knew that tone. He let out a groan of frustration. Then he heard a soft voice say his name.

'Ethan.'

'Alma!' He went to hug her, but she shook her head, warning him back.

'Not here. Not now.' He took in her trembling mouth, her pale face, and nodded.

'Come on,' he said, let's go upstairs.'

'Actually,' said Artos. 'I need to speak with Alma for a moment.'

'Come, Ethan,' said Cedran, fixing his son with a look. 'You can meet up again later.'

Ethan hid a sigh. All he wanted to do was be alone with Alma, but it looked as though that wasn't going to be an option, after all. Damn Deryck for showing up!

He stared into the Hall, frowning. Deryck turned as though he could feel his glare, his own brows lowering.

'Come on.' Cedran, who was already on his way out the doors, stopped and turned.

Ethan blew out a breath. 'I'll see you later,' he said, kissing Alma on the cheek. Deryck be damned.

She smiled, but it was faint. 'Okay,' she whispered.

He released her, turning back for one more look before he left the Foyer. She was still standing there. Artos, his hand on her shoulder, stared after him.

Then the doors closed behind him and she was gone.

~

'I'VE SPOKEN WITH ARTOS ONCE MORE,' SAID DENORIS, 'AND also with Alma.' He reached for another piece of chicken, tearing into it.

'I saw,' said Deryck, sitting opposite his father in the alcove. He was still recovering from seeing her, from being so close to her. 'Why didn't she stay? I wanted to speak with her myself.'

His father smiled. 'She's nervous, that's all. She wants to let Ethan down easy, before coming back to you.'

Deryck nodded. 'Of course. So, did she say when she might do that?'

'Oh, I think soon. But she'll need to choose her moment carefully, of course, so as not to anger his father. It helps that the boy doesn't live here.'

Deryck started to eat his own lunch. Alma *had* looked nervous as she passed him, close enough that he could smell her perfume, feel the soft flick of her hair. Yes, nervous. That was it. Touching the stone at his neck he breathed deeply.

'So, when will she be back?'

'Hmm?' Denoris looked at him. 'Oh, well, I'm not sure. I'll find out from Artos, next time I see him.' He sat back, wiping his mouth and hands with a napkin. Then he fixed his green gaze on Deryck. 'She will be yours, and soon enough. Remember that.' He got up and walked away, his black cloak billowing behind him as he stalked from the Hall, people moving out of his way.

Deryck watched him go. His mouth twisted, and he returned to his food. He *had* to believe his father. The other option was too hard to bear.

'Deryck.' The word was hissed, coming from behind the pillar. Deryck frowned, turning in his seat to see who'd spoken. It was Tomas, his brow wrinkled, hands twisting together.

'What are you doing? Come and sit.'

Tomas, glancing over his shoulder, scuttled round and slid into the seat opposite Deryck, keeping low.

'What's going on? You all right?' Deryck asked.

'I'm fine. But is your sister?'

'My sister?' Deryck sat back. He hadn't given Ellery a thought, even though he knew she'd been confined to her room, knew what his father had wanted them to do. It had been easier to block it out, to not think of it once he'd refused, dismissing it as a fever-dream. The stone had helped, a lot. Now dread rushed through him. But... his eyes narrowed.

'Why do you ask?'

Tomas licked his lips, leaning forward, his eyes darting to the side again. 'I haven't seen her in a week. Not *anywhere*. And I haven't been able to find you, either. Plus your father—'

'My father?' Deryck was beginning to understand why Tomas seemed so agitated.

'Yes. He told me, I mean, I went there, I had a gift for her and I wanted to see her, you know? He told me he didn't want her seeing me anymore.' His face twisted. 'Said she was dealing with a family matter. I just want a chance to speak to her, that's all, so she doesn't think I've abandoned her.' Tomas's brown eyes were bright with anguish.

Deryck felt a pang. He knew how it felt. 'I'm sorry,' he said. 'I'd no idea he'd done that. As for Ellery...' What could he say? He liked Tomas, but he didn't know whether he could trust him. 'I mean, she hasn't been well. That's all.'

Tomas frowned. 'Not well?'

Deryck raised an eyebrow. 'Do you think I'm lying?'

'No, no, I'm sorry.' Tomas sat back, rumpling his hair with one hand. 'It's just, I miss her. And I've been so worried.'

Deryck relented a little. 'I can tell her, if you like. Let her know you were asking after her.'

Tomas's face lit up. 'Really?' He rummaged in a pocket of his tunic. 'Can you tell her, well...' He ducked his head, his cheeks reddening. Then he met Deryck's gaze. 'Tell her I love her. And she's not alone. And give her this. Please,' he added, pulling a small box wrapped in wrinkled silk from his pocket and putting it on the table. 'Is there anything else you think I could do?'

Deryck blinked, his hand going to his tallus stone, darkness stealing over him, covering his sorrow, his memories of what it had been like to be loved. 'I'll tell her,' he said, reaching for the little box and tucking it in his pocket. 'Other than that, I can give you no further guidance.'

He rose to his feet and slid from the alcove. Tomas remained seated. The hope on his face made Deryck feel even worse. He nodded, then turned and walked away.

CHAPTER 24
COLD SHOCK

Someone was tapping on Ellery's door. She sat up, her head spinning. Her necklace was lying on the bed next to her, the clasp undone. Part of her wanted it, wanted the release of the stone, but she fought it.

'Who is it?' she croaked. The door was locked and Hilde and her father had the only keys.

'Ellery.' She recognised Deryck's voice and her eyes prickled with tears. She managed to get to her feet, though it was so hard, despite all the practising she'd been doing. She staggered to the door, leaning against it.

'Deryck?'

'Are you all right?'

Was she all right? 'What do you think?' she said and heard him gasp a laugh.

'Ellery, you have to stop fighting him.'

Her legs gave out and she slid down the door, sitting against it with a thud.

'Ellery!' Deryck sounded worried.

'I'm fine, just couldn't stand up.'

She heard a rustle as he sat down as well, the door moving as his weight settled against it.

'What do you mean, you can't stand up?'

'It's the stone, I guess. I've just been lying here. I don't even know what day it is.'

There was a silence. 'You've been in there for six days.'

Six? That was longer than she'd thought.

'But, you've been in here. I'm sure I remember... something. Right?'

'Oh, Ellery.' Deryck's voice caught. 'I'm so sorry. It was Father. He was trying to make me, to make us— I didn't want to. I didn't do it.'

Tears began to leak from Ellery's eyes. 'I know,' she whispered, her voice choked. 'At least, I think I do. Um, did you kiss me, for a while?'

'No!' Deryck sounded shocked. 'You have to give in. Even if you pretend, just do it. Just do what it takes to get out of there.'

'But, this stone... How do you do it?' she said. 'I can't even walk.'

'I don't know. Is it your human blood?'

'Father said something about it. I guess, maybe? Um, also, do you hear any, um, voices when you use yours?'

'No.' Deryck sounded confused, so she let it go.

'I just saw Tomas,' he went on, after a pause. Her heart lifted. 'You did?'

'Yeah. He was asking about you, said he was worried.'

Ellery closed her eyes, tears rolling down her cheeks. She wished she could see him, wished it with all her heart.

'What did you tell him?"

'What could I say? I said you were unwell. Otherwise he would have been here again—'

'Again?'

There was silence for a moment. 'He said he'd been here,'

Deryck said, finally. 'And that Father told him to go away and not come back.'

Ellery slumped down, sorrow curling through her like smoke. But beneath it was a flicker of fire, of rage.

'Ellery?'

'Yes?' Her voice was strangled with tears.

'He... he wanted me to tell you,' Deryck cleared his throat. 'Well, that he loved you. And you weren't alone. He, er, he gave me something to give you, for when you come out.'

Ellery curled over, sobbing, her mouth wide with grief. She smacked her fist into the door, but it barely moved.

'I'm so sorry,' Deryck said. 'Truly I am, for everything. Believe me, I know how you feel.'

Ellery doubted it. Then she felt bad. She knew what Deryck had been through, what he was still going through.

'Um, Deryck?'

'Yes?'

'Has father said any more to you about Alma?'

Deryck was silent for so long she wasn't sure if he had gone away. Then she heard his clothing rustle as he moved position.

'That he's speaking to Artos about the match.'

'And you believe him?'

Again he was silent. Then he spoke. 'What else can I do? I want her back so badly it hurts, even with this stone, even with giving myself over to it. She's all that's left. I don't think he would lie to me about this.'

'What do you mean, you've given yourself over to it?' Ellery felt sick. Of course their father would lie. He was very good at it. But this seemed the easiest question, the one least fraught with danger.

'It was when she came back, with the Cup. I tried to see her, but the guards turned me away, so I went riding, trying to get away, I guess.'

'Oh, Deryck.'

'I stopped on the cliff and it was near to where we once... where she... Anyway, I've never felt such pain, the stone didn't help at all so I grabbed it, you know, really hard, and let it take me. It was preferable, I guess, to feeling the pain.'

''But I don't understand. What did it do?'

'Well, now the pain is mostly gone, I just touch the stone and it's all okay. I don't care too much for anything, really. Occasionally something will jolt me from it, like when father was beating you. I'm so sorry, El, that I couldn't stop him.'

She smiled through her tears. He rarely called her that anymore, not since they were both small. But she was worried about him, about what he'd just told her. She'd known something wasn't right, but not this.

'It's okay,' she said. 'I know you couldn't.' Her mouth twisted, trembling. 'B-but, what do you mean, you don't care about anything? Is that why you joined the Hunt?'

Deryck sighed. 'Yes and no. I mean, it was exciting, I guess. But now I don't know.'

'And what about Alma?'

'That's the funny thing. When I touch the stone the pain goes, but all that's left is longing. And I'm not sure if that's worse.'

Deryck sounded so dejected. Ellery's heart clenched. Despite everything, he was her brother and the closest thing she had to an ally now.

'When I get out of here—'

'You'll be in thrall to your stone, just like I am.'

'Deryck?' She felt a thud, a reverberation as the front door opened and closed.

'I have to go. Just get out of there!' She heard him scramble to his feet, his footsteps receding down the corridor. Her father was back, she supposed. Then she stiffened. What if he wanted to come in and see her? He couldn't find her against the door like this. Her legs still wouldn't work so, using every last ounce of effort she dragged herself across the stone floor until she got to the soft rug where she lost her traction and got hopelessly stuck. Crying tears of frustration she looked around for something to help her.

Then the key turned in the lock and the door opened.

'WHAT WAS DENORIS THINKING?'

Alma, safe on the sofa in her grandfather's apartment, sat back, her arms folded. Her fear had gone, replaced by anger. 'Why would he just come up to me like that, like he's done nothing, like we're *friends* or something!'

Artos sat down in the chair opposite her. 'My dear, you need to be careful. By the Light, when I saw your hands sparking! I felt the very bones of the earth crack, you know, when you pushed it back!' He huffed out a laugh, shaking his head. 'I'm so proud of you, of what you can do already. But,' he went on, the smile leaving his face, 'it's better that Denoris doesn't know about it.'

Alma made a face. 'I think the cat might be out of the bag already with that one.'

Artos snorted. 'Yes, possibly. But, my dear, there's something else you need to know.'

Alma's stomach lurched. She waited for him to explain, chewing on her lip.

'I fear he may have been trying to engineer a meeting between you and Deryck,' her grandfather said.

Rage flared, her fingertips crackling. 'Why on *earth* would he think that was okay? He sent Deryck to get me already, and I said no.' She fought to keep a rein on her anger. But *seriously*. 'How many times does he need to hear it?'

'No is not a word that means much to Denoris, not when there's something he wants.' Her grandfather looked uncharacteristically stern, his brows drawn together.

'And what you're saying is that he still wants, that he wants...'

Artos nodded. 'Yes. There's something more afoot here.' He rubbed a hand over his face. 'I don't wish to worry you further, but I need to tell you something.'

He paused. He opened his mouth and closed it again, rubbing his brow.

'Grandfather?'

He blew a breath out through his nose. 'Denoris has made me a formal offer for your hand. For Deryck.'

Alma's eyes widened, a sick feeling inside her. 'What?'

'I know, I'm sorry, my dear, but I needed to tell you.'

'B-but Deryck knows, he knows I would never agree to something like that. E-even when we were together, I mean, we were too young and it's just—' She stopped, putting her hand to her mouth.

'I believe Denoris is lying to the boy, giving him false hope. That's the only explanation I can think of.'

'He's such an idiot! Ugh!' She spat the words. 'Why would he even think for a second that I would...! God!' She was so angry she didn't even know what to do with herself; angry at Denoris, but also, and this made her feel even worse, at the fact he was lying to Deryck, the small twisted part of her that still cared for him rearing its head. Artos came to sit next to her, taking her hand in his.

'My dear, I told him no. That it was not my choice to make, anyway. And now you're with Ethan...' He kept talking but Alma didn't listen. Cold horror washed over her. Ethan. Deryck had killed Caleb out of jealousy and they'd only been friends. What would he do to Ethan? She closed her eyes, tears falling at the memory of Caleb, defenceless on the green. Deryck had no mercy for him. She imagined Ethan in the same position and thought she was going to be sick.

'Alma. Alma! Are you all right?'

She opened her eyes. His concerned face was close to hers. 'Grandfather, I—' Her voice broke and she started to sob. He pulled her into a hug. 'I can't tell Ethan, he mustn't know about this,' she said, her voice muffled against his shoulder as he smoothed her hair, making comforting noises.

'I'm sorry, dear one. Perhaps I shouldn't have said anything.'

She lifted her head. 'No!' she said, fierce. 'No, you should tell me. And if I see Deryck anywhere, he'll be sorry. But Ethan can't know!'

Artos frowned. 'But—'

'Caleb,' she said, anger and fear choking her throat.

Artos' brow cleared, his hand coming to stroke her hair. 'Oh my dear.' He nodded. 'I understand. But are you sure? Keeping this from him may not be the best idea.'

'I can't put him in danger,' she whispered, wiping her face. 'Deryck can deal with me, if he has a problem. It changes nothing, this offer. I would never go back to him, even if I wasn't with Ethan.' She frowned. 'I told him this, when he came to me in Wales. I told him...' She trailed off, starting to feel calmer, though fear sat like a cold little weight in her stomach.

'Ah.' Artos nodded again, then let go of Alma and reached for the flagon on the table, pouring her a drink. She took it, grateful, sipping the cool, clear water. It cleared her head, clarifying her resolve.

'Thorion and I saw him, you know, when he came back through,' Artos said.

'You did?'

'It was obvious things hadn't gone to plan.' He shook his head. 'My dear, I understand you want nothing to do with him, but you need to be careful. There's more to this than one boy's obsession. Denoris wants you, for what I don't know. And Deryck – well, there's something different about him these days. I'm worried for him, if I'm honest.'

'Well, I'm not.' Even though she was, just a bit. And that made her even more angry. She put her glass down, folding her arms and glaring at the room in general. Artos smiled. He glanced at the portraits of his sons.

'So what do I do now? I need to still be here, to see you. And look for the Crown.'

'How do you know the Crown is here? Your father thought it may have passed through the Gates. He and Gwion were searching for it when he met your mother.'

'Yes, Thorion told me earlier.'

'He didn't find it, of course. But I think what he did find was of even more value.' He smiled, his eyes bright. 'So, perhaps you and that young man of yours could spend some time searching over there?'

Alma's eyes narrowed. 'Wait. Are you telling me to stay out of Ambeth?'

Artos screwed up his face. It would have almost been funny, if not for the pit of dread in her stomach. 'We-ell... not stay away, as such. But perhaps it might be safer for you to keep a low profile, for the next little while, let things calm down a bit.'

'Were you telling the truth, about my father? Or were you just trying to keep me safe?'

'Oh, my dear.' Artos hugged her again. 'I'm always trying to keep you safe.' He released her and sat back, wiping his face. His ice-blue eyes were bright with tears. 'I couldn't bear to think of it, you in his clutches.' He huffed. 'I don't want you to stop coming here, of course I don't. But I wasn't lying about your father, either. Neither the Sword nor the Cup were found in Ambeth – what makes you think the Crown will be?'

Alma reached out and hugged him. 'I'm sorry,' she murmured. 'My temper sometimes—'

'Gets the better of you? As I've said, you're so like your father.' He smiled. 'And where do you think he got his temper from? Believe me, I know what it's like.'

'You do?'

'Yes.' He took her hands in his. 'Come here if you want, but stay away from the hills. Don't tarry in the woods, or spend too long in the Hall. Cedran or I would be happy to look after you.'

'Cedran?'

'Yes. With Ethan helping you, and the current state of affairs, it seems we have more in common than perhaps we thought. He, too, is proud of you, and of Ethan, and he supports your search for the Crown.'

There was a knock at the door. Alma turned, running her hand through her hair. She knew it was Ethan, she could feel him. She gave her grandfather a fierce look. 'Not a word about Deryck, please. Promise.'

'I promise,' he said after a pause. 'Just be careful, dear heart. Remember what I said, about tarrying too long. I won't lose you again.'

Beran answered the door and Ethan came into the room, smiling, but his face changed when he saw Alma. She smiled back at him, but she knew he could tell she'd been upset.

'It's all right.' She got up. 'I'm... I'm fine. I'll tell you later,' she said, glancing at her grandfather.

Ethan came and hugged her, looking searchingly at her. 'Shall we go, then?'

She nodded, relieved that he wasn't going to push her. She had to tell him something, she knew that, but at least it gave her time to figure out what. All that mattered was that he was safe. She let go of Ethan and went to hug Artos one more time. 'I'm sorry,' she whispered. 'And I'll be back as soon as I can.' She looked at his dear face, so filled with concern for her, and she felt angry again, angry at Deryck for creating this situation. She kissed him on the cheek. 'I love you,' she whispered, meaning it. He hugged her again.

'I love you, too,' Artos murmured into her hair, then he let her go. 'Come and see me again.'

'I will, as soon as I can,' she said, heart sore.

Ethan came and shook Artos' hand. 'My Lord.' He bowed his head.

'Artos,' he replied, smiling. 'You're family, now.'

Alma and Ethan left the room, heading down the curving stairs in silence, hand in hand. Outside, the sun was shining and everything seeming normal, as though Denoris hadn't tried to just trap her, as though the Dark weren't still after her. Alma walked quickly, her head down, until they passed through a stone archway into an octagonal garden space, a small pond in the centre filled with golden carp.

'Hey,' Ethan said. 'What's going on?'

Alma stopped. 'I'm sorry—'

He didn't let her finish, backing her up against the rough stone of the wall and kissing her, his arms around her waist.

'Are you all right?' He pulled back a little, one hand smoothing her hair. He grinned. 'You don't have a very good poker face, you know.'

Alma grinned as well, unable to help it. 'I'm okay.'

'No you're not,' he said, leaning in for another kiss. 'And I thought maybe we might stay here a bit longer—'

'No! I mean, it's been a long day. And I was upset... It was just, we were talking about my father and, I don't know, it made me sad. I promise I'm fine now. Now that I'm with you.' That wasn't a lie. She kissed him again, pushing down the fear inside her of what she would do if she lost him. She couldn't bear to even think of it. 'I'm just still worried about Deryck, I guess. It was weird to see him again.' There. That definitely wasn't a lie.

'Huh.' Ethan snorted. 'Just let him try anything.'

'But that's the thing, Ethan.' Alma stopped him, her fingers on his lips. He kissed them. 'I don't want anything to happen. I can't bear it, couldn't bear to see you in danger like that.' She swallowed, her heart pounding. 'I care about you too much, to go through that again. And I just... I just want to go home.'

His face softened and he leaned in, his arms tightening around her.

'I'm sorry,' he said, his mouth close to hers, his eyelashes tickling her cheek. She breathed in his warm breath, feeling the calm he gave her, his strong energy mingling with hers. 'And I understand. We can come back another time, when you're ready. We can make our own fun back home.' He laughed softly and she felt a thrill at his closeness, his body pressed against hers. She kissed him again.

'We can.'

CHAPTER 25

AN UNFAMILIAR PLACE

'Oh, my lady!' Hilde came into the room, her worn face creasing with worry when she saw Ellery sprawled on the rug. She put down the tray of food she was carrying and came over, crouching down beside her. 'Let me help you.'

'Hilde, oh, I was just trying to get warm when I fell and I couldn't get up. Please help me before father comes, I was just so cold—' Ellery knew she was babbling but couldn't help it; her relief at seeing Hilde was overwhelming.

'And you'd best get yon necklace on before he comes,' Hilde said, nodding over to the bed as Ellery clutched at her. She draped one of Ellery's arms over her shoulder then stood with a grunt of effort, managing to get Ellery to her feet. She hung on to the back of a chair, her legs trembling.

'Thank you, Hilde. Can you help me get to the bed?'

Hilde put her arm around Ellery's waist and together they managed to reach the bed, where she sat down. Hilde draped a robe around her shoulders and Ellery slid her arms into it, grateful for the warmth. She picked up her necklace, careful not to touch the stone. The clasp had come undone again, just like it did every night. She frowned, turning it over between her fingers. Then there was a step in the hallway and her head came up, her eyes wide. Quickly, she put the necklace on, letting it hang on the outside of her robe.

She was just in time. The door opened and her father strode in, his black cloak billowing behind him. He was followed by Gwenene, her expression sly. She smirked when she saw Ellery, and slid her hands around Denoris' bare upper arm, leaning against him, all velvet menace.

'Having fun, are you?' she said. 'Such a shame about your human blood, making things so difficult for you.'

'I don't need your sympathy.'

'Oh, I don't feel sorry for you. I just think it's a shame you're so weak. But then your mother was the same, I suppose.'

Hilde, sitting by the fire, kept her gaze down, but Ellery saw her mouth tighten. She stared at Gwenene. 'You know *nothing* about my mother.' Her voice trembled, her whole body trembled, and she wished she could get up from the bed and scratch the other woman's eyes out.

'Now, now,' said Denoris, holding his hands wide. 'This is all very nice, but we have other things to discuss.' He shook off Gwenene's grasp and came over to the bed, sitting down and patting Ellery on the leg.

She fought the urge to recoil. He was smiling, his green eyes warm, and once again his beauty tugged at her, as though he could be the father she'd always dreamed of. But she knew too well now that whenever he was nice to her, something bad inevitably followed. She braced herself.

'You're looking thin,' he said, his hand coming to her chin, turning her face from side to side, but gently, as though she were made of porcelain. She tried not to cry, to steel herself, but it was so hard, and she was so tired. She felt for the anger from before, reminded herself of what he'd done to Tomas, but the world was slipping away again, grey stealing into her vision. 'You must eat,' he went on, releasing her chin, his fingers trailing down her neck. 'For we have things to do.'

'We do?' Her voice was a whisper.

'Yes, daughter. I have a surprise for you, a special trip. So I need you to be able to walk, to be strong again. Can you do that for me?' He leaned in close, his lips brushing her cheek, his scent of spice and leather curling around her. Revulsion and love mingled in her stomach.

'Yes, Father.' She bowed her head, partly because it was difficult to hold it up any more. Then she heard the voice again, the one she loved.

'Come on, lovely girl. Be strong, for both of us. You can do this, I know you can.' The voice was so gentle, so full of love and warmth. Her father could take Tomas from her, turn Deryck away, push everyone out of her life. But the voice was hers and hers alone. And for it, she would keep going. She lifted her head.

Her father was watching her, his expression uncharacteristically serious. Her heart lifted, slightly. Maybe he actually cared about what happened to her. 'Show me,' he said. 'Walk to the table, so I know you've been practising.'

Ellery blinked, swaying. Her legs were still shaking from before, but there was a glint in her father's eye. It wouldn't bode well if she refused.

'Come, my gorgeous girl, I will help you,' the voice said. It was as though a soft breeze swirled around her, a gentle hand beneath her elbow. She put her feet on the floor, making sure they were flat, that she could feel the stone beneath them. 'That's it,' the voice whispered.

Pushing her hands into the bed, she rose slowly to her feet, her gaze locked on her father. He nodded, as though encouraging her, and tears threatened again. Then Gwenene laughed.

'It will take you until Midwinter at this rate,' she said.

Ellery glared at her, anger giving her the impetus to move forward. There was still the feeling of a hand beneath her elbow, helping her to balance, and she managed to walk over to the table. The tray Hilde had brought was there. Bracing herself with one hand, she lifted the cover from the food. It was a bowl of stew, rich with meat and vegetables, soft white bread and butter on the side, and a bowl of sugared fruit. Her mouth watered at the smell of it.

A hand descended on her shoulder. 'Good.' Her father's breath was warm on the side of her face, his body against her back. 'Now eat. I'm out tonight, but Hilde will look after you. And tomorrow you must be ready. Will you be ready?' His fingers tightened on her shoulder. She flinched.

'Yes,' she whispered.

'Good,' he said again, his lips brushing her cheek, close to her ear. Then he was gone, Gwenene following, the door closing behind them both.

Ellery sagged forward and Hilde came to her, her hands gentle as she helped Ellery to sit down at the table. She moved the tray in front of her.

'Your father was right about one thing, my lady. You do need to eat. As for the rest...' Her wrinkled face creased even further as she glanced towards the closed door. 'Come now, eat up. I have my knitting and will stay for as long as I can.'

Ellery nodded, her tears falling into her stew. She took in a shuddering breath, wiped her hand across her face and started to eat.

Later, full and feeling better than she had in a while, she lay on her bed, listening to the crackle of the fire, the gentle clack of Hilde's needles as she knitted. She rolled onto her side. As she did so her necklace, which was still around her neck, slid down, the stone touching her hand.

But instead of marshmallow clouds and soft darkness, Ellery's body stiffened, convulsing as though electricity were running through her. It felt like that, too, as though lightning were coursing through her veins. She choked, saliva filling her mouth, her head going back and her feet drumming on the bed. Then everything went black.

When her eyes opened Hilde was bending over her, shaking her by the shoulder. Ellery's stomach convulsed and she rolled over, her dinner coming back up and onto the floor, spattering across the stones. Hilde moved out of the way just in time. Something was dangling from the maid's hand, catching the light. It was her necklace. She realised what Hilde had risked to help her.

'Oh, Hilde,' she croaked, reaching out, wanting the stone close to her again. 'Give it to me, it's all right.' She was sobbing, as was Hilde. Ellery caught the other woman's hand when she gave back the necklace, hanging onto it as though it were a rope and she was on the edge of a cliff.

'Oh my lady, oh,' cried Hilde. 'One minute you were all right, and the next you were all broken like. 'Tis a wicked thing, yon necklace.'

Ellery shook, tears coursing down her cheeks, curling herself around the stone. 'It is, Hilde,' was all she could say. But she knew she was wedded to it now, as surely as if she'd spoken vows. She was lost, and there was no one who could help her, no one at all.

SHE WOKE EARLY THE NEXT MORNING. NO LIGHT WAS VISIBLE yet around her shutters. Hilde was already bustling around; Ellery wondered whether she'd been there all night. Her floor was clean once more, the fire set and the dinner dishes had been replaced with a fresh tray, the smell of breakfast wafting through the room. It would have been lovely to wake up to, if not for the curling sense of dread running through her, the feeling that she was lost in a storm with no lifeline.

'Ah, my lady, you're up. Your, er, your father has been in already, bade me get you ready.'

Ellery sat up carefully. Her head was pounding and she didn't feel up to doing anything. But if her father had already been in... 'How long do I have?'

'Not long, my lady. Shall I help you bathe and dress?'

Ellery nodded. She hated feeling so weak, but she'd never be able to manage it herself. Hilde got her from the bed and into the bathing chamber, where she helped her to freshen up. She produced fresh bandages, wrapping Ellery's arm carefully before helping her into her gown.

'You must eat,' she said. 'And, I have something that might help you.'

'You do?' Ellery let Hilde lead her back into the bedroom, let her sit her down in a chair, let her brush out her hair.

'It's a drink, my lady. 'Twill perk you up no end, I swear.'

Ellery frowned. Her breakfast waited on the tray, porridge with honey and fruit. Next to the bowl was a tall glass pitcher, the contents a cloudy green colour. Hilde went to the tray and poured Ellery a glass of the green drink, handing it to her.

Ellery took it, sniffing the contents. It smelled fresh, like green leaves and citrus, peppermint and lemon. She hesitated, then drank it down, not really caring what it did to her. She was lost, after all.

'Not to me, you're not,' the voice in her mind said, the words full of love. Ellery blinked, the drink coursing through her. For a moment she thought she might be sick again, then the fog surrounding her lifted a little, the colours seeming brighter. Her stomach growled. She reached for the porridge and started eating, wolfing it down.

'Good to see you eating, daughter.' The door opened to admit her father, who was rubbing his hands together. 'But it's time to go. Come, now, finish up.'

Ellery did as she was told, scraping the bowl. Hilde helped her to lace on her boots and draped a soft cloak around her shoulders. Her necklace hung around her neck, and she felt an urge to touch the stone again. She followed her father out the door, with a glance back to Hilde, who nodded, her hands clasped together.

It was strange to be out of her room. The hallway felt like an unfamiliar place. Deryck was waiting by the front door and he smiled when he saw her, coming to take her arm.

'It's good to see you,' he whispered, and she felt him tuck something in her pocket, under her cloak.

The fresh air outside was a shock. Everything seemed too bright, and she squinted, hanging on to her brother, glad of his support, unable to move quickly. Their father walked ahead. They took one path after another, twisting through the gardens.

'Where are we going?' she said, looking around. She felt more alert than she had in days, but there was a sense that it was fragile, that she could collapse at any minute. She wondered whether she might have the chance to slip away, to find Tomas, before it happened.

'You'll see,' said Denoris without turning his head.

She glanced at Deryck and he shook his head. There were dark circles under his eyes and his arm was tense.

Denoris came to a stop at a curving stone wall. An ancient wooden door was set into the curve. She couldn't recall ever seeing it before, but the gardens changed so much she wasn't surprised. Her father unlocked the door and went through. Ellery glanced at Deryck.

'Just do as he says,' Deryck muttered as he helped her through the doorway.

She came through the other side and stopped dead. Denoris was kneeling on the paving stones, his arms braced against them.

'Wh-what's that?'

OUTSIDE THE WALL, MEREDAN WATCHED, HIDDEN IN THE shadow of the hedge. When the door closed he moved away, heading with purpose towards the Palace. Whatever was going on here, it looked as though Denoris was now involving his children. It was time to speak to Thorion.

CHAPTER 26
THE PIECES START TO MOVE

'The girl is unwell,' Meredan said. He leaned against the windowsill and folded his arms.

'What?' Thorion, who until now had seemed mildly amused, frowned. 'What do you mean?' Armour-clad, he paced up and down past the fireplace in his chambers, Adara watching him from her seat on the sofa.

'What I mean, Thorion, is that she's very thin and can barely walk.' Meredan shook his head, still shocked at his glimpse of Ellery leaning on her brother's arm. 'Yet I saw her not two weeks ago and she was fine then.'

'Is there something we can do?' Adara said, her golden gaze troubled.

'I doubt Denoris would look kindly on our interference,' Meredan replied.

'But if she needs help—'

Thorion held up his hand. 'A Gate is opening.'

'Again?' Adara frowned.

'*Again?*' said Meredan. 'Do you mean this isn't the first time?'

Thorion shook his head. 'The Dark, or should I say Denoris, have been travelling between the worlds since Alma returned with the Cup, despite the ban. Not often, though – it takes energy to open a Gate.'

'You would know,' said Adara.

'And you're not concerned?' Meredan frowned. 'I mean, I know you went after the boy, when he was sent through. But have you done nothing more about it?'

Thorion sighed. 'I am concerned, of course I am. But until now I hadn't thought there was much to it. After all, Alma is safer now than she ever was, claimed by Artos, and now under Cedran's wing through Ethan. We have the Sword and the Cup, and it seems as though Etras is gone. And, despite whatever intrigue Denoris cooks up, Alma seems able to evade his clutches. But...' His mouth twisted.

Meredan narrowed his eyes, his apprehension rising. Something wasn't right. He'd not felt it to be so for a while now, despite all their successes. 'But?'

'When Alma and Ethan were here yesterday, they told me about something they'd seen in their world. Darkness. Or, rather, dark energy, pure and raw, creating havoc among the humans. I've been pondering it since they told me, and I cannot help but think that Denoris is somehow involved.'

'But why would he squander dark energy like that? Surely the Dark need it, as we need the Light!' Meredan blinked. This was worse than he'd imagined.

'This is what the stars were saying, wasn't it?' Adara was leaning forward, her hands clasped together, a furrow between her brows. 'The Balance still tipping, and Daearen still obscured. That's what we couldn't understand.'

'I think so, dear heart.' Thorion shook his head. 'I think, perhaps, we need to track it.'

'But how?'

'I'll go to her,' said Meredan, his muscles already twitching.

'Alma.' Adara nodded her head. 'Of course. She'll be able to sense it.'

'There's something else, though,' Meredan went on. 'Something I've already mentioned to Artos.' He was keen to leave, but he needed to share this. 'You're aware, of course, that the boy has joined the Hunt. But the Hunt, as far as we know, are still after Alma.'

Thorion drew in a breath, his eyes turning the darkest shade of grey. He blinked and turned away. Adara went to him and rubbed his arm. The King exhaled. Meredan waited – he knew, they all knew, how hard the memory of that day was for the King, and why, perhaps, he would not want to revisit it.

'Because of the tournament.' Thorion ground out the words.

'Yes,' said Meredan.

'But they didn't get her!' Adara's expression was fierce, like a golden hawk. 'And it wasn't a threat, of course it wasn't, while she stayed away, but—'

'But now she's coming back here again, to visit Artos, but also with Ethan, to look for the Crown,' said Thorion, rubbing his hand over his face.

'Meredan, you must warn her!'

'I believe Artos already has. But I will mention it when I go through. Perhaps it's best if she stays away from Ambeth for a while.'

'I agree,' said Thorion. 'Though it will set back her search. Still, her safety is the most important thing.'

'So it's agreed, then? I'll go to her.'

Thorion nodded, his arm coming around Adara.

Meredan went to his own chambers, quickly getting changed into something more suitable for the human world and covering it with his cloak. Downstairs the Foyer was almost empty, but Meredan walked as though he were going nowhere in particular, internally on alert but externally relaxed. It was his gift to blend in, to seek out the pathways others didn't see, to read traps and tracers, to track those who were lost. Etras had been the same, but he had twisted his talent to hunt for his own desires, leading to his eventual downfall. Meredan had heard that he was now missing, though he doubted there were many who missed him at all.

He was soon through the gardens, crossing the meadow along the winding white path, heading through the woods to the door between the worlds. The pathways were deserted, though there were signs of those who had passed that way, if a person knew where to look and what to look for. A long red hair, caught on a twig. Several dark green threads from a velvet cloak on a large rock, as though someone had sat there for a while, waiting. Meredan's mouth tightened briefly. The Gate was up ahead, and he reached out with his mind, checking the tracers he'd placed there. Alma's signature was clear, as was Ethan's; they were the most recent to go through the Gate.

He stood for a moment, aligning his timing so he could pass through at just the right moment. Then he stepped between the trees and disappeared.

ELLERY FOLLOWED HER FATHER AND BROTHER OUT OF THE basement room and up the stairs, her feet dragging with tiredness, her head spinning from the passage through the Gate. It had been a shock to see it twisting in the morning air, the dark pool beneath swirling, menacing. But she'd let her brother take her through, hanging on to his arm, their father following. She knew where she was, now. The sounds gave it away, as did the air, heavy in a way that it wasn't in Ambeth. She was back in the human world.

At the top of the stairs was a wide hallway, dimly lit. Winter gloom lay beyond the glass around the front door. Denoris turned to his children.

'Deryck, take Ellery upstairs and show her where to get changed. We need to get going.'

Deryck nodded, once, then turned to his sister, his green eyes sympathetic.

'Come on,' he said, his hand at the small of her back as he shepherded her up the winding stairs. Her hand grasped the satin smooth banister. The effects of Hilde's drink were starting to wear off and her legs were shaking. At the top of the stairs was another hallway, lined with white-painted wooden doors. Deryck went to the closest, unlocking the door and ushering Ellery inside. It was a bedroom, the furnishings dark timber, the large bed made up with white linens. Ellery went straight to it and sat down, her head hanging.

Deryck went to the window. 'Ellery, come and see,' he said, pressing his face to the windowpane. 'Oh, there are lights everywhere.'

Ellery lay down on her side, wanting to curl up and sleep. The effort of fighting her stone had left her exhausted.

'Ellery!" Deryck came to the bed and sat down, one hand resting lightly on her arm. She had to fight the urge to shake him off, to move away – she knew he hadn't done anything to her, but the scars of her captivity ran deep.

'Hey.' His voice was gentle. She rolled over, looking at him through half-closed eyes. 'C'mon, Ellery. It's exciting here. The city is amazing!'

'I've been here before,' said Ellery quietly. Even talking was an effort.

'Oh, right.' Deryck sounded deflated. She half smiled, despite her exhaustion. 'Right, I forgot you lived here for a while.' His mouth twisted and he looked down for a moment. 'We do need to get changed, though. Father will wonder where we are.'

'I'm sorry,' she said. 'I'm just so tired, still.' Making an effort, she sat up and put her hand to her head. There was something hard digging into her hip – it was whatever Deryck had put into her pocket before they'd left. She pulled it from her pocket. 'What did you give me? Before we left?'

He was frowning, but at her question his brow cleared. 'It's a gift. From Tomas. Remember I told you?'

Ellery took in a breath. She turned the little silk-wrapped parcel over in her hands, her vision blurring. 'Oh.' It was faint, no more than a sigh. Her hands shook as she tried to undo the silk. Deryck took it from her, unwrapping it to reveal a small velvet box the colour of the sky.

'Is it really that bad, El?' He handed her the box.

She took it, frowning, unsure what he meant.

'How you're feeling. With the stone.'

'Oh,' she said again, looking down. 'Yeah. It's that bad.' A tear dropped onto the little velvet box, sitting like crystal on the lid before soaking into the soft fabric, leaving a mark. She opened the lid and took in a trembling breath.

Deryck leaned over and looked at the box, then sat back, touching his stone. He shuddered a little and his face closed down, becoming blank again; she could almost feel the distance between them grow. He stood up and went to the cupboards, rummaged around, then took out some clothing and disappeared through a door into an adjoining room, leaving her alone with her gift.

Which meant the world.

The inside of the box was lined with dark purple velvet. A small heart made of silvery card was tucked inside the lid. On one side of the card were the words 'Like your eyes'. She turned it over. 'I love you,' it said on the other side, with a letter T beneath. If that had been all the box held, it would have been enough.

But there was also a ring. Set into a little velvet cushion, it was made of twisted gold wire, with two tiny gold leaves almost meeting at the top. And, set between them, was a small emerald.

Like your eyes.

She took it from the box and slid it on her finger. Her vision was blurring so much she could hardly see, and she shook her head, tears flying. She had the feeling that someone was there with her, behind her, looking over her shoulder at the ring; someone who was almost as happy about it as she was. It was fleeting, but the warmth that came with it filled her from head to toe, her heart bursting with love.

The door to the adjoining room opened and Deryck appeared, dressed in dark jeans and a turtleneck. His face was still shut down, though. Ellery's good feelings started to fade.

He frowned. 'You're not ready yet?'

'Uh, no.' She tucked the box back in her pocket, the ring still on her finger. 'Do you know where my clothes would be?'

Deryck looked around. 'Huh, actually, I'm not sure. Uh, maybe in the drawers?'

She swung her legs off the bed, taking a moment to stand. Deryck just stood and watched her. She searched the drawers, one by one, until she found some leggings and a sweater.

Deryck stared at her. Then he blinked, stepping to the side. 'You can get changed in there,' he said, indicating the door.

She went past him. His pupils were so dilated his eyes were almost black. Her heart hurt to see him so. Somewhere under there was the brother who had laughed and cried with her, who she'd just been getting to know before their father's cruel gift took him away.

Through the door was a bathroom. She took a moment to freshen up, splashing her face with cold water. The urge to sink into her stone, to let it take her away again, was getting stronger. She leaned on the sink, her head hanging, taking in breath after breath until the urge lessened enough that she could get changed.

She emerged a few minutes later to the scent of chocolate. Two mugs sat on the dressing table. She raised her eyebrows. Deryck shrugged. 'You want one? Father sent them up.'

She went over and picked up one of the mugs. It was filled with hot chocolate, foamy and sweet, and she took a sip.

The bedroom door opened and her father was there, looking

strange in human world clothing, rather than the armour she was used to seeing.

'Come on,' he said. 'Let's go.' He seemed excited rather than annoyed, though. Ellery took another sip before putting the mug down and getting her jacket, which was red and down-filled and deliciously cosy, like wearing a sleeping bag. She slipped it on and followed Deryck down the stairs, hanging on to the banister.

'Deryck, help your sister.' Denoris had opened the front door, letting in noise from outside. Deryck came to Ellery and put his arm around her waist, but he was still distant. Ellery clung to him, though, as they went out the front door. The hot chocolate had revived her a little, but she was still finding it hard to walk, her legs aching. Her eyes widened when she saw the river, the familiar buildings, and realised where they were.

'I didn't know you had a house in London,' she said.

Her father was walking on ahead. 'Yes. I've had it for a few years now,' he said, over his shoulder.

Ellery frowned. So she could have been living here, but he'd chosen to place her with someone else, far away. Then she realised it was because of the Gate, and her frown deepened. Everything led back to Alma, to her father's plans. All Ellery was to him was a pawn in the game, to be moved around to wherever she could be most useful.

Despite the cold morning the city was busy, with people walking everywhere, traffic lining the streets, boats on the river. Shop windows sparkled with lights and glitter, more lights hanging from lamp-posts. It must be close to Christmas. A wave of nostalgia hit Ellery, for her old life in the human world, for the warmth of Christmas, and the freedom she'd enjoyed. She'd wasted her time here, though, longing for Ambeth, for her father's love, doing whatever he asked in an effort to prove herself.

Up ahead a couple embraced by the river. The girl had long red hair streaming out from under her woolly hat, and Ellery felt

Deryck tense up. His step faltered and his hand came up to his throat. Then the couple came apart. It was just another girl, not Alma.

Denoris stopped, turning back to Ellery and Deryck. 'Take one of these. You know how to use them, yes?' He nodded at Ellery, handing her a bit of blue and white plastic. An Oyster card, she realised.

'We're taking the Tube?'

Denoris nodded and headed towards a flight of stairs that led downwards.

Ellery and Deryck followed. She was starting to feel dizzy and hoped there would be a seat on the train. They passed through the underground station. Deryck let go of her so she could go through the turnstiles, then helped her onto the escalators. She realised something.

'You've been here before,' she said.

Deryck, ahead of her on the escalator, half-turned to face her and nodded. His pupils weren't quite so dilated and his expression was warmer. The effects of his tallus stone were wearing off. She was glad, but also shocked at how used to it he must be.

'So, do you know where we're going?'

He nodded again, then jerked his head towards their father, warning in his green gaze. Ellery bit her lip. That wasn't good, then. She clenched her fingers around Tomas's ring, holding on to the idea that she was loved, that she wasn't alone, using it to fight the urge to sink into her stone again rather than face whatever was coming.

On the train they were silent. Ellery was mildly amused by all the heads that turned to stare at her brother and father. She had to find some joy, somewhere. For, despite the glitter of the city and the warmth of her ring, she knew something bad lay ahead. If her father was involved, it could hardly be anything else.

But she wasn't prepared to descend to a museum beneath the city, or for her father to clear the room, his menace filling the air.

And she definitely wasn't ready when he took them through the wall into an ancient arena, hidden for millennia. Or for what waited there.

She stared at the machine, trying to keep the disbelief off her face. Was her father insane? Her eyes widened further as she took in the Crown suspended above the swirling dark pool.

'You took it?' Of course he did. It made sense, now, why he hadn't been as angry as she'd thought he'd be over Alma returning the Cup. He still had this card to play.

Her father smiled. 'Of course. I needed it. It's been here for over a hundred years, turning Light to Dark, sending this world into chaos.'

Ellery's stomach was churning like the pool. She hung on to Deryck. He stared straight ahead, his jaw tight. She'd seen the news, had lived in the human world long enough that she knew about all the suffering there. And to think her father was responsible! Though she knew that wasn't true, not entirely. Humans had their own capacity for cruelty. But it was her father who'd fanned the flames, as the Dark always had throughout history, trying to turn the Balance in their favour.

Her father had moved to her other side, and now he leaned in, his breath warm on her cheek. 'Would you like to see what it does?'

CHAPTER 27
THE TWIST OF LOVE AND HATE

I t was late afternoon, the winter sun striping the parkland with light, shadows growing beneath the trees. Alma leaned into Ethan, her arm around his waist. He turned to kiss her, seemingly recovered from the dizziness of crossing over. She pulsed a little bit of energy into him, just in case.

'Shall we go back to my house?' he said, kissing her again.

'Hmmm.' She smiled against his mouth. 'That sounds nice,' she said. 'And maybe we can—'

'Alma!'

The shout came from behind them, and they both turned. Alma's mouth dropped open. Meredan was approaching, dressed in jeans and a jumper, a cloak draped over one arm. He waved his arm, quickening his pace. Alma and Ethan stopped, waiting for him.

'Is everything all right?' Alma said, when he reached them. 'We only just left.'

'Yes and no,' said Meredan. 'Your grandfather is fine,' he went on, as she frowned, 'but I must speak with you both on a matter of some urgency.'

A short while later they were sitting at the café and Meredan had a coffee in hand. 'I miss this in Ambeth,' he said. 'The stuff we have—' he wrinkled his nose '—it's not quite the same.'

Alma glanced at Ethan and grinned. They were holding hands under the table. Alma didn't want to let go of Ethan, to lose the feeling of their energies being intertwined. Ethan seemed to feel the same way. He met her smile with his and rubbed the back of her hand.

'So, what's brought you here? Has something happened in Ambeth?' Alma and Ethan had only come through the Gate a half hour ago, but far more time could have passed in Ambeth since then.

Meredan set his coffee down. 'The situation is this. I have been monitoring Deryck for some time now, since the events of the tournament. And this morning I saw him and his father, as well as Ellery, enter the Garden of Shadows. They opened a Gate and passed into the human world.'

Alma felt sick. 'Th-that was how they did it before, when they sent Deryck, when he—' She looked around, fearful, as though Denoris might materialise suddenly out of thin air. It was a nightmare she often had, waking gasping in the night, it taking a moment for the shadows to resolve into familiar shapes.

'I don't believe they're coming through for you, Alma. Believe me, if that were the case, we would take steps to stop them. Plus, I think you can take care of yourself these days?' He quirked an eyebrow and reached to touch her bracelet stone. A couple of sparks shot from it. She gasped, coming back to equilibrium.

'So, if they're not coming through for me, why do you need to tell us?'

Meredan pursed his lips and glanced to the side before continuing. 'The dark energy you saw. Thorion has been considering it, and is wondering if, somehow, Denoris is involved.' He leaned forward. 'The stars tell us that there is a threat still to this world, that something is coming, and that it is coming from *here*. This is what we now believe your father and uncle were trying to track.

Thorion is hoping that you might be able to sense any more dark energy occurrences here, continue your father's work, and we can see if it correlates with Denoris visiting. Do you think you could do that?'

'But... it could happen anywhere? I mean, I'm not sure how I would—'

Ethan let go of Alma's hand, reaching for his phone. 'We could track it through the news, maybe. I know the thing at the fair was in the local papers.' He started scrolling through the newsfeed. 'So we could search for similar things happening at the same time, in other places?'

'But we would have to see an energy burst ourselves to know when to look.' Alma blew a breath out through her nose, folding her arms. 'I mean, I can try. But I don't know what Galen, what my father, was doing. I wish I could ask him.'

Meredan's eyes turned down. 'I know, dear one. We all miss him still. He would have been so very proud of you.' He paused for a moment before continuing. 'All we can ask is that you try. And—' he held up his hand, forestalling Alma's next question '—you can text Merewyn if you find anything, and she can let Thorion know.'

'Why can't we just cross over and tell him ourselves? We're probably going to be visiting a bit, now.' Ethan said.

Alma blushed, thinking of why they would want to go back there, what they would do.

Meredan's expression darkened. 'Well, as I'm sure your grandfather has told you, it might be wise for you both to stay out of Ambeth, at least for the next little while.'

'What?' Alma said. 'Why?'

Meredan blinked. 'He did not tell you?'

Alma shook her head, a lump in her throat. Ethan's hand tightened around hers.

'Deryck has joined the Dark Hunt.'

Alma swallowed. 'And?' Her voice was a whisper.

'And the Hunt, as far as we know, are still after you. I know, I know,' he said, raising his hands. 'It's a detail we all missed. The Hunt do not come to the Palace often, as they're banned from hunting within its walls. But Alma, they were called to catch you, and they failed. The contract remains.'

Cold prickled along Alma's spine as she remembered the terror of the chase through the woods. 'Th-that's what grandfather meant, wasn't it, when he told me to stay away from the hills and not hang out in the gardens?'

Meredan nodded. 'He didn't wish to scare you away, dear one. But yes. And, coupled with Deryck's involvement, we now think it a credible threat. So for now, stay away. They cannot cross into this realm.'

'What about me?' Ethan's voice was tense, his fingers woven tight with Alma's under the table.

'You're not prey,' said Meredan. 'But you did help Alma escape them, did you not? I doubt they would look kindly on you, were you to cross paths. Artos has spoken to your father and they are both of the same mind – that it's better for you both to stay here for now.'

'What about the Crown? Alma and I were—'

'That's what grandfather meant.' More things were clicking into place for Alma. 'Sorry,' she said to Ethan. 'It's just, he also said that maybe the Crown was here, not in Ambeth. And I think that's what he was trying to say. That we should stay here, but also search here.'

'So, what now? We stay away, but for how long?' Ethan sounded angry, but Alma knew it was about more than just the lost chance for them to be together without interruptions.

'We'll let you know, dear ones. But for now, stay safe. And do what you can.'

Alma glanced at Ethan and squeezed his hand. He nodded, but his mouth was tight, his brow furrowed. She got it, though, and she knew he did, too. It looked as though Ambeth was off limits for the next little while.

~

ELLERY THOUGHT SHE WAS GOING TO THROW UP. DERYCK PUT his arm around her and she flinched. He glanced at her, his brows drawing together, but let go. Chills ran through her and she rubbed her hands up and down her arms, hoping she wasn't going to faint.

Denoris was at the machine, standing in the hollow space beneath the Crown. His feet apart and legs braced, he took hold of the two thick metal rods driven into the ground. Ellery sucked in a shuddering breath. Deryck put his arm around her again. This time, she let him.

The machine began to move, the delicate metal pieces turning, twisting together and then apart. Their father's head was back, his eyes closed, teeth bared in a grimace. Strings of light appeared from all corners of the room. Ellery's eyes widened. She could feel what they were, the light inside her responding to their call. The strands converged above the Crown, forming into one single beam that passed through the circle and into Denoris. He began starting to shake, his muscles straining against his dark shirt.

'It's killing him,' she whispered. There was shame in her at the realisation that, if it did, she would be free. Denoris groaned as darkness rose from the whirlpool, passing through him.

'Stop it, stop it, make it stop!' Ellery lunged forward, but Deryck held her back, his grip like iron on Ellery's arms.

'He'll be all right,' Deryck said, though he didn't sound convinced. Tears were pouring down Ellery's face, her heart breaking as her father buckled and strained in the grip of the machine. Darkness poured from his eyes, his mouth, passing through the Crown to fuse with the strands of light, moving beyond the confines of the ancient arena.

'Father,' she screamed. 'No, no!' She sagged forward in Deryck's grip, and he put his arms around her, holding her close. Denoris groaned again, the sound rising into a shriek of pain. He released the poles and collapsed.

Deryck let go of Ellery and ran to him. Ellery dropped to her knees, sobbing and retching. She fell forward and rolled onto her side, curling herself up. She reached for her stone but managed to stop herself. Perhaps she would die in here. Perhaps it would be better if she did. Darkness knew she couldn't take much more.

A hand touched her shoulder, rolling her over. She opened her eyes to see her father bending over her. He was kneeling, and there was sweat on his brow, but colour was already returning to his face.

'Oh, oh,' she sobbed, 'you're all right.' Her heart felt as though it was tearing. Love and hate mingled inside her, an overwhelming relief that he wasn't dead mixed with regret that he'd survived.

Her father smiled. 'Were you worried about me, daughter?'

She nodded. 'Wh-what was that?' He sat back, crossing his legs, and she could see it took effort for him to do so. Her unease sharpened. 'What was it doing to you?'

'That, Ellery, was our future. The future of all the Dark, and of this world.'

'B-but, the Crown, it was—'

'It was doing what it was made to do. Channelling energy. And every time I do it, our power increases.'

Ellery pushed herself up to sitting, wiping her hand over her face. She was covered in dust. Cold dread was replacing her fear. 'So what happens next?'

'The pieces are almost in place. And, when they are, I will open a Gate and lead my armies through.'

'Your armies?' Ellery couldn't help her exclamation, or keep the shocked expression from her face. She flinched as her father cupped one side of her face, his thumb gently rubbing her cheekbone.

'Yes, my armies. I've had a thousand years to consider my plans,' he said softly, his breath warm on her face. 'And now they're almost complete.'

Revulsion and longing twisted inside her.

'When I rule here, Ellery,' her father continued, 'you shall be a queen. Or a goddess. There will be none who can stand against us.'

Rule here? Okay. That was it. She was going to be sick. She closed her eyes, swallowing desperately.

'Ellery, are you all right?' Deryck said.

She shook her head.

'She's overwhelmed, nothing more,' her father said. 'After all, she has a bright future to look forward to. As do you. Once you have Alma at your side, the two of you will be unstoppable.'

CHAPTER 28

OF LIVES LOST, AND DECISIONS
MADE

M ari bustled around her kitchen, wiping down the wooden counters, putting mugs and plates away. She lingered on one, engraved with leaves, her fingers tracing the curving indentations, remembering the hands of the one who'd made it, hands that had once held hers.

She'd never meant to come to Ambeth, let alone spend her life here. It had all been a lark, a game in the park so long ago, though she remembered it as though it were yesterday. The flowers in her hair, her white dress, perfect for dancing with fairies on Midsummer. She'd never actually thought she might go through to fairyland. But after several joints and a few bottles of red wine, Stephen had stumbled between two oak trees. She'd gone to grab him, laughing, the world spinning, but then he'd disappeared. She'd followed before she'd even had the chance to scream, travelling through mist and light to emerge in a winter woodland, where she found Stephen crying and shivering beneath a tree, his white shirt soaked and frozen. An hour, he'd said, he'd sat there waiting, even though for her it had only been seconds.

She'd helped him up and they'd wandered through the woods, calling for help. She shuddered to think of it now, of how lucky they'd been to meet one of the villagers, rather than some of the others who stalked the woods at night. The villagers had taken them in, offered them shelter and a place to stay, then told them of their fate – that they were trapped there now, unless they wanted to return to a world out of time.

Mari had dealt with it, in her own way. She had no family, at least none that she cared for, and the small cottage in the village was an upgrade from her dingy flat, from scraping by to make ends meet. But Stephen never got over it. He'd died a couple of years later, calling for the mother he'd left behind in the human world. The healer had said it was because he'd never recovered properly from the hour he'd spent waiting in the snow, but Mari knew better. He'd died of a broken heart. His longing to go home had never abated. He'd tried, of course, and she'd been pleased when he'd taken up pottery again, but more often than not she'd found him weeping in the small studio, broken shards around him.

He was buried in the small graveyard, beneath a simple stone bearing his first name and the word 'Beloved'. Mari's heart had been buried with him – she never loved another, instead dedicating herself to building a life of her own, using her jewellery skills to get by.

It wasn't a bad life, though there were times when she wished she could have had children, and worse times when the snow would fall and she would wander the woods, missing him. But the years passed and the world turned, and she remained, her art sustaining her for as long as the good Lord granted her.

There was a knock at the door and she jumped. Putting the mug down, she wiped her hands on the tea towel and went to answer it. The knock came again before she got there, but it was fainter this time and followed by a thumping noise, as though something had fallen against the door.

Frowning, Mari opened the door and was shocked when Ellery stumbled through it, almost into her arms.

'I'm sorry, I'm sorry,' she whispered, as Mari caught her arm, leading her to sit on a nearby bench. 'I had nowhere else to go.'

Mari was shocked by how desperately thin Ellery was. Her face was like carved bone, her eyes like two emeralds. She sagged forward and Mari caught her. Kneeling, she put her arms around Ellery's shoulders. The girl kept twisting a ring on her finger. Mari recognised it as one she'd made a while back for a young man of the Dark.

'It's all right, my lady, I'm here. Would you like to lie down?'

Ellery nodded, and Mari helped her up and through a nearby door into her sitting room. She settled her on the sofa with a pillow under her head.

'Can I get you something, my lady? A drink, or—'

'Ellery.' The girl turned her head, though Mari could see the effort cost her. 'Call me Ellery. And, some water, maybe?'

Mari went back into the kitchen and put the kettle onto boil. Ellery needed something stronger than just water. She reached for a jar of herbs and dropped a pinch into a mug along with a spoonful of honey.

When she went back into the living room a couple of minutes later, the steaming drink in hand, Ellery had her eyes closed. She was so still and pale that Mari's heart lurched. But then she sighed and moved, one hand coming out, and Mari realised she'd gone to sleep. She left the drink next to her, covering her with a blanket. With a gentle hand, she smoothed the hair back from the girl's brow, remembering doing the same for her mother almost seventeen years earlier.

She went into her studio and busied herself with work, wanting to give Ellery the space to sleep, but also to work out how she would handle this. Something terrible had happened to Ellery, that was clear, but she was also the daughter of Lord Denoris, and as such was valuable to him. He would tear the village apart looking for her. Mari frowned as she sketched out designs. There were difficult decisions to make – she only hoped she had the strength to make them.

After an hour she heard movement from the other room. When she went to check, Ellery was sitting up, the drink in her hand. There was a hint of colour in her pale cheeks, but she looked drained, as though some vital spark of life had gone from her.

'I'm sorry,' she said, putting the drink down. She tried to get up, but dropped back onto the couch, her face twisting.

'Rest a while, Ellery. Let me top this up, it'll help you.' Mari went and took the drink from Ellery. Then she paused, tucking the blanket around the girl once more. Ellery let out a sob. Mari's heart bled for her.

She went into the kitchen and topped up the drink, making another for herself. She had the feeling she would need her strength for what was to come.

For she couldn't keep the girl here. She would do all she could, though, to help her.

She returned to the sitting room. Ellery was still on the sofa, the blanket around her. She took the drink from Mari, taking a long gulp despite how hot it was.

'I shouldn't have come here,' she said. 'I'm sorry I involved you.'

'Involved me? What has happened, my dear?'

Ellery's face twisted again, tears trickling down her cheeks. 'Everything,' she whispered. 'I mean, it's all so awful, and I can't tell you about any of it. My father would kill you.'

Mari came to sit next to her, patting her on her knee. 'Well, there's nothing wrong with just sitting here for a little while. No one can get cross with us for that, can they?' Her heart was pounding, though. Her gaze went to the necklace around Ellery's neck. 'Ah, you're still wearing it,' she said. 'But it looks as though one of the leaves has come loose. Here,' she said, reaching out, 'let me fix it for you while you have your drink. It's the least I can do.'

But Ellery recoiled, spilling her drink. 'No!'

Mari snatched her hand back. 'Oh, my dear,' she said. Understanding washed over her. 'But, what happened to—'

'He destroyed it,' said Ellery, her voice shaking. 'The one thing I had from her, and he destroyed it.'

Mari swallowed, moving closer. 'It's not the only thing you have from your mother. She was strong, a fighter till the end. And I think you are, too.'

Ellery looked at her. Her lips trembled, more tears spilling down her thin face. 'I don't know if I can do it,' she whispered.

Mari bit her lip. 'I know you can't tell me about it, and I won't ask. Them lords in yonder Hall always say as how they move with fate, that the stars, and their nature, Light or Dark, defines what they do. You, however – though you're of the Dark, you're also human. And that means you always, always have a choice, right until the end.'

Ellery wiped her face, nodding. Then she leaned in and hugged Mari. 'I have to go,' she whispered. 'He doesn't know I'm here. It took me so long to walk here and I have to go back, I have to—'

'Let me see if someone will take you to the edge of the gardens,' said Mari, ashamed at the relief inside her. 'Let me do that, at least, if I can do nothing more.'

A short while later Mari stood outside her front door, watching the wooden cart rattle along the rutted road leading out of the village. Pieter raised his finger to his cap in salute before spurring his horse on. Ellery, sitting in the back, still wrapped in Mari's blanket, raised one pale hand. Mari returned the gesture, watching the cart until it turned from view. She went back inside and sat down at her workbench. Then she bent forward and burst into tears, sobbing as though her heart would break.

CHAPTER 29
GLOWING GREEN

'Ethan!' Alma opened the side door and stepped into his arms, kissing him.

There was a polite cough and they came apart to see Eleanor standing in the doorway, her arms folded, though her eyes twinkled with amusement.

'Hello, Ethan,' she said. 'Will you come in? Dinner's nearly ready. Unless the two of you would rather stay out here?'

Alma blushed, laughing as she let go of Ethan, taking his hand to lead him inside. He stopped and picked up a large square parcel leaning against the step. She raised her eyebrows. But he just grinned, squeezing her hand. 'You'll see,' he whispered.

They came into the kitchen together. The big pine table was already set and pots were bubbling on the stove. Alma's brothers were on the sofa watching TV. They looked up briefly before losing interest and going back to their show. But Eleanor was onto them. 'Come on, boys,' she said, clapping her hands. 'Dinner's almost ready, so you need to wash your hands. TV off.'

'But Mum—'

'But Mum nothing! We have company, so you can come and be

sociable. Come on!' She shepherded them off the couch and over to where Ethan stood with Alma.

'Gentlemen,' he said, holding out his hand. Tyler and Aidan looked at Alma, suddenly shy.

'This is Ethan,' said Alma. Aidan stared at him for a moment longer, then took his hand, shaking it as he said his name. Tyler was doing the same when their dad came into the kitchen, rubbing his hands together.

'Dinner smells good.' He kissed Eleanor on the cheek and ruffled the boys' hair. 'And you must be Ethan,' he said, holding out his hand.

'That's right. Nice to meet you,' said Ethan, shaking his hand.

'Right, dinner's just about ready, so why don't you all take a seat,' said Eleanor, bustling over to the table with a bowl of potatoes.

'Hang on a sec,' said Graham. He went over to the TV and switched it on. 'Just need to check something on the news,' he said over Eleanor's protests, flicking through the channels.

'Can you get the plates, Alma?' said Eleanor.

'Sure,' said Alma, but she didn't move, her eyes on the TV. 'Outbreak of riots and violence at temple,' the banner headline read, accompanied by images of men with bloodied faces and people being helped from the scene, their bright clothing stained.

'Where's that, Dad?' she said.

'India, I think,' said Graham, changing the channel again.

'Wait. Can you turn it back, just for a sec?'

Ethan took her hand, squeezing it.

'Sure, I guess,' said Graham. 'But why the sudden interest in India?'

'It's a school thing,' she replied, her eyes on the screen. There. Amid the chaos, the broken statues and struggling figures, something shimmered across the screen. Her eyes narrowed. She reached for the pulse inside her, the energy coming up through her feet. More shimmers became visible, like pale shadows, tentacles reaching in and through the rioting throng.

'What's in the parcel?' Someone tugged at her hand. She blinked, the spell broken, the shimmers fading away. She looked down to see Aidan. He jerked his head towards the package Ethan had brought.

'Just something for Alma,' said Ethan. 'I'll give it to her after dinner though, hey mate?'

'No, no, do it now. I'm still dishing up,' said Eleanor.

Ethan turned to Alma. 'You ready?'

Still recovering, she nodded. He leaned in as though he was going to kiss her, but instead he whispered, 'I saw it, too.'

She stared at him. 'Later,' he breathed. 'Right,' he went on, his voice back to normal volume. 'I guess it's time for presents.' He picked up the parcel, holding it out to Alma.

'What's the occasion?' asked Eleanor, who had paused from dishing up.

Ethan glanced at her. 'Oh, no occasion,' he said. 'Just something I thought Alma might like. And you.'

Alma tore off the brown wrapping paper to reveal a photo canvas.

'Wow.' Her eyes widened. For there was Ambeth. To anyone who didn't know it was just a photo of a curving path leading through a meadow to some woods, the rich green grass almost seeming to glow. But she knew. Tears came to her eyes, and she hugged Ethan. 'Thank you, I love it!'

Eleanor picked up the photo, studying it with an unreadable expression. 'This is lovely,' she said, her eyes bright. Alma knew she'd recognised it. 'Did you take this?'

'I did.' Ethan said. 'I have something similar at my house, and thought this was a nice image.' Eleanor nodded, seeming lost for words. Then there was a sizzle from the stove and her head shot up.

'Oh, the peas!' She rushed over, turned off the heat and mopped up the water. Alma saw her wipe her eyes as well.

Graham held the canvas up to the kitchen wall. 'This is great,' he said. 'The perfect spot for it, I think.' He winked at Ethan.

'No way!' Alma said. 'It's going in my room.' Ethan and Graham laughed.

'But seriously, d'you have any others? I'd like something like this for my office,' Graham said, studying the image. 'Beautiful spot as well. Is it somewhere local?'

'Er no, actually, it's near where my father lives.'

There was a clatter as Eleanor dropped her spoon. Alma went and picked the spoon up, put it in the sink and got another. She touched her mother's hand as she gave it to her, just a small pulse of energy but enough to calm her without Eleanor noticing anything untoward. She brightened straight away and went back to dishing up as Alma stirred the vegetables, turning off the heat. Ethan and Graham were talking about photography. She smiled to herself, listening to them talk, how easy it was. Warmth filled her; the warmth of love and family and life. She looked at her picture and her heart was full.

LATER, UP IN HER ROOM, ETHAN PULLED OUT HIS PHONE.

'Okay,' he said. 'I saw it, too, when I touched your hand. That was the dark energy, right?'

Alma nodded. 'I think so.'

'Okay.' He scrolled through his phone. Alma sat next to him, her chin on his shoulder as he typed and clicked, pulling up page after page, tweets and articles and images.

'Woah, slow down,' she said.

He turned his head, kissing her cheek. 'Sorry, I forgot.'

'Forgot what? That I don't speed read?'

'No.' He laughed. 'I just... I was using my power. Just like you used yours. You see the dark energy, I have a sense for danger.

So I was using it, letting it guide me to the right things. And look.'

He held up his phone and started flicking through its. 'A mass brawl outside a nightclub in Melbourne. A shooting in Alaska. And a group of people smashing up a supermarket in France. Based on the time differences, all of those happened at around the same time as the riots in India.'

'Do you think it's just coincidence, though? I mean, violent stuff happens all the time, right?'

He shook his head. 'No. No way. Because the one thing all these events have in common? Witnesses say they "came out of nowhere". Based on what Meredan told us about Denoris, it can't be a coincidence.'

Alma's mouth twisted. 'I guess I need to text Merewyn, then.' She picked up her phone and started to type.

It was evening in Ambeth. The scents of Spring drifted up from the gardens, the distant sea a smudge of blue. Adara leaned on the windowsill and breathed deeply, taking it all in. Despite all that was happening, despite the still-tilting Balance, she felt better than she had in years.

She turned, looking fondly at one of the reasons why. The main reason, really. Thorion, seated at the table, was bent over a silver bowl of water, his dark hair falling in wings around his handsome face.

'Yes,' she heard him say. 'So it confirms things, then, just as we thought.'

He paused for a moment, and Adara caught the sound of Merewyn's lilting tones, the girl's face drifting on the surface of the water.

'I thank you,' Thorion replied. 'And I think you might be right. Keep me informed, if you will.'

Merewyn's face dissolved, the water rippling as the connection was broken. Thorion sat back, letting out a sigh. He ran both hands through his hair and stretched.

'So it's happened, then? Alma has seen something?'

'She has. And it is as we thought. The times line up.'

'So, what do we do?'

'What can we do? I cannot stop him from opening Gates, nor do we have any proof of wrongdoing, only our own conclusions.' He rubbed a hand over his face. 'If the Crown is in the human realm, I only hope that Alma can find it before he does.'

'And if she can't?'

He pursed his lips, his brows drawing together. 'Then we open that Gate when we come to it. The stars, our very prophecies, indicate that she's moving towards it, as is Ethan. We cannot interfere in her choices any more than that.'

She came to him and sat in his lap, her arms around his neck. 'So we wait, then,' she said.

He nodded. 'We do.'

CHAPTER 30
WORDS OF LOVE

'Alma, Ethan, I thought you might – oh, I'm so sorry!' Dana put her hand to her mouth and pulled the door to Ethan's room closed again.

Alma dropped the blanket she'd clutched to her, reached for her hoody and shrugged it back on. Ethan pulled his shirt on, running his hands through his hair. Both of them were breathing hard. Alma thought she might die of embarrassment.

'It's okay, Mum,' Ethan called.

The door creaked open and Dana appeared again. There was pink on her high cheekbones. 'Sorry, I keep forgetting to knock. Shall I go and—'

'It's fine, Mum. We'll come downstairs.'

Alma, still dying inside, nodded.

'Oh! Well, all right. Dinner's ready, that's what I wanted to tell you, and anyway, um, right.' Dana closed the door again, and there was the sound of her feet on the stairs.

'Maybe I should go home,' said Alma, swinging her legs off the bed.

'I'm sorry, she just—'

'I know.' It wasn't the first time Dana had interrupted them. 'If only we could go to Ambeth.'

'Yeah.' He slid along the bed to sit next to her. 'I mean, we could.'

'Meredan said—'

'I know what he said. But he also said they can't hunt inside the Palace. So all we need to do is get there; we can head up to your room, and no one would know.'

Alma didn't say anything for a moment. She wanted Ethan so much it hurt, but neither her house nor his offered them enough privacy. But the Hunt waited for her in Ambeth. Although... She twisted her wrist, looking at her bracelet.

'I suppose I do have my power, if anything happens.'

'And I have my wings, plus my sense for danger. I bet I'd know before they even found us.'

'I don't know.'

He nodded. 'I get it. But, wow, I mean, it's not getting any easier, is it?' He laughed, but there was tension in his voice. She felt it in herself. It would be easy, she thought. After all, she'd gone to Ambeth to see her grandfather several times, not to mention the visits she'd made with Ethan, and the Hunt hadn't found her. Part of her hadn't minded not being able to go there; her worries about Deryck and what he might do to Ethan kept at bay. But at the same time, it had been difficult.

Ethan leaned in and kissed her, his lips lingering on hers, and her mind was made up. She wanted him, wanted to be alone with him. Surely they could go and be back before anyone noticed.

'All right,' she said. 'After dinner?'

'Hmmm.' He smiled against her mouth. 'Sounds perfect.'

A SHORT WHILE LATER THEY WERE THROUGH THE GATE, running through the woods as fast as they could, hand in hand. It was a bright spring morning and the woods were filled with blossom and birdsong. Luckily, no one seemed to be around. They crossed the meadow, taking the shortcut through the gardens, the Palace walls looming bright above them.

'Shit,' said Alma as they neared the entrance. 'What about the guards?'

'Leave it to me,' said Ethan, pulling her towards the doors. When they reached them he nodded to the guards stationed either side. 'You didn't see us,' he said, grinning.

Alma started giggling as the guards, both smiling, opened the doors and let them in. They raced through the Foyer, still laughing, taking the stairs up to her room two at a time. They emerged onto the landing gasping.

'I need to lie down after all that,' said Ethan.

But Alma's smile slid away. 'What's that?'

Letting go of Ethan's hand she went to her door and picked up the bunch of bright flowers tied to the handle. She brought them to her nose, breathing in the fresh spring scent. They were tied with a ribbon and a small card was attached. Alma turned it over.

'Love always, D'

She dropped the flowers as though they were on fire, the petals scattering everywhere. She leaned against her door, sickness running through her. Ethan picked up the flowers and read the card, then swore. She began to tremble. What would he do? She would die if he went—

'What the hell is this?'

She stared at him, unable to speak, fumbling in her pocket for her key. It dropped to the floor, her hand shaking. He swore again, not at her, and bent to pick up the key. She shifted to one side as he unlocked the door, her heart breaking at the cold anger in his face. When the door opened, Alma half fell into the room. Ethan went past her to the fireplace and, without a word, flung the flowers and card into it. He struck a match and held it to the card until it caught. The soft petals curled and blackened, and the card and its message turned to ash.

He came back to her and pulled her gently to him, his lips on her hair, her cheek as he murmured to her. 'It's okay. I got rid of them. He can't bother you, I won't let him. I'll speak to him.'

'No!' She pulled away, unable to look at him, hiding behind her hair. 'You can't talk to him. Promise me you won't.' She felt like guilt was written all over her in blazing red letters, even though she'd done nothing wrong.

'What's going on?' It was all he said, but it broke her. She groaned, going over to the bed. She sat down, wanting to get under the covers and hide from it all. 'Alma!' She lifted her head. He went to the door, closing and locking it. Her heart twisted at the worry on his face.

'Ethan, um, I have to tell you something,' she mumbled. He recoiled, his expression tightening. He looked like his father. Then she realised what he was thinking.

'No! I haven't... done that!' she said, feeling sick at the thought of it. 'Oh god, no, I would never. You're the only one for me, you know that.' He nodded, but his eyes were wide, as if he were frightened of what she was going to tell him. She swallowed. 'Um, but there is something. He er...' God, this was so hard. But she had to do it. She blew out a breath. 'He asked, or his father did, for my hand. In marriage,' she added. Ethan stared at her. Then he exploded.

'*What!?* When?'

'Um, a few weeks ago, I guess. I don't know exactly. He asked grandfather, made a big deal of it. But he said no, of course,' she added hastily, as Ethan's face twisted with fury. 'And it's nothing, it doesn't mean anything.'

'So why didn't you tell me, if it doesn't mean anything?'

Alma's mouth dropped open. 'I just... I didn't want to worry you.'

'But you've been worried.' It wasn't a question. She bit her lip. He knew her too well. She nodded. 'Is it because you're thinking of accepting?' Ethan's face was bleak. Her stomach dropped.

'*No!* How could you think that?!' Her fingers began to tingle, her hands tightening on the bed covers.

'Well, what am I supposed to think? If you don't trust me enough to tell me...'

'No!' She pulled back the sparks in her fingertips, though it took an effort. 'No, that's not it, not at all. I trust you with everything!'

'Except this.'

'Ethan...' She could feel tears starting. She shook her head, not wanting to cry. She had to tell him why. 'It's because of Caleb. What happened to him.' She let out a sob, the fear she'd been carrying getting the better of her. 'Ungh.' She covered her face, turning away, trying to hold it back. Her bracelet was throbbing against her wrist, its energy sparking through her. And then Ethan was there, his hands on her as he gathered her close, curving his body around hers. She sobbed in relief, that he wasn't angry with her any more, that he was safe. She clung to him, letting his touch, his energy, soothe her, until she could feel the surge passing.

'What about Caleb?' His voice was soft, his hands on her gentle, but she could still sense tension in his energy. She hated herself, hated Deryck, for making him feel like this. She took a breath, wanting to explain it right.

'Deryck killed Caleb because he was jealous. He, um, didn't always treat me right, and Caleb would defend me. They were always fighting. And then, when he got the chance, he killed him. I watched him do it, and I couldn't do anything.' Her voice was choked. She reached out to touch his face. 'I would die if he hurt you.'

'I can defend myself—'

'But it's better if you don't have to!' She sat up, pushing her hair back. 'I didn't tell you because it doesn't matter, it doesn't change anything between us. And all it would do is make you angry and then...'

She waved her hand around to emphasise her point. Ethan took it, turned it over and kissed her palm.

'And then I would call him out, demanding to defend your honour?' He quirked an eyebrow and she giggled, despite the situation. His energy was smoothing out and his smile grew deeper. He released her hand and pulled her close again, kissing her gently. 'I will always defend you, but I'm not an idiot.' She nodded, resting her forehead on his. 'So don't worry, I'm not going to rush out and do anything foolish.'

'It's just, there's something wrong with him, I think,' she whispered, looking down and playing with the ties on his hoodie.

'You think?' Ethan's tone was heavy with sarcasm.

'No, I'm serious,' she said, pushing him lightly on the shoulder. 'He seems, I don't know, different now. Like he's not all there. He didn't used to be like that. When he came to get me, you know, in Wales?' She was playing with the hoodie ties again. 'He had a stone, at his neck. He kept touching it, told me it was like my talaith, that it made him stronger. And maybe that's the case, but it seemed to be, I don't know, messing with his mind as well.'

'So you thought if you didn't say anything, it would all go away, just a misunderstanding, Deryck being weird?'

'Well, sort of. I was hoping, anyway. I told grandfather there was no way... Huh. Well, he knew that anyway.'

'I know you loved him.'

'I did, once,' she said, hanging her head.

'It doesn't matter,' he said, gently lifting her chin. 'There's no shame in loving someone. All it shows is that you have an open heart.'

'Oh Ethan, I don't love him anymore! I love—' She stopped, looking at him in wonder. 'I love you.' She touched his cheek, traced his jaw with her fingers.

He took in a breath, his face lighting up. 'I love you too,' he said. She smiled, then pushed him gently so he fell back among the soft pillows, laughing as she fell next to him. He raised himself on one elbow and looked at her. He was so beautiful in that moment she drew in a breath.

Then his mouth was on hers, and the world, and all her worries, disappeared.

LATER SHE WOKE, BLINKING AGAINST THE LIGHT FROM THE unshuttered window. The room was chilly and she snuggled closer to Ethan, pulling the blankets over them. He stirred, dropping a kiss on her bare shoulder. 'Back in a sec.' He got up and she rolled into the warm spot where he'd been lying, watching him set a fire in the fireplace. The remnants of Deryck's flowers went up in smoke as the kindling caught. He placed a couple of small logs on top and came back to bed. She reached for him and they lay together, face to face, arms around each other.

'You okay?'

She nodded.

'I understand, now, why you didn't seem as keen as I was to come back here. I thought it was something to do with me, that you didn't want to—'

'Oh, I wanted to,' she said. 'It was just stupid Deryck and the stupid Hunt and all the other stuff.'

He laughed. 'We're a team, right?'

She nodded. God, she loved him. If Deryck touched a hair on his head...

'So, whatever we do, we do it together. I can handle Deryck, don't worry. But no more secrets, okay?'

'Okay.' Her hands moved on him, and she felt him gasp. 'But let's not talk about him anymore, okay?'

DAY WAS SLIDING INTO NIGHT AS ALMA CAME OUT OF HER bathroom, towelling her hair dry. Ethan, already showered and dressed, was dampening down the fire.

'You ready?' He jerked his head towards the window. 'We really need to go.'

She nodded, fear beginning to curl in her stomach at the sight of the red-streaked sky. They'd stayed far too long.

'Hey.' Ethan came to her, his hands cupping her face. 'We can do this. Go straight to the Gate, do not pass go, do not collect two hundred pounds, right?'

She grinned, despite her fear. 'Right.'

She let him lead her from the room, pausing to lock her door. She would be back, she thought, her fingers lingering on the wooden panels. Deryck, and the Hunt, weren't going to take Ambeth from her.

As they descended the spiral staircase, the sound of voices came up from the Foyer.

'Damn.' Ethan stopped.

'What is it?' Alma peered over his shoulder. Her heart sank. The Foyer was full of people and, from the sudden heat at her wrist, they were all Dark.

'Is there another way out?'

Ethan shook his head. 'We're just going to have to go for it. Pull up your hood, and I'll do the same.'

'But our clothes are all wrong.'

'It's our only shot, if we're going to reach the Gate before night falls. Ready?' He pulled his hood up. Alma hesitated a moment, then did the same, making sure her hair was tucked away.

Ethan tugged on her hand and she took a deep breath. Then they plunged into the swirling crowd. Ethan pulled her towards the double doors. They were almost there when they opened.

And the Hunt entered the Foyer.

CHAPTER 31

A TALK WITH AN OLD FRIEND

E than reacted quickly, stepping back and pulling Alma to one side. But the crowd surged at the same moment and his hand slipped from hers. Momentum took her and she was shifted towards the edge of the room. As she passed one of the pillars she grabbed onto it, sliding around to the other side.

She leaned against it, panting, considering her options. The Hunt weren't allowed to hunt within the Palace walls, she knew that. So as long as she stayed in here she was all right. But what about Ethan? What if he'd gone outside, looking for her, and they followed him? She needed to find him, then they could figure out what to do next. But she couldn't let the Hunt see her.

She inched to one side, peering around the pillar, but there was no sign of Ethan. The crowd had moved forward again, leaving some space around her. The details on their fine clothing flickered in the light of the lanterns, in time with the burning at her wrist. And the Hunt were still there.

She pulled back behind the pillar and closed her eyes, wishing for Ethan, for anyone to come and save her.

'Alma?'

Oh no. Alma's eyes flew open. The carving of the knight

offering a flower to his lady loomed above her, carved into the pillar. This was where they'd first met. She remembered how she'd traced her finger along the design, before meeting him and throwing her heart away.

'What are you doing here?' Deryck said.

Taking in a deep breath, Alma stood straight, her chin up. 'I don't want to talk to you.'

Deryck came around the pillar. She moved back, trying to keep distance between them, and in doing so stepped further into the shadows. It almost felt appropriate.

'But why? Aren't you here to see me?' Deryck leaned against the pillar, his blond hair tousled around his angel's face, his green eyes warm. He was dressed in smoke-black armour. Red jewels glimmered at his neck and wrist.

'No. Why would I come to see you?' She blinked, annoyed at the effect he was still having on her. Then she remembered what his armour meant. She took another step back.

Deryck's expression changed. 'So you know.'

She nodded, her mouth dry.

He licked his lips and held his hands wide. 'I swear to you, I'm not here to hunt you.'

'So why are you here?'

'All the Dark are here tonight.' He came closer. 'My father will be along soon. Do you want to come with me? We can wait for him together. The Hunt have no sway within Palace walls. I'll keep you safe.'

Alma frowned. How many times did she have to tell him no before it sunk in? 'I'm er, already here with someone.' Perhaps he would think Artos was coming. But no such luck.

Deryck's mouth tightened. 'Your new boyfriend?'

She chewed her lip, not saying anything, not wanting to make things worse.

Quick as a snake, Deryck was on her, his body close to hers, his familiar scent curling around her. She turned her head away.

'I'm right, aren't I? So where is he? Why is he not here, protecting you?' She thought she was going to pass out when she felt his warm breath on her cheek. 'Truly, it is time for you to let him down gently, come back to me. My father tells me that's your plan, so why not do it now?' He curled a strand of her hair around his finger, the way he used to do. 'When you're mine again, I won't leave you alone like this.'

Anger sliced through her fear. She glared at him, digging her heels in and feeling for a pulse of power, her talaith hot against her wrist. 'I'm not coming back to you!'

'And she is not alone.' A hand came down on Deryck's shoulder. Behind him, fierce with rage, was Ethan.

Unarmed, unprotected Ethan.

Alma closed her eyes, tears prickling under her lids, her stomach dropping. This was all her worst nightmares come to life. The drama behind the pillar was beginning to draw attention, faces turning in their direction.

'Ethan, please don—'

But she was too late. Ethan pulled on Deryck's shoulder, turning him so they were facing. They were a similar height and build, blond versus dark. Deryck fronted up to him, his face hard.

'What's your problem?' he snapped. 'I'm just talking to an old friend.'

'Really?' said Ethan. 'Because she doesn't look like she wants to talk to you.'

'I had her first,' said Deryck. Alma gasped, outraged, as he put his arm around her waist, pulling her against him. 'And I'll have her again.' He looked into her eyes and she froze. It sickened her to be so close to him, a twisting sort of sickness that he could still affect her. Then anger kicked in and she pushed him, stumbling as she managed to free herself.

There was a crowd around them now, whispers moving like wildfire through the throng. And the Hunt had seen them. A woman with a long braid, her face fiercely beautiful, was closing in on them, as was a man with long dark hair and a hawk-like expression. They moved through the crowd like sharks closing in for the kill.

Ethan grabbed Deryck by the throat, his face cold and fierce.

'Do not touch her ever again.'

Alma couldn't breathe. Everyone became coiled energy lines, and light rose up the pillars and across the floor, intertwined with darker strands. The Hunt were black and silver, like their armour. Everything faded in and out, from people to energy lines again. Her wrist was burning, her talaith throbbing against her skin, the bracelet chain twisting.

Then Deryck pulled a dagger from his belt, and everything seemed to stop.

'Ethan!' she screamed. White light pulsed from her. The crowd stepped back, shocked into silence. Even the Hunt stopped their advance.

And then Cedran was there, his hand over Deryck's, forcing the blade up and away. Ethan stepped away and came straight to Alma.

'Focus,' he said, his voice quiet, his hand on her chin so all she could see was him. 'Breathe.' His touch made it easy to take hold of the reins of power once more, drawing it back into her so everything returned to normal.

'Oh Ethan.' She touched his face, patting him with her hands, limp with relief. 'Are you all right?'

'Don't worry about me.' Ethan's expression hardened as he looked over Alma's shoulder. She turned. Cedran had Deryck on his knees, his knife arm twisted up in a lock behind him.

'Do you submit?' said Cedran. The Dark Lord was like a statue, muscles standing out in his arms, rock solid as he held Deryck in place. Once again Alma was reminded of an ancient warrior. Deryck looked up at Cedran, his face red and angry.

'Do you submit?' said Cedran again. This time he gave the arm a slight twist.

Deryck cried out. 'I submit,' he muttered finally, hanging his head.

'Then release the blade,' said Cedran, his tone pleasant, as though discussing the weather. Deryck loosened his grip on the knife and Cedran took it from him, transferring it to his other hand. He released Deryck from the arm lock, keeping a strong grip on him as he helped him to his feet. Deryck stood before the Dark Elder, his head hanging forward.

The crowd around were rapt, watching the unprecedented turn of events. Alma sighed. This was news. It would be gossiped about for weeks, embellished and drawn upon until the very last dregs of the story were exhausted. That the son of a Dark Lord should draw a blade on another in the Great Hall, and over a daughter of the Light! And then to have an Elder intervene! Those who were there meant not to miss a single moment.

'I think it best if you stay away from my son,' said Cedran. His face was smooth, his manner even, but there was a dark glitter in his eyes.

Deryck, his head still hanging, nodded. 'Fine,' he muttered.

At this a murmur ran through the crowd. Cedran looked around, taking in the onlookers. He frowned.

'Thank you,' he said, 'for your concern. But the matter is dealt with, so please, go back to your celebration.' Once again he was mild, pleasant in his manner, but his dark eyes were powerful as they scanned the watching crowd. They began to disperse, though many kept an eye on the tense little group. The Hunt remained, too, all black and silver menace, staring at Alma.

'Ethan. You are unharmed?' Cedran said. His tone was still pleasant, but there was a slight undertone of urgency.

'Yes,' said Ethan, taking Alma's hand. Cedran fixed them both with his dark gaze.

'Then take Alma and go. Now. I will deal with this.'

Ethan pulled Alma behind the pillar, out of sight.

'We need to go,' she whispered, her voice trembling.

'We can't go outside, not yet. Not while the Hunt are still there.'

'So what—'

'We go back upstairs, wait a little while, then go.'

'But—'

'Shh.' Ethan put his finger to her lips.

On the other side of the pillar, Cedran was still talking to Deryck. 'I trust there will be no more... problems with Ethan and Alma in the future.'

Alma glanced at Ethan and he raised his eyebrows.

'No, sir,' said Deryck, his voice sullen. 'But she's supposed to be with me, and Ethan is just—'

'Ethan is my son, acknowledged and cared for,' replied Cedran, his voice steel and velvet. 'And he is Alma's choice. Do not think you will dispose of him so easily as you did Caleb.'

'I am *not* supposed to be with him!' Alma whispered.

Ethan, pressed against her, bit her ear gently. 'I know.'

Then another voice spoke.

'What is this?'

Alma's legs began to shake. She turned her head, peering around the pillar. Denoris. Another Lord was with him, clad in red, with glitter on his high cheekbones and in his dark hair. Ellery was also with them, but she seemed oddly vague. Her eyes were half-closed, her father holding her arm in a strong grip as she stumbled along.

She turned back to Ethan, and he nodded. He didn't need to say anything.

They ran for the stairs, and didn't look back.

CHAPTER 32
TWO ANCIENT HOUSES, ALIKE IN TREACHERY

'Cedran? What's happening here?'

Denoris had not expected to find his son in the Foyer, and especially not in some sort of altercation with Cedran, of all people! What was the boy thinking? It had already been a difficult evening. Trying to strike a balance where his daughter was well enough to walk, yet sufficiently under the influence of her stone, had taken some time, as had getting her dressed. And now this. Turning to Nevros, he offered him Ellery's arm. The other lord raised his eyebrows, yet took it. Ellery swayed and smiled at him, touching his dark hair.

The crowd that had seemed to be dispersing had now reformed. Conversation buzzed and echoed under the glass dome. Gossip. Denoris shook his head. This was all he needed. He went over to Cedran, smiling, though he would rather draw his sword and cut down the lot of them, screaming his rage to the heavens. Darkness knew he was tired!

'Your son just tried to stab my son. I stopped him from doing so,' said Cedran, an edge to his tone. He was holding onto Deryck with one hand, his knuckles white.

'Your son?' Denoris spread his hands. 'But where is he? Is he all right?'

Cedran's gaze narrowed. 'He's gone. As is the girl.'

Denoris felt like he was going to explode. Of course the girl was involved! He was so close to achieving his goals, and he didn't need his son messing everything up. He noted the presence of the Hunt, caught Simeon's eye. The Hunt leader nodded once, the movement slight. Denoris returned his attention to Cedran. He needed to clean up this mess – it was a night for celebration, after all.

'And you're sure Deryck tried to stab him? You must be mistaken, surely.'

'I am not.' Cedran released Deryck, giving him a little shove. He stumbled forward, his face sullen. 'I saw him myself. As did most of the people in here.'

'Why would he do such a thing?'

Cedran tilted his head, his arms folded.

Denoris snorted. 'Well, you can hardly blame the boy, can you, for wanting to protect what's his?'

'His?' A muscle moved in Cedran's jaw. 'I hadn't realised Alma was spoken for.'

Denoris kept his tone conciliatory. 'It's not yet official, but I have been talking to Artos. I expect to make an announcement soon. Perhaps you could let your son know that's the case?' He allowed an edge to creep into his voice.

Cedran's eyes narrowed, his lip curling. 'Is that so?'

Denoris paused. For the first time in a while, he felt as though he didn't hold all the cards. He smiled. 'Come now, Cedran. Tonight is a celebration. The Dark are here, gathering as they used to in the old days, and I have opened my cellars to stock the Hall with my finest wine. Come, drink with us. Just because you turned me down, doesn't mean you can't raise a glass with us.'

～

ELLERY HUNG ON TO NEVROS. SHE REACHED OUT TO TOUCH HIS hair. It was just like her own! But even more pretty, with all the glitter. He didn't seem to mind her touching it, so she lost herself in the dark strands, wondering why there was so much shouting going on when the world was so beautiful.

Underneath it all she knew something wasn't right, but she couldn't quite seem to grasp what it was.

'Wake, my beautiful girl, come on!' The voice in her mind, the one that loved her, sounded muffled. Oh, she loved the voice. She loved everyone. And she was awake, so what was the voice even talking about?

'Come on, child.' Ooh, Nevros was making her walk now, and it was so much fun, almost like dancing. Her skirts swished around her feet. She giggled, hanging on his arm. Oh, there was Deryck! She waved at him, but he just stared at her. And then her father had her other arm and she leaned her head on his shoulder.

'I'm so glad you're all right, that the machine didn't kill you,' she mumbled. He squeezed her arm, and it was a bit too tight, a bit sore, but the pain passed as soon as it came.

'Not here,' he said, his voice low.

Oh, oops! She'd forgotten it was a secret. But now she was being led through the crowd to the front of the room, where the thrones were. And someone was waiting there for her, smiling.

It was Rindor.

CEDRAN KEPT HIS GAZE FIRMLY ON THE HUNT AS HE ENTERED the Great Hall. He hoped to Darkness that Ethan and Alma had made it to the Gate. So far it seemed they were all here, though it was Simeon and Deryck he was most concerned with, and the woman, Floria. She caught his gaze as though she could read his thoughts and winked at him, rolling her tongue lasciviously.

And now Ellery was being dragged towards the front of the

room. He'd been horrified when he saw her, how thin she was, and obviously unwell, her pupils dilated so much her eyes were almost black. He wondered what Denoris was thinking, letting her out in that state.

Then he saw Rindor standing in front of the throne and stopped.

Surely Denoris wouldn't. Open treason wasn't usually his style.

But, it seemed, he would.

Ellery was brought up onto the dais and made to stand in front of the other throne. Denoris stood between Ellery and Rindor, holding onto Ellery, a wine glass in his other hand. He addressed the crowd.

'It's a pleasure to see so many of you here tonight, to feel our power growing in strength with each day. I trust you are all enjoying the wine.' He smiled, raising his glass. The crowd cheered, raising their glasses in return.

'Then join me in toasting my daughter, Ellery, who is now betrothed to Rindor, son of Nevros. Two ancient houses, joined together in front of the thrones. This is our future!' he roared, raising his glass higher. The crowd roared with him, drinking deep and calling out congratulations.

Ellery smiled and waved her hand. She giggled, trailing her fingers back and forth in front of her face. Rindor glanced at her, frowning. Nevros, standing nearby, jerked his head at his son. Rindor stepped forward, pulling something from his pocket – Cedran glimpsed the blood-red shimmer of ruby, the fire of diamonds.

'I present this ring, an heirloom of our house, as a token of my esteem and affection,' Rindor recited.

Denoris smiled and nodded, pulling Ellery around to face Rindor. A flicker of something crossed her face, but then Rindor had her hand, the ring slid onto her finger and the deed was done. He pulled her in for a kiss. Cedran was sickened by how his hands moved on her, the girl seemingly unable to stop him as the crowd cheered and whistled.

Denoris, still smiling, raised his glass again. 'To the happy couple!' His eyes met Cedran's for a moment and narrowed.

Cedran got the message. He turned, pushing through the crowd, glad beyond words that he hadn't subjected his son to such a spectacle. He needed to speak with Artos and let him know what had happened. At least Alma and Ethan would be safely through the Gate by now.

~

'It's all right. We're safe now.'

Alma was still shaking. Energy lines flashed in and out. She really needed to get a handle on her powers, she thought, shuddering as she regained control. Artos could help, perhaps, or even Merewyn.

They were back in her room, the door locked, the stars in the ceiling glimmering. Ethan steered her towards the bed and she sat down. She knew he was right, that they'd had no other option but to come back upstairs, but part of her just wanted to run home to the familiarity of her own room, her family.

Ethan had relit the fire and the kindling was already catching, throwing dancing shadows across the room.

'We'll just stay here for a bit,' he said. 'No pressure. If you want to sleep, I'll stay awake and make sure you're all right. And we'll leave early, at sun-up. The Hunt prefer the dark.'

He was so earnest, standing there, his hands open, and she knew he would do just that, would protect her to his last breath. Just as she would for him. The realisation relaxed her and warmth ran through her, the last flickers of power abating. If they had to stay for a little longer, so be it. Whatever came, they would face it together.

'I could sleep,' she said. Then she smiled. 'Or you could take off your shirt and we could make the most of our last night here for a while.'

His face lit up and he returned her smile. Then he pulled his T-shirt over his head and walked towards the bed.

LATER THEY LAY TOGETHER IN THE DARK, FEELING EACH other's heartbeats, hands warm on soft skin.

'Are you happy?' asked Ethan

'Yes,' said Alma.

'So am I,' he murmured. 'There is no-one for me but you.' His hands moved on her and she gasped, pressing closer to him as their breathing grew stronger. Through the window came the sound of the distant sea.

CHAPTER 33
NO OTHER CHOICE

Alma woke with Ethan's arm heavy across her. For a moment she wasn't sure where she was. Then she remembered and turned to snuggle into him, breathing in the scent of him, warm like amber and honey.

His eyes came open and he squinted at her.

'Hey.'

'Hey,' she said, her voice soft.

He rolled over and kissed her, then sat up, running his hand through his hair. The fire had died down and pale dawn light was visible through the open window.

'We should probably go,' he said.

Alma sighed, sitting up. She didn't want to leave. Her heart hurt at the thought. 'I know.' She slid out of bed, her hand lingering on the soft pillows, the feathery duvet.

When she came back in the room Ethan was already dressed. 'Ready?' he said.

She wasn't, but there was no other choice. She took his hand.

'As I'll ever be.'

Outside the gardens were misty and green, the cool air holding the promise of warmth to come. They were also deserted. Alma had tears in her eyes as she walked through them, trying to take in every turning path, every shaded nook. She hated not knowing when she'd get to return, when she'd see her grandfather, or Thorion, or Adara again.

They reached the last of the garden spaces, the white path through the meadow curving beyond. The garden was shaded by tall blossom trees and petals carpeted the smooth green lawn. Benches with tall carved sides sat around the perimeter. It was so perfect, so beautiful, that she stopped, wanting to soak up every last moment. Ethan stopped as well, putting his arms around her.

'We'll be back,' he said, but there was a roughness to his voice.

She nodded. It was all she could do.

ELLERY WAS CURLED UP ON A CUSHIONED BENCH, TRYING TO read her favourite book. Unable to focus on the page she gave up, closing the book and letting it drop into her lap. She twisted the little gold ring on her finger round and round, the small emerald catching the dawn light, reminding her of all she'd lost. On her other hand a ruby shimmered, red as blood, heavy as a chain. She had only fragmented memories of the night before. The whole thing was like some terrible nightmare. But the ring was proof that she was engaged to Rindor, of all people. Her mouth twisted, her eyes blurring. She wished she could rip the ring from her finger and throw it away, run to the Gate and the world beyond. But she could hardly walk, let alone run, and she had nowhere to go when she got there. Her father would hunt her down, anyway.

At the sound of footsteps she sank down lower on her bench, wanting to hide. Then she saw who it was. Alma and Ethan, holding hands, oblivious to anyone else. Ellery peered around the side of the bench to see Ethan taking Alma in his arms, kissing her. Once again she missed Tomas, the longing for him an ache inside her.

'I love you,' she heard Ethan say, his voice a deep murmur in the cool air.

'I love you, too,' Alma replied, her voice sighing, soft.

Tears started in Ellery's eyes. So their father was definitely lying to Deryck. What a surprise. Frozen, she stayed where she was. What was so important about Alma that Denoris would still want her, badly enough to lie to Deryck about it? He already had the Crown, in his stupid machine. Her heart sank and she closed her eyes, tears leaking down her cheeks. Of course. The machine. She'd seen what it did to their father. She also knew there were rumours about Alma, about the fact she could manipulate energy. It didn't take a genius to figure it out. She needed to warn Deryck, to let him know once again that their father was using him to get to Alma. She waited until Alma and Ethan left the garden. Then Ellery crept away, her heart sore.

It took her a while to get back to the apartments, but she was determined to keep practising, to be able to walk. She opened the door and went inside, hanging her cloak on one of the hooks in the hallway. She sat down to remove her shoes, trying not to sob. Deryck came walking past, a bunch of flowers in his hand. He stopped when he saw her.

'Are you all right?' He came to sit with her. Her heart broke to see him looking so well, his eyes bright, his expression eager. She knew who the flowers were for. She also knew they would mean nothing to her.

'Er, Deryck, um.' Her voice was choked with held-back tears. She could smell the flowers, sweet and fresh, like a small piece of spring in the dark hallway.

Deryck sat down next to her.

'Did father do something?' There. The perfect opening.

'He did, Deryck, oh, but not like that,' she said hastily, as horror dawned on his face. 'No, it is what he's been doing to you.'

Deryck's brow furrowed. 'To me? What are you talking about?'

'About Alma, Deryck. She's not coming back to you. I don't

remember much about last night, but I remember him telling you she would, that she loves you, and it's all lies!'

'What?' Deryck shook his head. 'You don't know, El, you don't know what's been going on. Father's been speaking to Artos. He's in favour of the match and they're making the arrangements. Besides, I saw her last night, and—'

'Did she seem like she wanted to talk to you?'

'Well, no, but that was because Ethan was there. And his father.' His lip curled. 'I don't think she wants to hurt him, you know, she's so nice. And now you're engaged to Rindor, maybe we can even make it a double wedding.'

Ellery didn't know what to say.

'C'mon, El, it's going to be all right.'

'It's not.' It came out as a whisper. Then her voice rose. 'Listen to me. Father. Is. Lying. To. You. Because he's the one that wants Alma.'

'He would never.'

Ellery rolled her eyes. 'Really? Oh, I don't mean he wants her for himself. It's for his machine. And the easiest way to get her back is through you.'

'That's ridiculous.'

'Think about it! He needs her powers to make it work properly. And he'll end up killing her to do it. If you still love her, Deryck, you have to stop him.'

Deryck stared at her, his face aghast. 'He wouldn't.'

'Of course he would.'

'But... no, Ellery, you're mistaken. And she still loves me, I know she does, despite what she says.'

Ellery swallowed, sympathy running through her. This was going to be really, really hard.

'I just saw her, Deryck. With Ethan.'

He went very still, his green eyes fixed on her. 'What do you mean?'

'In the gardens. I saw them kissing. And... and more. I mean, it's obvious how close they are. They're in love. I heard her say it to him, and him to her.'

Deryck went pale, his green eyes cold in his handsome face.

'I don't believe you,' he hissed, his hand going to his neck, touching his stone.

'If she wants to come back to you, why has she been avoiding you? Why hasn't she thanked you for the flowers? I know you leave them every day. Come *on*, Deryck, stop fooling yourself!'

'No, you're lying, Ellery. You're lying! Why would you lie to me, after all I've done for you!'

She flinched. 'Deryck, I swear—'

'No. She told Father she loves me, she *told* him! And she *is* coming back to me.'

'She's not—'

'Ellery, shut up!' He got to his feet, shaking with rage, flower petals dropping around his feet. 'You never liked her, and now you're trying to spoil things just because you're jealous!'

'Deryck, please.' She grabbed his arm but he shook her off.

'No wonder no one loves you!' he hissed. She recoiled as though he'd slapped her. 'Maybe Father was right about you after all.' He turned and marched away, trailing leaves and petals as he went, bright spots of colour on the pale floor. The door slammed behind him

Ellery felt sick, so sick she couldn't even cry at first, her shock and pain so deep she couldn't move. Then the voice was there, the one she loved. 'Come, my darling,' it said. 'Be strong. You have to keep going, to the end. You can do this.' Ellery shook her head, leaning back on the bench with her eyes closed. Tears ran down to her chin, dripping on her bodice. She wept for Deryck, for herself, for everyone in the sorry mess her father had created. Then she sat up. There was only one thing left to do, only one person left for her to turn to.

CHAPTER 34
COLD HEART BETRAYED

A dara woke early. The sky outside was only just starting to pale, the fire a warm glow of embers. Beside her Thorion slept, his dark hair around his face, his mouth curved, utterly relaxed. She gazed fondly at him, pulling the covers around her shoulders against the early morning chill. What had woken her? She listened, wondering if something outside had disturbed her, but all she could hear was the ocean's distant roar. She frowned, looking around the room, but could see nothing. Starting to shiver, she slid back under the covers, curling up next to Thorion's warmth. Then she felt it. Deep inside, a flutter like butterfly wings, like magic awakening. It was unmistakeable – a new presence just starting to stir. She reached down one hand to her stomach. It was flat as always, but she could sense an energy that hadn't been there before, a glowing spark of life. Thorion stirred and rolled over. One muscled arm came across and pulled her to him. He kissed her softly on her forehead.

'Thorion,' she whispered, her voice shaking.

'Adara?' He opened one sleepy blue eye to look at her. 'Are you all right? Was it a dream?'

'I'm fine,' she said, starting to smile, twining her hand with his. 'We're fine.'

He opened both eyes, then, the dark brows raising slightly. 'We?'

'We.' She placed his hand on her stomach.

'Adara, what—?'

Then understanding dawned on his face. He wrapped his arms tight around her, burying his face in her shoulder as he shook against her. She could feel his tears, hot on her skin, as she held him close.

'Can it be true? Are we so fortunate?' His voice broke. He smoothed the curls back from her face with one warm hand. She smiled at him, wiping his tears with a delicate touch.

'We are, my love. I am with child.'

ELLERY STUMBLED THROUGH THE GARDENS ONCE MORE, HER cloak pulled tight around her. She'd left her father's house as soon as she was able – she wondered whether she would ever go back there again. For she was about to make a choice that would change everything.

She passed through the Foyer, barely nodding at the guards as they bowed, and made her slow way up the stairs of one of the towers, stopping every few steps to lean against the wall, her heart pounding. One of the guards in the guard room came out to offer help, but she waved him away. She would do this, even if it killed her. A while later, her breath coming fast, she stood in front of the closed door, fighting tears, her hands sweaty against her skirt. For a moment she considered turning around and leaving. But she couldn't. No more. It was time for her to take a stand while she still could. She reached for her stone, then stopped herself, groaning with the effort. She needed to be herself to do this. She reached out and knocked on the door.

Thorion came through into the sitting room. Adara was seated on the sofa, concentrating on a piece of embroidery, the soft light turning her curls into a halo around her head. Thorion's eyes filled with tears, his heart swelling with love. Their child. He couldn't believe it, that such joy was to be theirs. At his step she lifted her head and smiled.

'Oh Thorion.' She laughed. 'The whole world will know if you keep welling up every time you look at me.'

He sat down next to her, leaned in and kissed her, holding the moment, enjoying the sweetness of it. 'You've made me so very happy, my love, I cannot help it.' He grinned, ducking his head.

She put her embroidery aside and slid her arms around him. 'Not as happy as you make me,' she whispered, kissing him again. A discreet clearing of the throat announced Edric's arrival with tea and breakfast. They came apart, Adara flushing pink.

'Thank you, Edric,' she said. 'Just what I need.'

'Tea?' asked Thorion, leaning forward to pick up the pot.

'Please,' she said, leaning back on the sofa. He passed her a cup before pouring his own, his heart light.

Then there was a knock at the door.

The door opened.

'Yes?' Thorion's servant, Edric, peered around the door, his eyes bright in his bearded face.

'If you please, it's Ellery, to see King Thorion. If he's free,' she added hastily, part of her hoping he wouldn't be. But then the High King appeared behind Edric.

'Who is it?' His gaze came to Ellery and his face changed, sorrow and pity moving across it. He took her hands and led her inside the small vestibule.

'What is it, my dear?'

Tears prickled against Ellery's eyelids – she was so close to losing it she could hardly speak.

'Lord Thorion,' she managed, her legs shaking. 'I need to talk to you.'

'Of course, dear heart. Come.' He took her arm and led her through to a sitting room. Adara was seated on the sofa, but she got up as they entered.

'Ellery! Are you well?' She came over, more glowingly beautiful than ever. 'Oh my dear,' she said, pulling Ellery into a hug. 'It's all right, you're safe now.'

Ellery resisted briefly, then to her great shame started sobbing as though she would never stop. Ugh, she hated this, hated feeling so weak. But Adara's gentle touch, the way she so obviously cared, reminded her of the voice in her mind, of Tomas, of the small share of love she'd had in her life.

Adara led her to the sofa, sitting her down and handing her a napkin to wipe her face. 'Tea, I think, Thorion dear,' she said, tucking a blanket around Ellery and sitting next to her. Thorion poured a cup of tea, added a liberal amount of honey and gave it to Ellery. He sat down opposite. Ellery took a gulp of tea. Then she put the cup down on the table and sat up straight, wiping her face. She was a Princess of the Dark and she needed to stay strong.

'Lord Thorion, Lady Adara,' she started, her voice husky. 'I need to tell you, er.' She looked down. This was it. This was when, possibly, she signed her death warrant. But what did she have to live for any more? She raised her head. Thorion was watching her, his eyes changing from blue to grey. Adara squeezed her hand. And, from somewhere, she found the strength to continue. 'I know where the Crown is.'

There. It was done. Adara gasped, but Thorion said nothing, his face like carved stone.

'I also need to tell you about my father, and what he's doing.

Please, will you help me?'

AFTERWORD

If you enjoyed *Light And Dark*, please leave me a star rating or review on Amazon, come and see me on Goodreads, or visit me at my website, www.helenglynnjones.co.uk

Thank you for reading.

Want more?
Join my mailing list for release news, sneak peeks, competitions and more...
eepurl.com/c9lzRD

Volume Six, the final chapter of the Ambeth Chronicles, is coming soon...

ACKNOWLEDGMENTS

This has been quite a journey so far, and there have been some wonderful people who've helped me along the way. Thank you once again to Lucy York for her editing expertise, and to Rich Jones at Turning Rebellion for the beautiful cover design. To my beta readers, Lucy and Angelika, friends met first virtually and then in real life, thank you for your support, your insight and for sticking with me on this writing journey - may your light always shine bright. Thank you also to my family and friends for their love and support, and, finally and always, to my beloved Marcus and Isabelle, for coming on this journey with me.

ABOUT THE AUTHOR

Helen Glynn Jones is a prize-winning author of six novels.

Born in the UK, Helen has lived in both Australia and Canada. A few years ago she returned to her native England where, when she's not writing stories, she likes to hunt for vintage treasures, explore stone circles and watch the sky change colour. She now lives in Hertfordshire with her husband, daughter, and wonderfully chaotic cockapoo.

Hills And Valleys

Volume Three of The Ambeth Chronicles

'Sometimes things call to us until we can no longer ignore them. And Ambeth is calling you, Alma.'

After the events of the Harvest Fair, Alma is finished with Ambeth - they can find the missing Cup and Crown without her. But Ambeth is not finished with her. First the mystery of her dead father comes back to haunt her, then the Dark reach out, hoping to trap her once more. And then there's the strange power she seems to have...

Under Stone

'This is one of those rare books I simply couldn't put down.'

'Highly recommended for those who like strong female characters, coming-of-age narratives, and true love -- just keep the tissues nearby!'

A Thousand Rooms

Available on Amazon as an e-book or paperback